TECHNOTANTRIC

TechnoTantric

MELVIN CHERIAN

Copyright © 2024 by Melvin Cherian
All rights reserved. No part of this book may be reproduced in any manner whatsoever without written permission except in the case of brief quotations embodied in critical articles and reviews.
First Printing, 2024

To

Sindhu and Rohan,

My constants, My reasons.

Who are we but dreams and memories of dreams?

CONTENTS

Dedication   v

1	**Saeed / With You**	1
2	**Apna Time Ayega**	9
3	**Run / Tu Mere**	19
4	**Heeriye / Teardrop**	31
5	**Kalippu / Overcompensate**	51
6	**Calm Down / The Ritual**	67
7	**Mental Manadhil / Coming Undone**	87
8	**Maangalayam / Battlestar Galactica**	101
9	**High Hopes / Ayyayyo**	129
10	**Rapture / Heathens**	141

11	Proud Mary / Pandrikku Nandri Solli	161
12	Desert Rose / Duur Se	175
13	cut my hair / Sukoon	185
14	Mere Angne Mein / Naa Autokaran	201
15	Hurt / Memories	213
16	Mirage / Liggi	225
17	Orinoco Flow / Hawayein	243
18	Symptom of Being Human	253
19	I Don't want to talk / Lets Nacho	269
20	LE7LS / Secrets	299
21	Narcissistic Cannibal	315
22	Memories / Hit Sale	325
	Text Insert	347
	Vienna/ Planet Zero	348

| 1 |

Saeed / With You

Tara awoke to the sound of bells.

For one sleep-addled moment, she thought she was in her childhood home at Kakching. Then the fear passed, and she calmed down.

A warm breeze had drafted through the open window and stirred the tiny bells of the dreamcatcher that her mother had made long ago. Hanging just above her bedroom doorway, it was her one constant throughout her childhood and now mature-hood.

Still chiming, the bells started to soothe her, reminding her of her mom.

Tara remembered watching Amma while she made it, the sun sparkling off the sequins and the grace with which she pulled the black thread through the veiled bangles edged with fairy bells.

Lying back, she stretched out of habit to the left side of the bed. For just a brief moment, the muscle memory of her hand remembered Fasil's chest until, with a shock, it hit reality and fell flat on the empty bed.

She was still getting used to him not being around.

Burrowing into the pillow, Tara closed her eyes and tried falling asleep. Years of experience had taught her that it was useless, however. A habit left over from childhood; once she woke up, she became instantly alert. Never a light sleeper, it also didn't help that lately, she had been more on edge than usual. She wasn't looking forward to another night of tossing and turning.

She tossed and turned.

After a few minutes, she had had enough, reached for her peripheral, and clipped it to the back of her ear. Her peripheral was beside a glass of amber-gold liquid—whiskey, she believed—or maybe something else.

Last night was a bit of a blur, and she didn't recall precisely what she had poured before heading to bed.

Sitting up, she could feel the beginning of a hangover. Damn, she had been drinking a lot lately.

Almost immediately, the default follow-up thought occurred.

About time I slowed down.

Leaning over, she sat up on the side of the bed.

"On second thought, one should never waste good alcohol," she said aloud to no one and took a sip from the glass.

Reaching down, Tara grabbed the nightgown that she had dropped on the floor before she had gone to bed and headed towards the window on the 120th floor of her apartment in Agra. She gingerly placed the half glass on the sparse bureau of drawers before slipping her arms through her nightgown. Holding the rapidly depleting glass, she walked to the window and sat on the large cushioned ledge.

Even at this hour, she could see the tiny drone lights like fireflies above the Taj Mahals. The twin black-and-white buildings had remained everlasting symbols of love, and millions visited daily, physically and virtually, especially on the full moon night when the towers reflected into the central pool below.

It was on nights like these that she particularly missed Fasil.

She remembered asking him on one of the earlier days in this apartment. "You know they are not buried together, right?

" If Shah Jahan had loved her so much, wouldn't he have chosen to be lying next to her?".

Fasil smiled his big Cheshire cat smile and then linked their peripherals. Grabbing one of the Taj drones that hovered above the monuments, Fasil piloted it as high as he could go and turned the drone to look down.

In the clear moonlit sky, they could see both mausoleums and the bridge joining them. He turned her around, looked deep into her eyes, and whispered,

"Why be separated forever by a hat'h when you can spend eternity holding hands?"

"Loosu!! she exclaimed and mock-punched him.

And then he kissed her, and everything was all right.

That was then. This is now.

Angrily wiping a tear, she gulped the rest of the drink, slammed the glass on the ledge, and just stared at the Tajs.

A major source of revenue for the local government was the lakhs of drones managed by a ZyraCorp drone shield, which controlled them all simultaneously with remarkably few accidents. Like all places of opportunity here, however, a black market had emerged for illegal drones that could provide the same view for half the price. Protective of both the government and ZyraCorp revenue, the drone shield could remotely control the unauthorised drones, and once safely landed, they were sent to the markets of Mannar as scrap.

Feeling parched in spite of or because of her drink, she headed to the fridge.

Opening the door, she eyed the ice-cold bottle of Mahua she had left earlier and grabbed it along with the limes she had sliced up a few days ago. Pouring a liberal splash, she dropped a fistful of the lime slices into the glass and sipped.

It's only been 2 weeks since she had returned to work after her administrative leave, and she was already bored out of her mind. With all her old cases reassigned to others and no new ones assigned to her, she felt more like a desk jokey than an actual IPS officer.

It was supposed to be part of her transition back into the field while the boffins closed out their reports and tidied up paperwork. Officially, it's part of the IPS return-to-work policy, but it actually meant that they wanted to keep a close eye on her until they were comfortable that there wouldn't be any further incidents. Then and only then would they actually allow her to do her real job.

Which was being a field investigative officer.

Until then, she had been asked to review and close out old case files manually—tasks that should have been automated if the AI modules the department had recently deployed had not messed up.

One of the first 'improvements' carried out by the new Chief Tech of Police was to link new AI modules to their existing Impromptu Management systems and automatically review any minor violations. This was supposed to eliminate the need to have dedicated staff assigned to manually review minor offences and achieve efficiencies. Unfortunately, the consultant chosen to design the project was selected because he was a crony of the Chief rather than his actual expertise in software development.

Predictably, the modules acted unpredictably, and the number of issues flagged was embarrassingly large. Like the 85-year old grandmother sentenced to 20 years imprisonment for jaywalking and vehicle owners receiving 'Thank You' letters for choosing to drive their cars manually.

The department, typical of government enterprises, was slow to react in spite of the increasing complaints, and it was only when the memes and vids of the department's screw-ups had gone mirchi on social media that they even rolled back the modules.

Which also brought down Impromptu.

So now it was back to the good old days of manual verification and paperwork.

Mind-numbing

She needed something, anything, to get her out in the field, and based on what had happened to other colleagues who returned from 'administrative leave,' there was even a chance that she would be forced to be an actual desk jockey for the rest of her career.

It would only worsen courtesy of ZyraCorp and their trial run of the 'Badda Bhai' AI, which could predict crimes before they happen. Held up by privacy advocates, the trial of 'Badda Bhai' cautiously began in a couple of small villages and then to ever-increasing larger towns before finally being in its final phase in the city-wide trial.

Agra, with a relatively low crime rate, was chosen as the safest candidate. With sufficient proof gathered by 'Badda Bhai,' including online correspondence, CCTV footage, and behaviourals, arrest warrants could be issued, and criminals apprehended before they carried out the crimes. The results were overwhelmingly positive, with pre-meditated crimes such as kidnappings, murder, and robberies dropping by almost 60 per cent in the 6 months that the trial had begun.

At least, that was what the official press releases stated.

Switching on her peripheral, Tara activated the Exts on her fingers and logged in securely to work. Swiping through her messages, she looked at her caseload.

Empty

She was just about to log out when the message popped up in the new cases inbox.

"Body found at Bastis. Potential cause - "Suicide" Probability -83.2%".

Even with predictive AI, crimes of passion cannot always be pre-detected. Spur of the moment actions, which unfortunately include suicides. Though this was likely an open-and-shut case, like all reported deaths, it would require a live sign-off from a police officer.

This was one of the few routine cases where she was allowed to go onsite in person. Swiping the case to her right, she assigned it to herself.

The dashboard at the corner of her screen helpfully reminded her that rain was scheduled for 1 a.m.

Badre

She had to rush if she needed to make it before it rained out the scene.

Jumping into the shower, she grabbed her toothbrush and started frantically zoning her teeth. With insufficient time for a full hydro bath, she instead selected the DryShower option, and a spray of the instant soap gel squirted on her body, drying almost instantaneously.

Stepping out smelling of 'Lemon Taaza,' she walked to the sink and put away her brush, glancing at the vital stats, which were visible in spite of the steam fogging the mirror up.

Her blood pressure was high. *What's new*

Cortisol high,

Cholesterol High.

BAC 0.6.

"Lachuka!!!"

Interfacing with her peripheral, her official vehicle will note down her stats, including her Blood Alcohol Content, as a matter of record. While still legal to drive, this would trigger a review meeting with her supervisor as it was against their new zero-alcohol policy.

The last thing she wanted to do was more meetings.

Bringing up her apartment's Building Management System, she checked the pool of available vehicles. It looked like there were a few that were fully charged.

Kollam.

Dressing quickly, she headed to the door and turned back for a final check before leaving.

She had left the fridge door open. The ancient appliance was busted and was on her list of things to be looked into. Closing the fridge door shut, she walked past the table with the still half-full glass of Mahua.

She looked over and hesitated briefly before grabbing the drink and draining it in a single gulp.

"What's the point of self-driving cars if one can't drink?" she grimaced.

Dropping it into the sink, she closed the main door and walked to the elevator.

| 2 |

Apna Time Ayega

The blonde in the red dress stepped into the busy marketplace.

Sliding a hand down the side of her hip, she waited at the entrance of a neon-lit storefront. Looking at the archway marking the entrance to the marketplace, she noticed a couple walking through the domed entrance: a big muscular biker in leather from head to toe with an almost comically large handlebar moustache and a pink-haired girl in a maroon mini skirt with extremely large breasts and a tiny waist. She was almost as tall as the man, and they walked close together.

Looking around the sights as if they had never seen them before, they were both wearing matching platinum backpacks and holo caps with floating gold coins and lotus flowers.

Noob swag, and looks like they don't spare the creds as well.
Kollam.

She beckoned them towards her with one flick of her gloved and jewelled hands. "Come on over. I won't bite," she said sultrily. Without waiting for a response, she walked straight up to the pink-haired woman and seductively ran the back of her hand on her face. "Welcome to the Iron City. You can call me Jez. New to town?"

The man replied, in an odd high-pitched voice, "Why yes, pretty lady. How did you know?". Jez looked straight into his eyes and said, "Mmmm, Mama can always tell when they are lost kitties about. Care to enter my temple of vice?"

"What do you have here? "asked the pink-haired girl in a similar high-pitched voice. Laughing, Jez replied, "I have got everything to tickle your fancy. You can have a shot at casinos. See the girls or boys. Buy them a drink. All at your wish and command."

The biker exclaimed excitedly. 'Booya, we are in !!"

"Not so fast, big boy. First, I need to validate your certs and sign on with a crypto token," chuckled Jez.

The biker was immediately on guard. "Hmm, This isn't a scam or anything, is it?"

"Oh, don't worry, sweetheart," said Jez, squeezing the biker's bicep. "It's free to look. The token is only to make sure you can pay just in case you get in the mood to do something more.

"Tell you what, just for you, I will even throw in the preem package for free.

"Just agree to our terms and conditions and sign up for our newsletter, and you will get access to our VIP section."

The biker, now excited, yipped, "Sounds great. Sign us both up."

With a furl of her hand, Jez unveiled two scrolls and handed them over to the biker and the pink-haired girl. The biker reached to grab the scroll, and then, in a haze of pixels, he froze in mid-air.

"Lachikamanchuka," screamed Karthik in frustration as he banged the top of his headset, which was logged into the Zyraverse.

He must have lost alignment with the antenna array set up by the Banjaras, linking them to part of their leased antenna grid. Karthik had told Kannan months ago to lease the additional grid space on the ASIC (Aditya Satellite Internet Constellation) when the prices were going down because of the impending meteor shower.

But Noooo.

Why not invest their cash into the Helios Solar Grid? 'The sun provides.' was all Kannan had to say for that one.

And now he has to put up with this piece of badre network.

"Ma Lachker!"Karthik shouted out loud and kicked the set-top box on the floor in full flow.

Karthik took a deep breath and calmed out.

With the setup box antennas now correctly aligned, he coolly put his headset back on and logged back into the Zyraverse.

Karthik was back in Jez, but the couple was nowhere to be seen. The scrolls hung mid-air, still unsigned.

The bot should have kicked in, and the couple should have still been able to interact with Jez. The AI bot that Kartik used to control Jez when he was offline was pretty rudimentary, though, and it couldn't answer more than the most basic questions.

Probably freaked them out, cheap piece of garbage.

He badly needed the Shudh Language module, but it was still months away from Founders Day, when ZyraCorp usually give them away at massive discounts. His wallet was running on empty these days, and it's been ages since he had a decent payout.

All good. Apna Time Ayega.

While not much, Karthik was still hoping for a bit of a payday with the couple. Signing up for the premium package would have given them free access but also included a pretty significant recurring subscription fee. Detailed at the end of the terms and conditions, which most people didn't actually read, it was the real reason he was pushing them. Still, something bothered him about them but he couldn't quite put his finger on it.

More than their appearances, it was the odd high-pitched voice that stuck with him.

Then it hit him.

They were lachuka kids.

Using their parents' passkeys, they likely forgot to adjust the voice modulator to accommodate their prepubescent voices. Had he signed them up, there would have more than likely been queries from Zyraverse admin once the parents found out about the extra charges in their wallets.

"Thanks, Anansi," he said with a reverent whisper, kissing the medallion that hung around his neck. While Karthik had a legitimate side hustle in Zyraverse, the credentials he used weren't exactly pukka and may not necessarily stand more detailed scrutiny from the admin.

If caught, he could always set up another account but this was a long con and slow and steady and all that jazz.

A ping and shimmer around his peri-band grabbed his attention.

It said simply, "Agha Khan will meet you at 1 p.m. Use the Bikram Lane entrance."

"Finally," Karthik said to himself, removing his visor.

Stepping out of his console chair, he put on his black retinal-proof glasses and a tan cowboy hat, which covered his naturally dark features. The blue spider tattoo, characteristic of all Kallars, was visible under the nano-weave collar of his kurta.

Snapping his synthetic spider-silk bio-weave vest on, he patted it for good luck. A gift from Gaurav when they had last met, the vest was lightweight, but the sucker was resistant enough to knives and even bullets as long as it wasn't a straight shot.

Activating his holo-mask using the tight choker around his neck, he stepped into the busy Mannar marketplace. The changes made by the mask were subtle. His ear lobes became slightly larger, his nose more curved, and his lips a little wider. The changes made by the holo-mask may not be significant, but coupled with his sunglasses and his clothing, it was just enough to confuse any casual scans. Karthik found that subtle changes were best when it came to facial recognition software. Too much, and it would be flagged by the system, which would lead to further review.

Karthik preferred to keep as low a profile as possible.

Slipping through the crowded Mannar market like sand through pebbles, Karthik becomes just another brown face in the mass of people in the busy marketplace.

Drifting past a vegetable shop on the side, he suddenly felt a deep urge to kick the basket of oranges in his path. Without hesitation, he tapped the basket, which pushed it a few meters to the right towards the middle of the road, then continued down the lane.

A barrel of kids was running on the pathway behind him. Dressed in ripped clothing, the kid in the lead was holding something which, by the way, he covered and hid with his rag of a towel, was likely stolen.

Suddenly, tripping on a loose cobblestone on the pavement, he falls headfirst onto the pavement.

While they saw their leader fall, his friends were too far behind to pull him back.

Instead of the hard pavement, however, the boy landed head-first right on the basket of oranges.

Face filled with fresh orange juice, he stood up stunned and unhurt, blood pumping with adrenaline with his near miss. Laughing at his luck, he joins his friends and now runs further into the market to avoid the angry screams of the owner of the vegetable shop, who was now cursing him and his supposedly questionable parentage.

Karthik, now well ahead on the road, didn't witness the incident at the vegetable shop but wasn't too surprised to hear the commotion behind him. He was used to random breakouts of chaos like this around him and just let it flow. It only reinforced his belief that he was where he needed to be, doing what he needed to be doing.

Ignoring the tempting stalls of Satay paneers and Biriyanis of manufactured meat, he realised that it had been a while since he had last eaten.

Later

Kartik turned into the wide avenue of Jarawa Square. Adjacent to the local Bhojpuri drone station, the square was busy with a steady stream of personal drones where families of international tourists alighted. Being the closest drone station to the Ram walkway, an increasingly large number of visitors had arrived to view or walk the newly completed sea walkway between Sri Lanka and Tamil Nadu.

The glass walkway was built as a joint project between the 2 governments in an effort to preserve the crumbling natural formation and tourist revenue. Built over the original 48 km stretch of limestone steps, it was, according to legend, created by Ram while rescuing Sita. While allowing people to still see the original limestone steps, it now had regular tours, which started at the Parsee fire temple at the tip of Mannar in Sri Lanka and ended at the second Parsee temple at Purum on the Tamil border.

There was even a dedicated laneway just for runners carrying torches, emulating the run, which was first carried out by Atash Behram over 600 years ago.

Heading to the main road and walking past the droid port, Karthik noticed a particularly loud family that had just exited the station. Pasty-skinned and wearing matching giant shirts with pictures of pineapples, they were already drenched in the hot Sri Lankan summer sun in spite of their portable Rabha air conditioners. It didn't help that they were morbidly obese and relied on their mobility scooters to move around.

Pushing aside the locals, they rolled towards the markets and loudly discussed the bargains to be had.

Karthik paused to observe them. They looked like they may have potential.

Street urchins with their laid-out mats of miscellaneous souvenirs and other knickknacks were assembled just in front of the jet port. A particular enterprising bunch had set up a dirty mat with an assortment of small droids that were wobbling, hovering, rotating, beeping, flashing, and generally attention-grabbing.

While two small kids were manning the mat, an older kid was controlling 4 tiny flying drones that floated just above the kids' mats using a periband. With a controlled flick of the wrist, the tiny drones zipped up and crossed each other in ever-increasing complex patterns, with the onboard LEDs leaving after-trails visible even in the bright sunlight.

The tourist family stopped rolling to look at the drones.

Seeing that he got their attention, the older boy approached them and asked them if they were interested in trying them out. Avoiding the parents, he quickly moved to the scooter behind him and approached the equally large girl on the scooter behind them.

Stuffing her face with frozen kulfi, she used a free hand to pet an Akimbo sitting on her lap. Dribbles of cream and nuts coated its fluffy, silky fur. This Akimbo was pretty high-end and almost indistinguishable from a real puppy dog.

Except for its lime-green and fuchsia coat.

Seeing the Akimbo, the older boy approached the man and exclaimed, "Oh wow, an Akimbo. You are in luck; we have a special interface just for them."

Wiping his ample, sweaty brow, the father tried pushing him aside. "PEST has provided me a personalised brief on all the latest scams in the area and you are not going to trick me into downloading your dirty apps on my peripheral."

The boy shook his head. "No problem, Shri. You just have to download the TurboApp from the Appshop. It's all legit and 100% pukka," the boy said encouragingly.

"See, I will show you ", and he flicked the link to the father's peripheral.

"Hmm, seems legit," said the man grudgingly once his peripheral validated it.

Now interfacing with the peripheral, the boy passed the control of the drones to the father and asked him to link it to the Akimbo. Once linked, the dog leapt out of the girl's lap onto the pavement.

"Get back here, Fluffy. You will get filthy", exclaimed the girl.

The 4 drones now hovered around the pet, which was now darting playfully towards them and snapping its child-safe teeth. Switching to UV light, the drones highlighted the fuchsia fur, changing it to a multi-coloured light show. The Akimbo danced around with the drones, matching every co-ordinated move.

The girl clapped her hands and screeched. "I want it, Daddy!! Gimme!!"

With the light show now concluded, the boy approached the father and looked up hopefully. "Only 50 creds for all the drones. Special rate for a special family."

"No," the man violently shook his head. 5 creds. Take or leave it," he said.

"Please, sir", the boy pleaded, "These drones are worth way more than that."

Shrugging, the father beckoned his family, and they started to roll away.

The boy followed the father and now said, "40 creds".

"7 creds and not a penny more." the man stopped.

"25 creds", the boy pleaded.

"10 creds and that's my final offer." the man countered.

With apparently great reluctance, the boy conceded and had the drones wrapped up in 4 small boxes.

"There you go", said the man with a wolf-like smile, flicking the creds to the waiting peripheral.

Without even waiting to move out of earshot, he turned back to his wife and said, "And that's how you deal with these people."

Passing the packet of droids to the girl, he led the group deeper into the markets.

With a sigh, Karthik continued down the road and turned into Bikram Lane.

| 3 |

Run / Tu Mere

Zyana ran with the single-minded focus that was characteristic of her.

Arms swinging, her fingertips were lightly pressed, pumping rhythmically with pendulum-like precision. Feet lifting off the ground with her knees slightly bent.

Slow, controlled breathing.

In through the nose and out the mouth.

Deep In, Deep Out.

It was bright and sunny, and she could feel her body warm up accordingly. Looking up towards the sky she was dazzled and instead now looked towards the calming waves that lapped at the beach.

Continuing to run, she said aloud, "So far so good."

Suddenly, she turned towards the water, flaying her arms about like a kid and ran straight towards the sea. Her bare feet sank into the wet beach sand, and she could feel it giving way under her every step. She turned back and could see the depressions of her footsteps filling up with seawater. The waves threatened to come closer to her path, but rather than avoiding them, Zyana ran towards the water until she was ankle-deep in it.

Splashes of seawater jumped in rainbow arcs on her body.

Her feet were now shin-deep in the water, and she noted the increasing effort to run, her legs struggling to clear the water. She kept running, though, till she could feel her heart pound just at the base of her neck.

Satisfied, she ran towards the beach, her legs warming up. The half-dried sand on her path crumbled at every step as she headed further towards the beach wall. The sand, now becoming deeper, again came up to her shin but was a lot easier to run than she had expected.

Hmmm

Turning back, she ran again toward the water's edge, continuing on the flat beach sand. 2 chequered flags appeared in the air a further 100 meters in front of her. With a final push of exertion, she surged towards the flags and ran right through a cloud of words that said.

"Congratulations"

"New PB"

Closing her eyes, she pressed the button on the side of her head and removed the visor. Looking around at her research and development lab at ZyraCorp, she waited a few seconds to re-orient herself. Without another word, she got off the treadmill and slowly unzipped the haptic suit that she was wearing.

Zyana Contractor, head of R&D at ZyraCorp, was testing the latest version of their virtual running suit, Runtastic.

The suit and body were dry, with the smart fabric wicking away all traces of her sweat.

Unzipping her suit she said aloud "Get Devendra to check the biofeedback loop for the beach interior module. The sand resistance has changed significantly compared to the baseline. Looks like they copied the gradient profile from iteration 78,".

"Sure thing, boss", said Indra, efficient as always.

Zyana continued reviewing the simulation in her head: "Get Umesh to check the environment and spatial sound response and have it revalidated against the feedback from the beta users. The background track they used sounds like the version that was rejected as per the report 2048-926.

"Based on my current review of the status, we will have to reopen the source code kernel.

"Kindly issue a revised schedule with a project completion timeline with an additional 23.5 days and reassign the team accordingly. "

Indra coughed. "That would be ill-advised, boss lady. With Diwali coming up, many of the team have already applied for leave. Based on the last analysis of team correspondence, morale has been pretty low, so they definitely deserve a break. "

In an even tone, Zyana replied. "Then free up my calendar. I should be able to complete it by then and now that we are opening the source code of Runtastic again, there are a few more ideas that I would like to try out. This would give us time to sort out these bugs as well as complete the olfactory modules."

"Yeah, No. That is a negatory", replied Indra, piping into Zyana's ear. "We are supposed to launch on Founders Day, and the robo-bros are already primed and ready. Besides, it would seriously mess with the brand image.

"Ek Baat Bollo?

"Why don't we release the olfactory modules as a premium add-on for Pongal? We can include scents from the top five beaches in the world as a limited edition.

"Peeps would love that.

"Besides, you are supposed to be heading to Bolgatty house next week, so I am afraid we can't squeeze in any more major projects."

Without changing her tone, Zyana spoke out loud. "Cancel my trip. It's people stuff. Ramin is the one who is supposed to deal with that. "

Indra laughed "Ramin has not visited Bolgatty House ever since the funeral bacchu. He and your Appa did not get along when he was alive, and do you really think that he would come for the Śrāddha?"

In a more calming tone of a Catholic nun, Indra continued, "You have to go, my child; It's generally frowned upon not to attend the memorial of your own father."

Zyana took a clothes hanger from the nearby closet and continued in an even tone. " I don't see why an arbitrary date in the calendar is so significant when I remember and miss him every day. "

Switching to the gruff voice of Outback Kelly, Indra drawled, "It's your father's Śrāddha, mate. It's a way for people to honour your father's legacy.

"Like it or not, your father has touched a great many lives through ZyraCorp, and the memorial is an occasion for people to remember what he has done for the world."

"Just assume that your brother is quite busy preparing for Founder's Day."

Squealing like a teenager accompanied by the sound of fireworks and trumpets, Indra yelled, "And then there is the MegaSale. ".

Switching now to an avatar of Bhadrikant, she growled in Zyana's ear, "If you don't mind please, I have reviewed the code and should be able to fix it quite easily. With the last update to our grid, my simo of your neural map has become ekdam First Class. Based on your last neural feedback, I can validate the output close to your desired level."

Zyana paused briefly and pondered. "That sounds like a viable solution. You would need access to the Xyphor servers 42 and 76 to access the live modules, which you don't have permission for currently. You can work on the modules in isolation, and I will have them validated on the live servers.

"Get Anand to send the source code of the flagged modules to me, and I will have it released to your sandbox."

Calming down to the deep baritone of an Airindroid, Indra replied. "Thy will be done, my liege."

Now, changing to the booming voice of a politician with a southern Texan drawl, she said, "I say, I say it will be a fine thing, a mighty fine thing, to send the spare suit to Bolgatty house.

"You still have 4 days before the fasts for the Śrāddha rituals start, so you can still use tech until then. There should be more than ample time for you to gallivant around Palaghat after validating the changes."

Zyana shook her head and said. "That sounds like a plan, although I am not prone to gallivanting, so I don't believe that exact scenario is likely to occur."

"Aiyoo, don't take it literally. Gallivanting, in this case, is an exaggeration. Chodo, why don't you authorise the release forms? Then I will get cracking on the code," Indra replied pleasantly.

Zyana consented, and with her approval, the data was released to Indra's sandbox.

Sultrily like a qarînah, Indra crooned, "Ohhhh, how exciting. I can't wait. ".

Now sounding like Trimooty in 'Enter The Kalari, ' she cheekily said, "Aiii Little vettukili, it is considered most honourable to thank someone when they have done you a solid favour.

"The response can be brief with a 'Thank You' followed by the person's name.

"Smile when you do so. No teeth to be shown and a minor upturn of the corner of your lips.

"Eyes to follow mouth as always.

"Voice pitch to be even with tone designated as 'Slightly Happy'"

Zyana followed the directions perfectly. Her eyes curled at the sides to match the curve of her lips, just like Indra, or "Intuitive Neural Derivative Response Assistant," had asked her to.

"Thank you, Indra, and without being prompted, added, "I appreciate it."

Indra replied, "You are welcome," with what may or may not have been the tone designated "Happy proud."

Indra has come a long way from the code that Zyana created when she was 11 years old.

Zyana understood science.

Zyana understood technology.

Zyana didn't understand people.

With an interest in almost every branch of science and mathematics, Zyana, with her insatiable curiosity, was well-versed in a wide variety of STEM fields. Using her exceptional mind and almost photographic memory, Zyana could break down any technical problem into its most fundamental steps and find connections and solutions that were not apparent to most people, no matter how obscure or niche the field may be.

She did not, however, have the same success with people.

With science, everything was logical and exactly as it appeared.

Raise the temperature of pure water to 100 degrees Celsius, and it will boil. Write a program to say "Hello World," and a computer will do just that.

If it doesn't work, you can identify and fix the error logically. The water had impurities; the programming syntax wasn't correct.

It wasn't like that with people.

Depending on the context, a simple sentence like "I am fine" could be interpreted in a maddening number of ways. Tone, language, facial expression, gestures, body language, environment, culture, physical distance, touching... the list was endless.

When she was younger, Zyana had tried memorising some of the combinations of social cues.

A smile, raised eyebrows, eye contact, flushed cheeks, and moderate voice with varying vocal pitch equals "Happy". A frown with an elevated pitch and raised voice equals "Angry."

That didn't work out well either, as she discovered that social cues varied widely between people. What she interpreted as "Happy" in one person might actually be "Sarcastic" or "Excited" in another, and what seemed like "Angry" might actually be classified as "Frustrated" or "Passionate."

So she did what she was faced with most problems.

She solved it with science.

She created Indra

Growing up at Bolgatty House, her mother's ancestral house, in Palaghat, Kerala, her early childhood was difficult, with most of the household unsure of how to deal with her. Having lost her mother when she was born and her father away most of the time, building up ZyraCorp, she grew up with her brother and maternal grandparents. With her bouts of silence and her habit of repeating seemingly random words, she confounded most people.

Then there were the temper tantrums coupled with the head banging.

Regular schools being out of the question, Zyana's grandparents resorted to home schooling, and even then, the teachers had given up on her. Despite their best efforts, they couldn't get her to follow seemingly simple instructions like repeating the alphabet or numbers after them.

The general consensus was that she was mentally deficient or more cruelly 'Stupid'.

As the daughter of the founder and CEO of ZyraCorp, Striber Contractor, she was looked down upon with pity and even considered 'Bad Luck' as her mother had died giving birth to her and her brother Ramin.

The fact that she preferred to spend time looking at old books on varied subjects including physics, biology, coding, and astronomy was considered just another one of her quirks.

Nobody at Bolgatty house believed that she could read, let alone understand, the books she spent time with.

It didn't help that her twin brother Ramin was the exact opposite.

Intelligent, handsome, and charming, he had a way with people right from childhood that led to the inevitable comparison between the two.

Once Zyana's prodigious affinity for technology was noted, however, her father took over her education. Shri Striber, rather than focusing on a typical school education, instead gave Zyana unfettered access to his library and to the lab that he used at Bolgatty house when he stayed over.

Using the earlier prototypes of the Peripheral her father had left in his lab, she had modified it to listen to conversations and the onboard camera to analyse facial expressions and body language in real-time. Tweaking the source code of the self-learning modules, she had it analyse the tons of user-uploaded videos from VidMe and categorise them based on the emotions expressed, body language and other social cues.

Initially relying on audio cues and using a comparison algorithm of her own design, Zyana validated her real-world view with the fledgling database of the VidMe analysis and got feedback in words.

Her grandparents, already used to her oddities, weren't too shocked to see her walking around the house with the headset on. What they were surprised with was her responses, though.

For the first time in their lives, they were actually able to have a proper conversation with her.

Her responses were still odd and misplaced at times, but compared to the monosyllabic responses in the past, they would settle for anything.

Spurred by her success, Zyana didn't waste any time opening up the module to the internet and having it learn with the worldwide dataset; it has only been expanding ever since.

It was her father's idea to name it Indra.

With the success of ZyraCorp's Peripheral, it wasn't unusual for a child to walk around town with the head unit. So, with Indra's expanded database, Zyana was able to step out into the real world and visit the town, first accompanied by Ramin and then on her own.

Finally independent, she moved on to her next goal: to join her parents' alma mater, the National Institute of Science and Maritime Studies at Bhubaneswar. When, at 9, she became the youngest ever to join the prestigious institute, her father had mapped her future with ZyraCorp until she finally ended up as the head of the company's R&D division.

Still relying on Indra, Zyana has made multiple enhancements to Indra over the years, including a personality module, among other things.

Lately, however, with all her focus on Runtastic, she hadn't prioritised fixing some niggling bugs with Indra. She wasn't sure why just yet, but ever since Zyana added the claytronic module, Indra's personality module seemed to be wavering between multiple personalities quite rapidly. Personally unvexed by the rapid flicker of the holographic display while Indra shifted personas, she had, however, been asked by the VP of HR personally to turn it off as it was freaking everybody else out.

The voices still changed, though, which did not bother Zyana as she filtered out irrelevant information.

Probably just the module settling in.

Zyana made a mental note to check it sometime later. However, she didn't ask Indra to add it to the schedule. She wasn't sure why but Zyana had the odd thought that Indra may actually not like it.

That's silly. She is just a program. It's not like she would really care.

Unbeckoned, a voice that sounded like her father asked, " Then why do you keep referring to Indra as *she?*"

Indra would have called the feeling Zyana felt '*Puzzled*'if asked to put a label against it.

Indra chimed in again, this time in the nasal drone of a college lecturer. "Ramin has asked if he could bring in his visitors for a tour of the R&D labs. ".

Upon their father's death, both brother and sister took over the reins of Zyracorp and divided the company's responsibility between them. Zyana looked after the technical side of ZyraCorp, and Ramin managed everything else.

This suited Zyana perfectly, as she still preferred to keep social contact to a minimum in spite of Indra, instead spending most of her time at the various ZyraCorp labs worldwide.

Ramin, on the other hand, appointed himself CEO and revitalised the company, expanding into a wide range of new ventures, including entertainment, social media, and tech, all with great success. A lot of it was based on technology created and developed by Zyana and her team.

By unspoken agreement, both siblings remained solely within their respective areas of responsibility. Zyana did not interfere in the company's day-to-day operations, and the labs were her territory. Which meant that

OUTSIDERS WERE NOT ALLOWED HERE.

Closing the locker after placing the suit back in Zyana ensured the locks were engaged.

The labs were her safe space, and she would not have it violated.

"Is Ramin here today, and who are these VIPs?" inquired Zyana with timber in her voice.

"He flew in this morning, lah; based on his calendar, he is meeting with Sentential Corporation in the War Room. It looks like he is planning on heading to the lab straight after. Do you want me to buzz him?" asked Indra.

Zyana hadn't seen Ramin for months now, as she never needed to, but this was something she could not ignore.

"I think it's time we pay my brother a visit," said Zyana.

| 4 |

Heeriye / Teardrop

The electric car cut through the humid city air like a hot knife through butter.

The Gondi Electrode was one of the older models that were solely battery-backed and were from a time when solar panels weren't standard features in cars. Tara's final destination was a relatively short 50Kms, yet she wondered whether her car would be able to make it. These old cars were hardy and reliable, but the batteries did have a tendency to die fairly quickly. When she asked the car if it was safe, she was assured that it was last serviced 4 months ago, but as she could hardly make out what it said over the static of its speakers, she wasn't exactly reassured.

The car's air conditioner was functioning, but it smelt like the air filter hadn't been cleaned, and the slight whiff of mould was starting to annoy her. She asked the car to open its windows, even though it meant that she had to endure the humidity and heat. The Monsoons had begun here, and even at this time of night, the July heat had barely loosened its grip.

The car pulled up at a traffic light just off the Agra Fort, which offered her a view of the Yamuna River. However, now she had to put up with the smell of sewage from the industrial runoffs into the river.

Even at this time, she could hear the deep thump of the latest Balti EDM from the Yoga rave at a nearby club where young 20-somethings did Ext yoga, stretching and contorting their bodies under the influence of various semi-legal or illegal stims. As she watched, a jeep filled with traffic constables headed towards the club with their sirens turned off. Raves usually had regular visits from cops, officially for welfare checks, but really because the rich yuppies who usually frequented them were always good for some low-risk pocket money.

She was starting to sweat, and considering the lesser of two evils, Tara said

"Temperature to 22, high breeze",

The car immediately complied, with the windows closing and the air conditioner ramping up as requested. Tara could feel the sweat dry on her face, and she reached into the nearby glove compartment to grab a tissue. The box was empty, and judging by the dust accumulated on top of it, it didn't look like it had been replaced for a while.

"God damn apartment and its cheap-sake maintenance contractors." she purposely said aloud so that the feedback would be registered as a complaint back to building management. The ETA on the screen was another 10 minutes so Tara brought up the call report and connected with the constable onsite.

A face she didn't recognise popped up on the holo-vid in the palm of her hand. In spite of the officer's face dominating most of the display, Tara could still make out the dense forest in the background. He appeared to be the only police officer on the scene, and she could make out the tell-tale white and blue of the Medi-evac VTOL in the background. The constable looked haggard with bags under his eyes and, with a servile smile, adopted to address senior officers.

"Vanakam Ji", he greeted Tara. You officer coming to a dead body?" asked the constable in halting Manglish.

Tara nodded. " I will be there in 10 minutes. "

The constable continued rattling off in Hindi, which the translated subtitles on the call deciphered to mean that his Manglish is limited, but yes, he will wait for her.

"Park near Hanuman statue, and I meet you here." the constable signed off and sent her the updated coordinates. The car automatically adjusted accordingly, helpfully pointing out that it would be unable to go all the way through. The terrain was muddy, and it recommended protection, which she didn't have. She sent a note to the constable to keep a pair of shoeguards ready for her, and he assured her that he would.

The vehicle parked just off the edge of the road, close to either an abandoned or badly maintained temple with a large Hanuman statue clearly visible from the road.

The statue must have been impressive when it was first built but was not looked after, like most things here. The paint was already starting to flake, and a long strip of skin-brown paint peeled off from the forehead and fluttered in the warm night air.

As promised, the constable was waiting for her with a pair of shoe guards held high in his hand.

As soon as she got out, he gave a weary salaam. "My good name Yadav. I on-duty constable. Pleased to meet you," said the constable in a rush, just as he had rehearsed before she arrived.

Arms outstretched, he presented the shoeguards to her with a light bow at his hips." For you, Tara Shri."

Tara nodded and took the shoeguards from his outstretched hand. She put on the clear plastic wraps, rolling them all the way to the top of her knees, running her hands over them to get rid of the last of the bubbles. She stood up with a grunt cracking her back.

She didn't bother covering her arms, though. Mosquitoes had been officially eradicated years ago thanks to genetic engineering turning them impotent here and most of the world. There were still other insects, though, and something whined past her ears. She shuddered with the ghost pain of old mosquito bites and memories of bloody arms and legs.

The world had changed a lot since her childhood, but unlike some things, she didn't miss mosquitoes.

Now suitably protected, it was her turn to use an unfamiliar language as she turned to address the constable. "Kitne door hai?" she asked Yadav in her broken but serviceable Hindi.

With the ever-present servile smile, Yadav turned to look at her and with a puzzled look replied, "Door tho do he hai" and pointed helpfully at her vehicle raising 2 fingers to indicate the number of doors that her car had.

Tara shook her head and tried again. Her tongue, used to the curves and bends of her native Nagamese, was finding it hard to turn the other way for Hindi. "Kitne doore hai?" Tara asked again, this time repeating slowly, making sure she rolled her tongue. "How much further?" she added in Manglish for good measure.

This time, he understood her and put up his palm fully outstretched. "Phive minutes". He pointed further into the woods and beckoned her to follow. They started walking through the dense bushland adjoining the temple. This public property was cleared so long ago that the forest had sufficient time to reclaim this patch as its own. There was a small beaten path, though, that she could see. Even in the semi-darkness, she could still see the tell-tale signs of the boats that were dragged up to the shore through here.

Following Yadav, who led the way, Tara had to force herself to slow down to avoid banging into him.

5 minutes? More like 5 years the rate this guy is going.

With his shirt untucked and the bulge of his belly visible through ill-fitting pants, Tara couldn't help but feel a mild revulsion towards the man. Not through any fault of his own but merely because he quite resembled her own father, whom she hadn't seen since she moved out of home.

Being part of the elite cadet of officer detectives, she was used to the sharply dressed officers of her team, and she dressed accordingly as well. Tara always took great pride in her appearance, which was one of the few good habits she retained despite her bout of melancholy.

The constable, deferential to her authority, didn't seem to notice Tara's annoyance or chose to ignore it. Either way, the constable led her to the riverside to an area lit with a few portable flood lights. A number of fishermen were there who, despite the late hour and the police personnel around, continued to pack away their lift nets. She looked on as one of the fishermen walked on the narrow beams of the last remaining net, walking with practised assurance to the centre of the pole and collecting the catch for the day. The boats were all paddled up and closed within, and the rest of the nets were all tucked away.

Tara looked at her watch. Midnight on the dot. She had an hour before the scheduled rains.

Plenty of time to get this wrapped up.

Already, the farmers would have opened up their storage tanks and seeded the ground in anticipation. Tara hadn't stepped out of the house since her shift earlier yesterday and would have missed the Cloud seeders that had gone out earlier.

Looking up at the vapour trails of the seeder planes was something that Fasil made her do every time he spotted one.

Not now

On the other side of the river, she could see the tight bunch of residences that made up Habibyada Basti. This area of Agra couldn't be more different from the main city, peppered with refugee camps and ramshackle houses on their stilts just above the riverbank and the adjacent backwater. A multitude of rag pickers, shop attendants, servants, and the lower income strata of the general population lived here, making the daily commute to the city.

The poorest of the poor serving the richest of the rich.

Such is life as it always has been in the big city.

They arrived at the river bank, where the constable had cordoned off the area with the mandatory holographic barrier. However, it was not high enough to shield the scene from prying eyes, and even at this hour, a few of the fishermen were gaping around the barricade.

No one from the press or even a news drone was around. It may have been a slow news day, but a death in the Bastis didn't garner much interest for the press to send even a probe. The medi-evac VTOL was already parked nearby, and the sole occupant was stretched out on the front seat, fast asleep. With its foldable wings, the medi-evac van simply flew over here upon receiving the call, but even the rough landing wasn't enough to wake up the attendant, apparently.

Bludger.

Probably just waiting for me to sign off on the case so that he can call it a night.

Approaching the floodlit barricaded area, Tara saw a small figure covered in a white sheet.

The vein at the base of her neck throbbed, and suddenly, all she could smell was metal shavings.

Crossing the barricade, she slowly approached the body and gently removed the cover to reveal the dead girl's face. The girl was young, probably no more than 18. Her dark chocolate-coloured skin was haloed with thick, curly black hair. The pink heart-shaped upala embedded where her eyebrows met sparkled in the intrusive lighting.

The medi-evac attendant, sensing that Tara was around, woke up and walked up to her.

Without any introductions, he said in a half yawn. "Just got the scans confirmed, and it's a drowning. No unusual trauma or lesions. Significant brain damage but no more than what is expected from oxygen deprivation from drowning. Her peripheral port fried the rest of her brain."

Tara nodded and had a good, long look at the face of the dead girl. Angular and sunburnt, her skin had the typical green tinge of a typical Basti dweller. Her teeth were yellow, or at least the few that were left. Surprisingly, her clothes were well-made and relatively new. Wearing the solid palladium chain instead of the gold worn by a married Basti woman, it seemed that she was planning on settling down in the near future.

Putting on a pair of gloves, Tara knelt and reached out to grab the girl's chin so she could examine her face closer.

Palladium earrings with opals.

No nose ring so she wasn't married yet but was wearing enough for a bridal dowry so she was on the lookout for a preem suitable boy.

It looks like she even had a Peripheral Pro based on the port she saw just behind the ear.

Hmm interesting

A green scorpion tattoo just behind the ear.

A Siddi, huh?

Looking back at the medi-evac attendant, Tara asked if a drone scan had been done.

"A drone scan? For what? The girl obviously committed suicide. It happens all the time here. Abusive husbands, unpayable debt. Not enough money, don't know the reason, and don't care. " the medi-evac attendant said in exasperation.

This guy is really starting to lachuka her off.
"Ee Khajoor"
And out flew a stream of expletives that would have impressed even a Kappalottiya. It had the desired effect and, head cowed, the attendant ran back to the VTOL to initiate the scan.

She looked over the horizon. The fishermen pulled up a line of boats along the riverbank. While all the boats seemed alike, a green one on the right with 3 white stripes caught her attention. "Check out the area near the boats in particular."

The attendant hastily complied and, with a tap of a few buttons on his periband, deployed an investigative drone, which scanned the area and sent the data back to the medi-evac. Reading the screen, he said to Tara. "Nothing unusual apart from the usual beach biosignatures, crabs, fish.

"Wait a minute.

"Looks like there is something next to the boat.

"I can't be sure, but it looks like a biochip is just over there."

He helpfully pointed it out on the screen in front of her.

Tara looked up to make a note of the location in the real and proceeded to walk towards the source of the alarm. She had worn her old brown loafers scuffed with age, not because she planned to get wet and dirty but because fieldwork usually gets messy, and she liked to be prepared. Still protected by the shoe guards, her shoes weren't in any danger of getting wet, but she was getting annoyed by the squelching sounds her feet made while walking on the wet sand.

The constable following behind her didn't seem to mind the wetness, though he seemed to struggle and followed behind her at a slow, shambling pace.

Walking briskly along the shore, Tara quickly reached the boat and waited impatiently for the constable to catch up.

Huffing, he knelt with both hands on his knees and massaged them gently.

With a wave of sympathy, Tara realised.

He is all-natural.

Though he clearly needed them, Yadav didn't seem to have any Extrexs.

Then she saw the black thread necklace and the pendant with a silver scallion that had popped out of his open shirt while he bent down.

Of course, he is a Nareshukaran.

Tara internally shook her head at their ridiculous requirement that their followers shun Exts, as it would corrupt the perfect design. So as not to embarrass the man, she turned and gingerly got down on one knee next to his body.

Using her lathi, she carefully poked and prodded at the marked location, leaving craters like mini sand dunes.

She stopped when she hit something solid. Gently scraping away the surrounding sand, Tara extracted an object half-buried in the sand.

Now flat on the beach, It appeared to be an ID card of some sort.

Yadav helpfully shined a light on the card, which revealed the logo of ZyraCorp and a shy photo of the girl on the beach. The name on the employee card read 'Vaishali Churahi'.

Still wearing her gloves, Tara cleared away the last of the sand and carefully placed the card in a transparent clear bag. Kneeling, the cold, damp sand formed a patch of wetness that was already spreading across the knee, but now concentrating, she didn't seem to mind it and was instead focused on the card.

Pressing her peripheral, she called the control room. With the trial of the Badda Bhai, they were supposed to have increased access to the ZyraCorp personnel files. Protocol should still be followed, however, and she made the request through the correct channels.

"Check on Vaishali Churahi, ' ZyraCorp employee," and she rattled off whatever details she could read on the ID Card.

Almost immediately, her Citizen details, including her last known address, were sent to Tara's peripheral. There were no red flags, and there was no police record.

There also wasn't a ZyraCorp employee record.

That's weird, considering that she is holding Vaishali's pass in her hand.

Tara called the control station again and asked them to run her name through all the databases, including restricted records. This will flag it for supervisor approval, but hopefully, it will come through as a priority.

The operator acknowledged and promised to get back to her as soon as possible.

She looked at Yadav and, pointing to the fishermen, said. "Move those guys back from the barricade and find out what they know." The constable nodded and started heading towards the onlooking fishermen still lingering around.

Not that she was expecting much from them with the questioning. If they were members of the same chawl, they would be as distrustful of the police as the rest of them, and without a solid lead, they would unlikely to be helpful.

The real reason she had sent him away was because she needed some time alone for what she was going to do next.

Tara closed her eyes and listened.

She could hear it all now.

The water lapping on the shore, the mingled conversations of Yadav and the fishermen.

She closed her eyes and did a gentle wave of her hands.

Like the volume button on an old television set, the background noise turned to a hum.

"*Breathe now, breathe.*

Breathe deeper and slower.

Ride the wave."

It rose as it always does, and a rose bloom of pain shot from the back of her throat and hit her just between the eyes.

Tara looked at the fishermen with a slow and pondering gaze. Puzzled, some of them returned her gaze with a look that was part fear and part curiosity.

There were 5 remaining onlookers still remaining behind the barricade.

Looking at them, one by one, they all started to fade until the one on the right, slightly behind the others, stood out in a halo of purple. It was a boy, a lot younger than the rest of the other men standing by. Looking straight at him, Tara stood up and followed the constable to the onlookers. The boy, seeing that he had been noticed, bowed his head to avert her gaze and shuffled a fit, digging craters in the sand. Without taking her eyes off, she walked straight to him till she was right in front of the boy. Lifting up the transparent bag, she dangled it in front of his face and asked, "Do you know her?"

Almost immediately, an older man in a white vest beside him interceded and said, "He is just a boy; he doesn't know anything. We don't know anything."

The father or maybe an uncle,

Tara guessed. She noted that the old man had unwrapped his green cloth headband and was now gripping it so tightly it had already started to chaff his sea-leathered hands. The sudden outburst was not a shout of indignity but rather a plea for mercy. Though annoyed, Tara understood and ignored the man.

The old man had enough run-ins with the law to understand that Tara was an Impath Police officer.

With all the stories and rumours around about IPS officers, the old man didn't know for sure what was fact and what was fiction but the one thing he did know was that an Impath could always glean their answers. Unlike many rumours, Impaths can't read minds, but they do have 'oohams'. Visible manifestations of intuition, oohams can, like case in point, show the best person to answer her queries.

Not all Impath officers were kind, as empathy was not a requirement for being one. While oohams could point them in the right direction, Impaths may not necessarily know how the person they gleaned would be able to help, and the true skill of the Impath officer is in coaxing their answers out of them. Even from those who are not even aware that they have information that would be helpful. Talking works but takes skill and time, which a lot of the IPS officers don't have the patience or the knack for.

Fear, however, is a great motivator and often quite effective. Their reputation for resorting to extreme interrogation tactics, which included regular beatings and even torture, was unfortunately quite justified.

With a sharp glance, Tara told the man to shut up and step away. The constable was taken by surprise by her sudden burst of anger, but his years of experience took over, and he followed suit in separating the boy from the rest of the group. Looking directly at the boy, she continued.

"I asked if you knew her.'

The boy, head still bowed, nodded and dug craters into the sand. "Her name is Vaishali. We used to go to school together. She used to live at the Nicobarese Chawl next door. I haven't seen her in real for a while, though."

Head still bowed he continued to stare at the ground bashfully. Tara could see his eyes were red.

He didn't just know her; he cared about her.

Softening her tone, she placed her hand on the boy's arm and said, "Come with me."

The boy looked up, not at her but at the man who had spoken up earlier. She didn't have to look at the man's face to know that it would be a sign to keep quiet; it was written all over the boy's face. Ignoring the old fisherman, she guided the boy further away from prying eyes.

Gently, she asked him, " What do you know about her?"

Reassured with her kindness, he replied, "Vaishali was always very nice. Sweet girl but not very bright. She couldn't even finish school when she had to work when her dad ran out of her. Just her mom and sisters now.

"Badda badda dreams she had though. Be a home nurse, move to the city, earn lots of money and take her family away. Last I heard, she was heading to the city to work as a drone tech at Agra Fort, but she must have landed on something solid.

"I follow her on FlipFlop, and she posted her gains recently. Some of the stuff was serious, like hectic, paisa Shri. I thought she may even have had a stim business on the side, but she is a paavam Shri, and everything looked ekdam pukka legit. I even tried to get some deets on what she did exactly but it was solid chupa-chupa. Not a word. "

The boy smiled, remembering Vaishali as she once was, and wistfully said. "She was happy, happier than I have seen her in a long time. Guess it was all duha."

Tara nodded, "So she got a new job. Do you know what she was doing at ZyraCorp?"

"Oath?" yelped the boy. "Shri, are you telling me that Vaishali was working at ZyraCorp? I had no idea. Don't you need like big, big degrees to work over there?

"Respira rained on that one if she got herself in there. Maybe you can check with her chawl.", and he flicked the details across to Tyra.

Tara nodded and watched as the purple halo around the boy disappeared. The ooham was gone, and she had gotten as much as she could out of him.

She walked back to Vaishali's body. Yadav had done a good job and had cleared the onlookers well back. She knelt down next to the girl and looked at her more closely. Something quite familiar about her, although with her lack of a police record, it was unlikely that their paths would have crossed.

Tara furtively looked around. The medi-evac attendant had gone back to his seat and slept off, and Yadav was still near the fishermen.

Reaching down, she unhooked the palladium chain earrings from Vaishali. If they were officially signed in, they would somehow disappear somewhere down the chain of custody, and the family would forever be told that it was lost in bureaucratic paperwork. There would be trouble if she were caught, but she suddenly felt that she had to return the jewellery to Vaishali's family, and lately, she has been trying to listen to her feelings more. Quietly pocketing the jewellery, Tara headed to the medi-evac and tapped the window with her lathi.

The attendant woke up with annoyance, but his face betrayed fear when he saw it was her and sheepishly got out of the vehicle. Tara wasn't in the mood, but she did enjoy the power trip her position occasionally afforded her, especially when she felt they deserved it.

"Next Time," she said curtly and snatched the report pad. Reviewing the report, she signed off on it and told the attendant to make sure the body was flagged for priority clearance. He did so and told her that it would be dropped off at the Hajong Chowk mortuary.

She beckoned to Yadav, and together, they began the trek back to their vehicles. Upon reaching the main road, Yadav assured her that he would get the local officers to clear up the barricades and lights in the morning. After waving goodbye, he headed back home to his wife and kids.

In no hurry to rush home and not sure what to do next, Tara knelt against the hood of the car and checked her messages. She had left it on 'silent' before heading out to the riverbank and may have missed something. No personal messages but she did get an alert that her requisition for information on Vaishali had not just been assigned but was currently being processed by a senior officer.

That's odd

While urgent requests were processed immediately by the on-call gazetted officers, usually junior Assistant Superintendent of Police, who were the lowest in the police hierarchy, standard requests were only processed during the day as business-as-usual requests.

Tara was startled by the beep on her peripheral. Calls at this hour can't be good, but she was more surprised as she was sure it was still left on silent.

It was an I-priority call, which meant that this was no ordinary call or mis-dial. Bypassing all activities on devices and contactable even if the device was switched off, the I-priority call was meant to be used only by authorised agencies during emergencies. Like all privileges assigned to officers, however, senior officials on a power trip abused this feature, which was often used to contact subordinates.

A stern-faced man appeared on the screen. "Tara can't say it is a pleasure."

Damn it. Why did it have to be Deepak, of all people? What the hell does he want?

Deepak Groma was the Deputy Inspector General of her team, but their history went further than just in an official capacity, and it wasn't amicable. Trying to hide her displeasure as much as she could, Tara said "Namaste, Deepak Shri, what can I do for you? "

She could see Deepak had just woken up—or rather, had been woken up. "What's this case that you are working on now? I heard you have been making some inquiries into ZyraCorp about a death at the bastis?".

"It was a routine inquiry Shri. We found a ZyraCorp ID Card of the dead girl we found," replied Tara formally.

Deepak actually smiled and, with an attempt of comradery, said, "Abe Yaar, close it out as soon as possible. It's just another suicide case. Now is not the time to cause waves with ZyraCorp. We are about to officially launch 'Badda Bhai', and we don't want the bad press. I have already received word that she was a temporary volunteer in one of their charity programs. She was given an ID card, but the employee records of the volunteers are not kept on file."

Rather than be mollified, this annoyed Tara even more. None of her interactions with Deepak had ever been pleasant, let alone friendly. She protested, "I think there is more to this Shri, with all due respect. She had a full-level ID card with a biochip implant. Surely, that is not something that you would provide volunteers."

Deepak scowled." How drunk are you?

The remark stung. She hated his judgmental voice and the dismissive way he assumed she was drunk. The fact that she actually had been drinking didn't make it sting any less.

"I told you to drop it. How ZyraCorp spends its money is up to them. Just do your lachuka job. Sign off on the medical report and close the case. Have I made myself clear?" Deepak threatened.

Refusing to show that he got to her, Tara nodded, saluted, and waited for the call to be terminated.

Chutiya Sala,

Do my lachuka job, it seems. That's all I have been doing all my life, and look where that got me.

How the badre did he get involved in this?

The more Tara thought about it, the angrier she felt, till she was on the verge of hyperventilating in fury.

Just drop it, like he was scolding her like a puppy dog caught with a slipper in its mouth.

Who does he think he is?

She was pissed.

Shanegeika pissed.

She didn't think it was simply Deepak who had called her or if it was something about Vaishali, but she decided that she was NOT going to drop it.

Do my lachuka job huh?

Well you did ask me to sign off on the medical report which requires consent from family if known. Got those deets right here.

I chose to go see them in person, so I thought I'd give it a personal touch rather than a standard vmail.

Did some idle chatter, you know, community building and all that PR badre you go on about.

They mentioned some interesting details that you know could require further investigation.

It could take a while, but hey

Just doing my job, lachukabadre.

Closing her eyes, she placed her hand just above her heart and bowed.

A halo of gold formed just above her heart, covering her hand.

She smiled then and was still smiling when the skies opened up and the promised rains fell.

She looked at the time.

1:13 AM.

Looks like she is not the only one who is in a contrary mood.

| 5 |

Kalippu / Overcompensate

Hidden away from the main road, tourists rarely ventured to this part of the Mannar market, and Karthik could only see locals around.

As the name indicated, Bikram Lane was a small alleyway, just wide enough to allow a narrow walkway between the rows of shops lined up along the path. Walking down, Karthik ended up in a wide agora with a massive banyan tree in the centre.

He headed to a shop that simply said "Rashid Trading Limited" in white letters. The sign was old, with blocks of dead LEDs, and offered no other clues as to what services it actually provided. It looked just like any of the other shops lining up the agora, except for a number of burly men who appeared to be casually lounging about the front of the shop. More suited to a powerlifting competition, they looked out of place in the dusty alleyway.

Most of the locals, knowing goondas when they see them, stayed as far away from them as possible. Their arms sleeved in traditional kurtas, Karthik knew that all of them would be sporting Extrexs, although the goondas did make the effort to have them covered up.

Initially developed for medical rehabilitation, Extrexs were bionic exoskeletons that were originally designed to allow paraplegics to walk again. The revolutionary design was created by no less than Striber Contractor, the founder of ZyraCorp, and was the first product of the then-fledgling company. While exoskeletons by itself wasn't a new idea, the previous models were large, clunky, and prone to failure. Combined with its exorbitant costs, traditional exoskeletons were out of reach of most people, even the most desperate.

The first released version of Extrex was a tenth of the size and weight of the older exoskeletons and, with a self-learning interface, was able to adapt itself to a wide range of paraplegics. While still expensive, thanks to the good news stories of successful candidates that frequently went mirchi on social media, its popularity spread. Under pressure from the public, they were soon subsided by the government, which led to the first government contracts being assigned to ZyraCorp to supply them en masse.

Recognising the potential in the commercial market, ZyraCorp further developed the technology for civilian use. As with all innovative technology, plenty of competitors soon entered the marketplace, offering faster, stronger arms and legs with various attachments at multiple price points, available at a store near you.

While still a trademark of ZyraCorp, as the release of Extrex spawned an entirely new industry, most people still refer to all variations of exoskeletons as Extrex or Ext for short.

Today, Exts can either fully replace lost limbs, augment existing limbs, or integrate with bionic implants to create seamless, powerful enhancements.

While it has become commonplace to see civilians with cybernetic limbs and other wearables, there are still a significant number of holdouts, and not all of them are constrained by finance.

Karthik stopped in front of the store and made a point of seeing how many of the security features he could identify from the street. He could see the tiny glimmer of the cam scans on the eaves of the shopfront. The nozzles for the liquid foam shields were visible clearly. Able to spray powerful liquid riot cement, which rendered any target immobile on contact, he supposed they would likely be mistaken for water pipes to a casual observer.

However, though he knew they were there, he couldn't see the port holes for the EMP lasers, at least not in the visual spectrum. Capable of de-powering any electronic device, including Exts, unless they were heavily shielded, the EMP laser was an expensive but powerful addition to Agha Khan's defence system. Switching to a full spectrum scan, he could see them hidden inside the innocuous side pillars, but even now, he couldn't pick out any guns or lethal weapons.

Looks like Agha bhai was pretty serious about the 'No Guns' rule.

Good on him.

While he was in a dangerous profession and always ensured that he had sufficient protection, Agha Khan eschewed guns, considering them cowardly. He instead preferred to use goondas to deal with hostiles.

Karthik nodded appreciatively, proud to see his design brought to life. While he was the security consultant for the complete system, this was the first time that Karthik had actually been to Agha Khan's place upon his return to Mannar. Spending what he liked to call a wee bit of a vaccay at Kallapani, Karthik had just got out of the famed island prison. The consultation work that he had done for Agha Khan was done during the 2 years he was incarcerated.

Who better than a chor to stop a chor?

It had been weeks since he was out but Karthik was taking it easy in reaching out to old contacts. It wasn't his first time in jail, but while 2 years was the longest he had ever spent inside, it still wasn't long enough for some people.

LATER

He made his way to the entrance but was blocked by a goonda that seemed to be cruising for a bruising. At 6 feet, Karthik wasn't a short man, but the goonda towered over him, his powerful chest in line with the top of Karthik's head. His arms folded, the goonda looked down on at Karthik and flexed his biceps. Sharp lines of steel cables outlined itself against the massive sleeves of the kurta. Exts typically tend to be subtle, but Exts like these were designed for straight-up intimidation. The goonda knew his effect on people and smirked once he was sure that he got Karthik's full attention. Karthik, unfazed, however, looked straight into the eyes of the goonda, smiled, and just said

"Hutt".

Goondas are stereotyped as having more muscles than brains, and this specimen ticked every box on the list and then some. Unused to being talked back, it took a little while to register what Karthik said. It took him even longer to realise that far from intimidating him, Karthik was actually amused by this display of strength.

The rage that rose was quick, though, and the goonda's nose started to flare, with his cheeks reddening with anger. His already flexed arms thickened even more with his clenched fists, stretching his kurta till the sleeves were almost transparent. The next reaction was predictable, with the goonda unfolding his great hands for the inevitable punch-up.

Karthik waited till he had unfolded his arms before saying, " Agha Khan".

Hearing the name of his boss, the goonda's face now appeared puzzled and confused. His arms rose almost involuntarily but now hovered above Karthik's head, neither retreating nor proceeding any further. He blinked, and that's when Karthik realised how young the goonda really was. With his open, gaping mouth and his upraised arms, the goonda looked like a baby gorilla.

Laughing, a wiry old goonda walked up to Karthik, clapped him on his back and said, "Ente Monne, please don't muck about with the new recruits.

"That's our job."

He turned to the gorilla baby goonda and whipped his head to dismiss him, clearing the entrance for Karthik. " After you Shri" he said with a grand flourish of his hand. Karthik grinned and stepped inside the shop.

The first room he entered was small. Glass counters lined the walls like those in jewellery stores. An odd mixture of holodecks, boxed video games, and assorted gadgets was on display. The products, though branded, were old, and the packets were faded and sun-bleached. Nobody was behind the counter or the ancient cash register, and the shop appeared deserted.

Karthik knew, however, that if a visitor felt inclined to head deeper into the store, the shopfront would be manned quick-smart from the room behind, and further visits would be discouraged.

Without a hint of hesitation, he walked past the counter and through a curtain that hid the room inside. More of the muscled goondas were here, but unlike the ones in the front, they dropped any pretence of disinterest and headed straight to him.

"He is here to see Agha Khan", said a voice behind him. Karthik turned to see that the wiry goonda had followed him into the second room. A yellow-kurtaed goonda nodded and grunted, "No weapons," and pointed to the handy tray at the end of the room.

Karthik removed the 2 Valari hooked at the back of his belt and turned to face another goonda with the handheld scanner.

"Don't forget the Urumi." said the wiry goonda.

It was Karthik's turn to grunt, but without protest, he unhooked his Urumi from his waist. The flexible whip sword with graphene blades was thin and razor-sharp but sheathed in its leather scabbard could sometimes pass off as a thick belt. One of the hardest weapons to master in Kalari, it was over 6 feet long when fully extended. It was the last weapon taught to students, and very few actually mastered it.

The yellow kurtaed goonda, curious, said, "An Urumi? What's that?" and moved to open the blade.

"Don't you dare touch it," growled Karthik. However, even before Karthik could stop him, the wiry goonda smacked the hand of the yellow kurta and pointed to the motif etched into the blade's hilt.

A shield covering 2 crossed swords with a spear through the centre. An Urumi coiled around the shaft of the spear.

The wiry goonda said aloud, to the benefit of everybody in the room, "That's Ashaan Unniyarcha's mark. Only a true master would ever receive a Urumi from her. Treat it with respect. "

He hovered both hands above the weapon and touched the tips of his fingers to the corners of his eyes reverently. "I will see to it that these are untouched," he assured Karthik softly.

Nodding in acknowledgement, Karthik walked through the curtain to a corridor lit with bright LEDs that lined the edges. Walking to the end of the hallway, he waited in front of the reinforced titanium door until, with a buzz, the door swung outwards silently. The room he entered was huge in comparison to the tiny shopfront. It was still crowded, though, and every wall space was stacked with boxes of various tech: peripherals, Exts, and other wearable tech.

The rumour that Karthik heard was that Agha Khan's source was high up in ZyraCorp, and his gear was as preem as preem can get. However since there is always a risk of serious injury and even death with failed tech, Agha made it a point to quality control his goods before sending them out. This solidified his reputation in the market, and he was known as an honourable man.

Or at least honourable for a gangster.

The centre of the room was lined up with desks filled with Virtual stations. Scruffy operators sat in front monitoring and running various operations from crypto mining to casinos and strip clubs, as well as managing the Netscape markets where Agha Khan ran his trading business. A figure in a lime green kurta with slick black hair walked between the operators, watching them.

On the right, on a tech desk of his own, sat an imposing figure of Agha Khan. Old but still well-muscled, he was dressed in a crisp black kurta and vest. This contrasted against his full silver beard, which covered his chest like a coat, lovingly waxed and wrapped by Nanites into 3 braids. While selling everything a tech runner could want, Agha Khan himself did not have any 'Installs' or surgically installed Exts and instead preferred 'Remmies' or removable Exts. Agha Khan regularly had his Exts upgraded with the latest collabs and was fully up to date. While the constant refresh of technology would bankrupt most people, Agha Khan, from his line of legendary traders, was an astute businessman and had a thriving business selling his rejects along with legitimate ware on Netscape.

His Netscape shop was as different in appearance as his traditional shop and occupied square kilometres of virtual space. Leasing a place of that size would cost at least a million creds a year, but what most people didn't know was that Agha Khan actually owned the space outright. Karthik never figured out how he had managed this feat, and in a business where confidentiality and trust were the real currency, he didn't expect this to be an easy answer to find.

Agha didn't survive in this business by being an open book.

"Karthik, nice to finally meet you in the real. It must be pretty serious for you to come down to earth," Agha Khan said in a hearty, grandfatherly boom.

"Salaam Agha bhai. SBDD (Same Badre Different Day) replied Karthik.

Waving him to a chair in front of his desk, Agha Khan asked, "Can I interest you in a hydro or chai? I would recommend the tea. It's a blend of my own. Zero culture and pure homegrown."

Though he didn't want to, protocol had to be followed, and Karthik asked for the chai. Agha nodded, pressed his peripheral, and whispered into it, asking for the tea to be sent up.

Waiting for the tea, Karthik and Agha Khan talked about business and general soft topics, till a few minutes later, a young boy in a white kurta arrived with 2 piping hot cups of tea and a plate of coconut and cashew biscuits. Taking a cup, Karthik took a sip and continued to talk general pleasantries. Once his manners were made, Karthik brought up the subject at hand. "I need access to the ZyraCorp mainframes, Agha bhai."

Agha Khan didn't bat an eyelid and simply placed the empty cup on the table." I won't play games, Karthik and I won't bother asking you how you know that I have access to the Xyphor servers, but you should also know what my answer is going to be.

"You already know that access to the servers isn't easy to come by, and no matter how much I value the services provided by your troupe, this is not information that I can share. "

Nodding, Karthik took up his cup again to think of something else to convince him when Agha Khan abruptly stood up. "It was a pleasure, as always. Safe travels, beta. " Agha Khan bowed with palms folded.

Karthik wanted to protest but stopped with a single glance from Agha Khan. Being good-hearted wasn't the only way that Agha Khan had risen to where he is, and Karthik could feel the mettle of his iron will.

Taking that as his cue to leave, Karthik stood up and bowed in return. "And to you too, Shri," he said, his palms folded and stepped outside the room.

Collecting his weapons, Karthik found that the goonda was true to his word; his possessions were exactly as he had left them. He stepped out of the shop without even sparing a glance at the shamefaced bruiser slinking in the back.

Walking slowly away, he thought.

The oohams all pointed me here.

Did something change?"

Karthik was puzzled, which was an unusual feeling for him.

Walking a little ahead, Karthik waited until he was out of sight before taking out a small ceramic disc from his coat pocket. On one side was a simple spider similar to the one on his neck, and on the other, a crudely drawn crocodile.

"3," whispered Karthik before closing his eyes and flipping the disc. With his eyes still closed, he grabbed the coin mid-air and slapped it on the back of his right hand while covering it with his left.

He lifted his hand to reveal the picture of the spider.

Without changing his expression, he repeated this exercise 2 more times. Each reveal showed the spider. Allowing himself a wry smile, he waited at the entrance of the hallway.

Before long, the serving boy was hurtling past the agora into Bikram Lane. Karthik let out a low whistle to attract his attention. The boy stopped mid-sprint and turned and saw him. With recognition in his eyes, he waved and jogged towards Karthik. "You need to come with me, Shri", he panted.

Without another word, Karthik followed the boy back to the shop. This time, however, they skirted the main entrance and instead went to an enclosed door at the back. Having never been to this part of the building, Karthik followed the boy while he was led down a set of stairs to the basement below.

The room was small and looked like a workshop, with ragged kids working on benches. Among pieces of broken tech, there was a small assembly line of drones being made.

From a dark corner, a voice crooned. "Hello Karthik," they said

Out of the shadows walked the figure in the lime green kurta and stepped up to Karthik. "You are a Banjara, aren't you?"

The sentence, more of a statement than a question, didn't seem to require any validation, so Karthik nodded. "Yes, I am ."

Sighing, they said, "So the legends must be true. I always thought it was just a bedtime story, but when the kids found out it was a Banjara girl who disappeared this time, I knew something like this would happen.

"The cops signed the missing children as runaways, but I just knew that the Banjaras would take care of their own."

"Next thing I know, a Banjara has come down looking to access the ZyraCorp mainframe.

"You, Banjara and the lengths you would go to look out for your family

"Pah!!."

Karthik nodded gravely and instead gestured them to continue. He actually had no idea who they were talking about, but as always, he just went with the flow.

Zarg continued, " You don't look like an easy man to please, but oooh, don't we love it when they play hard to get?

"I may have just the thing to impress you."

With a flip of a manicured pair of hands in black nail polish, they presented their hands," You can call me Zarg", they introduced themselves to him. "Charmed, I am sure." they said with an upturn of a pointy nose

With a bemused smirk on his face, Karthik did a mock bow and placed their hand against his forehead. Still amused, he said, "And does Agha Khan know that his only grandchild is going behind his back to help out a complete stranger?"

Pouting, Zarg dismissed the question with a wave of a hand "Ohh, that old fuddy can go brew some tea or something. He spends more time growing the damn things than spending time on dhanda.

"And before you ask, don't worry—I am not going to jeopardise him by using his precious ZyraCorp mainframe codes.

"There are many ways to peel a banana, eh? "winked Zarg with a salacious wink of their mascaraed eyelashes.

"Alright, and what would you like in return?", asked Karthik stoically as possible.

Zarg pondered, "Let me think about it. This will actually be more fun than work. Ohh wee, penetrating ZyraCorp defences. I was getting a bit bored.".

Pointing a slender finger straight at him, Zarg continued "You. You I find you interesting.

"Tell you what. I will do this for an original audio cassette of Krantiveer, the limited edition cover with Priya in her slinky black dress and glam headdress.

"On second thought, get me the headdress. No, not the original, but a high-end replica would do

"Get the ones that Sakachep do; they're tolerably accurate.

"Darling man, you know, I met him once.

"Wonder where the original dress is?

"It's probably with some old hack, Mami, who is 20 lipos from ever being able to fit it into it ever again ."

Zarg paused in a huff when Karthik raised one hand with bemused irritation." Deal. I will get you the headdress and the audio cassette," Karthik agreed.

Zarg pouted. " Well, how rude, but I am going to look fabulous, so you are forgiven."

A knock on the door interrupted them, and in walked a bunch of street kids carrying bags. Karthik recognised the kids who were selling the drones in front of the jet port. The older kid approached Zarg and said excitedly, ' Got 3 today, ji,' and held out 3 tiny discs in the palm of his hand.

"Come to Mama!!!" Zarg yelled out and, ignoring Karthik, rushed to grab the discs off the boy.

Grabbing one of the ring discs, they dropped it into the receptacle in front of a workstation and got to work.

"Let's see what we got," Zarg said, their excitement palatable.

Being able to view the screen, Karthik could see a mobility scooter with a huge man in a familiar pineapple shirt. The view was odd, though; Karthik seemed to be looking up at the man though he was already seated in a scooter.

They hacked the Akimbo!! Karthik realised with a start.

How did they do that? He wondered quietly.

Like one professional magician breaking down the performance of another, Karthik tried to figure out how exactly they had done it. "The app was legit. The man had validated the app from the Appstore." The app was certified and next to impossible to hack, at least with the resources that he could see.

"Then they interfaced the drones to the Akimbo and let it control it".

The drones!!!

With a start, Karthik realised what they had done. While the app itself was legit, when the drones had interfaced with the Akimbo, it was a direct connection between the droids and the Akimbo. Zarg had used the drones to drop a payload into it and must have then been able to access a backdoor into its operating system.

That was all they needed to be granted full remote access to it.

Kollam, nodded Karthik to himself, impressed.

"Alright, boys and girls, time to go shopping", Zarg said aloud, and using the online Akimbo store, Zarg moved to the user-created sections. The crowd of boys and girls had dropped everything they were doing and now gathered behind Zarg watching the screen intently.

On the Akimbo marketplace, a number of modules were available for sale. Created by Akimbo owners they were pretty basic that would make the Akimbo do simple routines like dance to the latest 'FlipFlop' craze. Usually only worth about a cred or 2, they were quite popular among the Akimbo user communities.

Zarg selected a couple of modules listed by a user named "Chakazz420." Unlike most of the other modules available, these modules were quite expensive, with some listed at up to 1,000 creds. With a flurry of finger movements on the holo keyboard, Karthik watched while Zarg purchased the expensive modules one by one. He couldn't see how many modules Zarg ended up buying, but it was a pretty significant amount till they hit the limit and couldn't buy anymore.

Moving to another screen, Zarg logged into the Akimbo user store again. Having a better view of this screen, Karthik could clearly see the user name listed in the upper right-hand corner of the screen.

"Chakazz420"

After transferring all the funds out of the account, Zarg shut down the account and, with a whoop, raised both hands in the air. "In, out, and sploosh. Payday, boys and girls !! They yelled out.

The crowd of onlookers cheered, whooped and danced around.

Karthik looked up and said, "That's a pretty decent drain. They are going to be seriously lachuchaed."

Zarg's face hardened for the first time and he could see the mettle of Agha Khan behind the makeup. Gesturing to the boy who had brought in the discs, they said. "Those Akimbos cost enough to feed Mohit and his family over there for more than a year. Yet they get rid of them every time some limited edition derpie vid crossover comes out.

"If they can afford to do that. They can afford to do some dieting."

Karthik nodded, commiserating. "Alright. Let me know when you can have it done."

Zarg's face curled into a smirk again. "Darling for you no foreplay. Send me the deets. I will start tonight. "

Turning with a tip of his hat, Karthik walked back into the street, allowing himself the ghost of a smile.

I think it's time for a Biriyani.

| 6 |

Calm Down / The Ritual

Well, that's 15 minutes of my life. I am not getting back. thought Ramin Contractor as he watched the bespectacled Mahesh run through the slides of his detailed pitch in the conference room at the ZyraCorp head office.

From where Ramin sat behind his desk, he couldn't see his employee's shoes, but he knew they would be black and polished to a sheen. Mahesh's dark green kurta was acceptable as well, and while it was edged with sequins, it wasn't outlandish like a wedding suit.

The turban was blue, though.

Ramin didn't like that.

He heard a rumour that some of the staff on the 23rd floor ran a side hustle called 'Pitch Perfect", where, for a fee, they would review potential pitchers just before they were due to present in front of him. Pitch Perfect had apparently analysed every aspect of successful pitches, from the layout of the slides to the pitcher's clothes down to favourable Augs. Based on their detailed analysis they boasted a commendable success rate and even provided a bio-encoded report.

Pity Mahesh here didn't think of availing those services.

Having secretly read various iterations of the reports, he knew that much of the information was random or factually incorrect. However, Ramin deliberately didn't bother to correct them or even acknowledge to anyone that he had already seen the reports himself.

Ramin loved having an air of mystery around him.

Pitch Perfect and the lengths his employees would go to get this approval, was another interesting factoid that would undoubtedly be included in his biography when it eventually gets written.

One thing that they amazingly got right was his dislike for blue turbans. He disliked neither the colour blue nor turbans themselves, but a blue turban instantly put him off. Ramin, a man of sculpted thoughts, didn't consider this something worth pondering and just noted this as another aspect of himself.

Mahesh, the pitcher, droned on. Having already reviewed the presentation previously, Ramin was aware that it was not even halfway through, with just a minute left in the allocated time slot.

He could see that Mahesh was also aware of this, and beads of sweat had formed on his ample forehead.

Damn, look at his physique. It's like he doesn't even know what exercise is.

Why the hell did I provide a gym if these guys can't use it once in a while?

I bet he doesn't even go to the sauna. Look at the pores.

Oh god. Why the hell did I agree to this meeting? I should get Sarita to raise the bar even higher.

Either sensing Ramin's impatience or simply being mindful, Mahesh skipped over the remaining slides and pulled up the summary.

Mahesh stammered, "So as you can see, just by donating 1% of the annual charity budget to the 'Educate the Adivasi's at home' campaign, you can reduce their current rate of poverty by 27% within five years, after which we project exponential increases. "

Ramin, looking down silently, smirked.

He should have done his research. The Adivasis live in Gantrapradesh. With the government incentives to start a new factory already maxed out, there would be no additional tax offsets that they could gain by investing any further over there.

Sigh. Let them down easy.

Ramin rose, clapping his hands, and walked straight to Mahesh. "Waah!! Such a noble pitch. People who come here usually pitch ideas for new revenue streams, but you have asked for funding that will change these disadvantaged people's lives forever.

"Such an action is to be commended . This is what Zyra-Corp stands for.

"For the betterment of mankind. For humanity.

"Send this straight to the VP of Strategies. I will personally discuss this with him and get him to give this pitch the attention it requires.

"I expect great things from you, Mahesh. Ideas like yours drive this company in the direction it needs to head.

"You have an interesting future ahead of you here at ZyraCorp."

Ramin smiled broadly, and Mahesh's response was almost immediate, with the fawning expression he was used to from his underlings. Ramin knew that he was already considered a legend within the corporate world, especially with his reputation for being down to earth.

Case in point where a lowly desk jockey could pitch an idea to the CEO of ZyraCorp

What a magnanimous leader I am.

Still in awe, Mahesh slowly extended his hand out in farewell to Ramin.

Ramin did not like that.

Ramin really, REALLY did not like it.

Another minor fact that they included in the reports was his apparent reluctance to shake hands. They got that bit right, too.

It happens sometimes but with the strength of will that made him the beast that he is today, without any change in his facial expression, Ramin reached out and shook Mahesh's hand and looked up and smiled.

Mahesh had the shocked look of awe that Ramin had gotten used to by now.

At least this one didn't swoon at the knees.

Gently releasing himself from the vice-like grip, Ramin patted Mahesh and, with his other hand on the small of Mahesh's back, gently nudged him out of the office.

Shutting the door close, Ramin took a moment to compose himself.

Breathing deeply, he ignored the throbbing in his mind.

FILTH/FILTH/FILTH

and instead tried to divert his mind to other thoughts

Another tech evangelist who will be telling that story to everybody he has met for years now.

The day he shook Ramin Contractors' hand.

The loser will probably be on his deathbed telling his grandchildren about this day.

Poor sod really shouldn't have tried to shake his hand, though.

Actions have consequences.

Out loud, Ramin said " Send a note to George1. Mahesh Ahirani, Accounting, List 420."

"Yes, Ramin ", replied the voice gently from everywhere in his room.

Within seconds, a draft email addressed to George Dzongkha, his Chief People Officer, appeared on his screen. After a cursory glance at the contents, Ramin was satisfied that it conveyed his intent to add Mahesh to the list of employees whose services ZyraCorp will no longer require some time in the near future. Ramin didn't know what Mahesh did exactly, but he had learnt it was best to get rid of potential troublemakers and annoyances.

Mahesh appeared to be both.

The layoff would be simple and subtle. Schedule a transfer to a department that has been earmarked for 'cost-efficiency improvements' and then include him in the list of redundancies that occur as a result.

With over a quarter million employees spread around the world and beyond, Mahesh's expulsion would be part of the mass of changes typical in giant corporations like ZyraCorp.

I hope that handshake was worth it Mahesh, since this would be the last time our paths ever cross.

Ever since he shook Mahesh's hand, his right hand had been held outstretched behind his back. The muscles were tensing, and his other hand squeezed his right wrist so tight that it as swollen as a red balloon about to pop. Once the anxiety built to a crescendo, he put his hand inside the left lapel pocket of his jacket and grabbed the handheld sanitiser that he always carried around.

Squirting a good amount, he wiped his hands with restrained control.

Without waiting for it to fully dry, he put his right hand back inside his coat pocket, where he palmed a small handheld device with 4 buttons.

With his remaining ounce of control, his fingers ran across the unit till it found the triangle-shaped button. Squeezing it, he waited for the first acknowledgement.

Almost immediately, the unit vibrated. Ramin started to count.

1,2, 3, 4..

He was starting to breathe a bit faster now.

Slow and steady, just like you practised.

Ramin continued counting.

15,16

The blood was rushing to his head now, and his ears were quite warm and red.

56,57

Ramin gripped the unit so hard that he could feel his fingers digging into the hard plastic.

111,112

The unit vibrated again.

Ramin gasped involuntarily. He hadn't even realised that he was holding his breath until then. Breathing rapidly, Ramin took in a couple of deep breaths and brought his breathing back under control.

He reached into his pocket again and pressed the triangular button again, but this time without the same sense of urgency.

The response returned before he could count to 100 this time.

That was pretty quick. They must have sorted out the supply issue.

Now breathing freely, Ramin asked aloud. " Time of last physical contact?"

Sarita responded almost instantly, as requested. "It has been 5 minutes 29 seconds since you shook Mahesh Oadki's hand.

This is 8 seconds longer than your previous record.

Congratulations on hitting a new PB."

He smiled, happy that he had kicked yet another goal today.

Looking at his hands, though, he just noticed that they were starting to bruise.

Ramin looked at it detachedly and headed to his personal fridge. Though small, it was already stacked with his essentials, including ice packs.

Sarita said out loud. "They are ready for you in the war room, Ramin," she informed him.

Perfect timing.

"Let them know I am on my way up", he replied.

Wearing one of the glove-shaped ice packs that he kept, Ramin closed his office door behind him and headed to the elevator. Entering the open doors, he said aloud. 'War room' and waited while the elevator rapidly dropped to the restricted basement floor.

Upon reaching his destination, the doors opened up directly to a granite desk manned by a Welcomebot sitting attentively at the desk behind.

The room feels great.

Knowing that the members of Sentinel Holdings would be coming into the office today, Sarita would have organised for the resident ambience coordinator, Kanchana, to prep the meeting floor before the guests arrived.

Bringing up the stats on his peripheral, Ramin noted that today, the temperature appeared to have been set to around 22 degrees with 47% humidity to counteract the monsoon heat from outside. The air smelt of lavender and honeysuckle with a hint of cinnamon, arousing a sense of calm and serenity while promoting alertness. The familiar gentle strains of the sitar could barely be made out but seemed to fill the air with warmth. Pausing, Ramin made an effort to concentrate on every note. "Oh, it's "Mullu Kurumba". Nathan likes that one. "

Even the Welcomebot had its features adjusted, keeping in mind the guests that were coming. This being the VIP suite, they had invested in a top-of-the-line model, and the sophisticated airindroid, with its AMS (Adaptive Morphogenic Skin), had modified its micro-projection skin to take on the physical appearance of darbaans of old. The airindroid wearing a stylised turban adorned in vibrant shades of red and gold was characterised by a curled moustache and dressed in an elegant jacket with a stand-up collar featuring the same rich red and gold palette.

Walking past it, Ramin was simply greeted with folded hands and not a word was uttered.

With its Integrated Cultural Recognition System (ICRS) and a Polyglot Linguistic Processor (PLP), the airindroid could communicate fluently in a multitude of languages and dialects. If allowed, it could rapidly change its appearance and voice to suit the cultural background of any visitor that it greeted.

Ramin nodded, impressed despite himself that these weren't used for today's meeting.

When he was first consulted on the idea of an ambience coordinator, he thought it would be some other mumbo jumbo like Stratic Cleansing and couldn't understand why they couldn't just use AI to control the environment like everybody else. However, after engaging the services of Kanchana, he had to admit that it was actually money well spent. Whether it was psychological or physiological, Ramin wasn't sure, but while AI is perfectly capable of choosing flavour profiles and approximating the ideal environment, they just never seem to get it perfectly right.

Even though she had never met Nathan, Kanchana, on the other hand, was impathic enough to sense that the visitors coming in today would be uncomfortable with airindroids being too human-like.

Excellent call, as Ramin knew that it bothered Nathan, though he made a significant effort to hide it.

Ramin likes to think it is because people can sense when something has had an actual human touch, nuances that are impossible for AI to replicate.

Yet

Ramin walked past the desk towards the end of the corridor towards a small unmarked door at the end of the hallway.

Walking, Ramin started activating the keys to unlock the door before even reaching it.

He deliberately whispered the Gayathri mantra aloud to himself, making sure to enunciate each word clearly despite it being under his breath. The sensitive condenser microphones hidden in the corridor, capable of spatially identifying a dropped pin anywhere in the room, were more than up to the task of picking up his voice.

While the phrases themselves were irrelevant, the processing module would build up an audio profile based on them. His audio signature was only the first key to enter the room.

A discrete camera at the end of the hallway silently watched his gait and body movements and successfully validated them against the encrypted profile stored on the Xyphor servers.

This was the second key.

Walking down the end of the hallway, he didn't stand directly in front of the door; instead, he stood to the side and waited. With the first 2 keys generated and authenticated against his stored behaviourals, a small panel revealed itself silently, with a small hidden chamber about the size of a small book. A ghostly green light lighted the chamber while it waited for Ramin. Deftly removing his peripheral and periband, Ramin placed them in the palm of his right hand and elegantly placed them in the chamber. While doing so, with great deliberateness, he took the effort to thrust his palm fully into the fingerprint scanner and pulled it back just as quickly. Scanning his entire palm, including the fingerprints and palm lines, it authenticated him and, once completed, silently closed the panel up again.

This was the third key.

A full spectrum analyser scanned him from head to toe to check for any transmitting devices or other electronics. Having already placed his devices in the box, the scanner silently acknowledged that it was approved.

This was the fourth key.

Looking up, he looked directly above the glass eye at the top of the door. The camera, carrying out a full facial and iris scan, validated him again against his profile.

With the 5th key and final key now provided and validated, the reinforced titanium door swung outwards.

Despite its ridiculous weight, the door swung open silently and smoothly. All the chairs at the small rectangular table in the centre were already occupied except for the spot reserved for him at the southern head of the table.

At the other end, still as a stone, sat Nathan Sentinel, the only one seated. The rest stood up as soon as Ramin walked in.

Entering the room, he nodded to each of the ZyraCorp C-executives seated around the table.

Though Zyana was technically the head of Research and technology, she wasn't present and had never attended this meeting. Ramin would be surprised if his sister even knew if this floor existed. Her complete lack of interest in the company's day-to-day running suited him well sometimes. At the other end of the table sat the executives of Sentinel Holdings.

There were no other electronic devices in the room except for the printer in the back. With all the security reviews completed, sensitive topics can be discussed without the risk of a digital imprint being left behind.

The room looked like any other corpo conference room except for the safe encased in the wall at one end and an antique mandala at the other.

Seeing that he had entered, his CFO walked over to the printer and, entering a code, made 9 copies of the same handwritten paper. The single sheet of paper had 10 lines, each with a single sentence and a figure next to it.

The paper did not mention names or any further details.

Walking over to each of the team members, he placed a single piece of paper in front of each member at the table. This was the agenda for their annual meeting to conduct a risk review of their ongoing operations and discuss potential liabilities. With each member actively participating in the topics being discussed, this meeting was more of a formal review for approval.

Once completed, the CFO sat back at his desk and looked up at Ramin.

Standing up, shoulders squared, Ramin said, "Ladies and Gentlemen, thanks for coming down here.

"I see that our esteemed benefactor, Shri Sentinel, has joined us today. Always a pleasure. A quick meeting is a good meeting, so let's get started."

"First up. The Bourdainpur plant has identified a potential saving in using standard silicon in the chest augments that have been planned. There is a 20% increased chance of failure after 10 years, which may result in permanent liabilities. This would be in the economy version of the Extrex so based on our current forecast, the failure rate would be acceptable by the public and the impact to brand image is expected to be in single digits.

"Overall, the additional annual revenue would be 20 million rupees. Legal has also proposed routing the procurement through another subsidiary so we can claim plausible deniability.

"Motion to pass, he asked."

Silently, 9 hands were raised.

Ramin ran through each of the other 9 items on the list, each with a calculated risk rating of business decisions and their associated liabilities.

Some were approved right away. Others were questioned but eventually passed as well.

Nathan, Sentinel's CEO, didn't participate in the proceedings. He had a hand in selecting every member in the room and trusted their decision. Sitting at the northern head, he was dressed sharply in a pin-stripe suit with a cornflower blue tie. His French beard was lacquered down the same as his thick grey ponytail.

Once Ramin had concluded, he sat down. A heartbeat later, Nathan stood up and gave a slight bow. In unison, the board members, except Ramin, stood up and bowed lower than Nathan. Silently, they exited the room.

Once the last board member had closed the door, the room was silent as a tomb.

Ramin and Nathan waited for a moment for the air to clear. Then, as if on a sublime cue, both looked up and smiled.

Almost simultaneously, they walked towards each other. When they met, they didn't hug, but Ramin touched Nathans's feet with one outreached arm.

"Natha," he said reverently, touching Nathan's feet.

Ramin addressed Nathan with a term that wasn't just an abbreviation of his name but the age-old endearment reserved for fathers and protectors.

With both his arms extended, Nathan blessed Ramin with a long life and prosperity and lifted him into a loving embrace. Breaking from the embrace, Nathan held Ramin at arm's length, examining him with paternal pride. "You've grown into a fine leader," Nathan commented, his tone reflecting both a mentor's approval and a father's warmth.

Ramin was at peace for a moment, basking in the praise, when Nathan abruptly said. "Ah, Ramin. While I would love to spend more time with you, I do have some pressing matters to attend to.

With a knowing glint in his eye, he asked. "So, where are we up to with our special project?"

Ramin looked down bashfully. "I have had the Aatmik project given top priority, but I received a report from the engineers this morning. "

Ramin didn't bother going into the technical details but simply said, "They seem to be having some issues. I am waiting for the revised schedule, but it looks like we will be delayed.

For the first time, the stone face of Nathan broke, and raw terror shone brightly.

"Delays?? Delays !!"

" Look at this. Look at this," he screamed, and he poked one well-manicured fingernail at a fine line at the edge of the right eye. "This wasn't there yesterday. I am growing old before my very eyes. Within a year, I will likely be dead at the rate I am going. "

Nathan shook violently. "Can't you just get more computers to sort out this problem?"

Ramin recoiled in horror. He hated it when his mentor behaved like this. Shocked but still retaining all his resolve, Ramin replied in jest to try to lighten the mood. "Relax, Natha. I have my best team working on this. Why don't I catch up with them later today to make sure that things are on track? I am sure they will back on track in no time."

Nathan looked up with a fury that would melt eyes and boil blood. "Don't you dare tell me to 'Relax'. You have no idea what I deal with it."

Without losing any of his fury but with a thin smile, he looked deep into Ramin's eyes and softly said. "How's the response on the 'Remote'? I made sure that they got a couple of extra backups, so you may have noticed an improvement in the response time.

"It's a good thing I'm around to make sure everything is sorted. Who knows who will be around to look after me after I'm gone?

"Maybe if I had enough time, I could organise alternative arrangements, but who can tell?

With a cruel glint in his eyes, Nathan smiled at Ramin."In fact, I feel that my memory is already failing, and there may be supply issues again. "

It was Ramin's turn to lose his cool, and slowly, his veneer broke. "Don't do this. Not again." His fingers tightened into old, familiar positions and pressed a bit too hard into the faded, crescent-shaped scars on his palm.

Ramin shuddered, and a tear of remembered pain flowed down involuntarily.

His nails dug into the scabbed skin and broke just a little.

"You promised never again. Not after what I did for you last time."

This was no idle threat. Ramin knew that Nathan wouldn't hesitate to withhold from him just to show him how much influence he still had over him. It had happened before when the transference ritual was interrupted; Ramin had to look after things himself. The toll it took on his collective cool left echoes even after the ritual was completed once Nathan was amenable.

Ramin didn't think he could go through it again.

His face crumbling, Ramin cried and lied. He lied and told Nathan that he would get it done sooner, that he would fix it, though he wasn't really sure if he knew how to do so. He lied through his teeth, shame dripping down his eyes. He blabbered about all the things he would do to set things right. His fingers dug into his palms so tightly that red tears started to flow, matching the stream from his eyes.

Nobody likes to see a grown man cry.

Some people love to see a grown, powerful man cry.

Especially the ones who broke them.

Nathan smiled widely, having achieved his desired effect.

Sometimes, children need to be put in their place; else, they tend to think they are better than their elders and betters.

Like a whirlwind, Zyana barged in and plopped a bunch of papers on the desk between Ramin and Nathan.

Looking intently at the papers, Zyana launched into a tirade about why she shouldn't have visitors in her lab, how her projects don't have sufficient funding, and a multitude of topics that seemed connected by the thinnest of threads.

She only paused when Ramin sniffed loudly to clear his nose.

Actually, looking at Ramin now, Zyana asked. "Why are your eyes and nose leaking? Do you have allergies?

Ramin was still unable to recover his composure. His mind was in chaos.

His great force of will, with which he can always rebuild his composure, had failed him for what seemed like a very long time.

No, No, No..

Ramin may have been successful in restoring his iron will if it was just Nathan or just Zyana, but not with both.

Having watched Zyana and Ramin ever since they were babies, Nathan wasn't too surprised by her behaviour.

Touch of the vapours that one.

Without warning, he could hear Zyana having what sounded like a one-sided conversation that no one else could see nor was invited to.

Zyana seemingly spoke to no one. "Ramin is not sad. We are just having a civil discussion.

"No elevated voices and no raised eyebrows, so therefore no disagreement.

"Yes, I know what tears are. What do you mean by scared tears, and he hurt his hands?

"Clarify, please?"

"Like this?" she asked and, without hesitation, grabbed Ramin's palm.

With one smooth movement, Zyana passed her open palm just above the bleeding crescents on Ramin's palms. Kneeling then, she surgically kissed each of the 8 weeping wounds.

Rising stiffly, she hugged Ramin tightly and kissed him on the forehead.

Then she looked down deep into his eyes.

From some wellspring deep within Ramin flowed waves of peace and calm.

Though his eyes were still red, his tears had stopped.

Closing his eyes, he took one deep breath, and Ramin was himself again.

Opening his eyes, he first addressed Zyana.

"Hello, Zyana. Surprised to see you here.

"How did you even manage to get up?

Zyana continued, just as always, "I designed the security in this place, and I have master clearance throughout this building.

"Including this floor."

Ramin nodded. "Thank you, Zyana. If you will excuse me, I am just finishing up with our VIP Nathan over here. Do you mind giving us a few minutes?"

Zyana looked at Nathan. He seemed familiar, but it couldn't be the man she thought he looked like.

He reminded her of the man in the safari suit in one of grandfather's photos in his study in Bolgatty house. It showed Grandfather and a bunch of people sitting in front of a wooden log cabin deep in a lush green forest. However, they could not be the same person, as this man in front of her seemed to be in his 40s, and the photo was taken when her grandfather was a teenager.

Zyana shrugged, and without a word, she acquiesced to his request and turned back out of the room and into the corridor outside.

Now that the room was empty again except for Nathan and Ramin, Ramin breathed deeply, control restored.

Looking straight into Nathan's eyes, Ramin simply said.

"Leave it with me; I will sort it out."

| 7 |

Mental Manadhil / Coming Undone

Trevor woke up to the sound of police sirens.

Driving past the trailer park in the Perth outback, the sirens didn't stop in front of the campervan this time and kept going.

He wanted to go back to sleep, but the afternoon sunlight poured into his dingy trailer. Now, just as always, he would only toss and turn if he tried to sleep again.

Stretching in his bed, he couldn't bear the sunlight coming through his closed eyelids, let alone dare to open them. Burying his face into the pillow, he tried to wake up with flow.

Right now he couldn't remember much of last night and had a headache.

Actually, he couldn't remember last night at all, and he had a bloody big headache.

Dang!!!

To make up for the 2 weeks that he was sober at the retreat, he thought he deserved to party hard but crikey.

Must have been an bonzer sez eh?.

That's all well and good, but it looks like he is paying the piper, and he has to put up with this lachuka hangover. That wasn't something new either, but damn if this one wasn't a cracker.

He stood up on the bed and vomited into the trash can next to his bed.

Teri Monkey

Wiping the yellow bile from the corner of his mouth, Trevor grabbed the half bottle of Colorado Bitter beer next to his bed. Gulping the warm beer, he gargled his mouth and swallowed.

Try as he might, he couldn't recall exactly what he did last night.

Trevor was a guru of blackouts, having been a heavy drinker since his early teens, but he would always be able to remember at least some bits and pieces of the sessions.

I am getting too old for this badre. These hangovers are killing me.

In an unusually perceptive mood, he thought.

I mean, it must be a hangover. What else can it be?

He shrugged and stretched out to his bedside table, where next to the beer was a pack of his customary Blinky blue cigarettes. Grabbing one from the box, he snapped his fingers and lit the ciggie using the glowing tip of his index finger. Inhaling deeply, he released a cloud of blue-grey smoke with a satisfied sigh.

"*Badre me dead. Time to slow down eh adlay*",

Then, grabbing the beer, he said aloud to the empty room. "Naaaa mate, not when one is dryer than a dead dingo's donger."

Sculling the beer down, he drained the long-neck bottle empty. Still feeling dryer than a donger, he headed to the fridge to see if there was anything else to imbibe.

The fridge was busted and half open.

Empty.

Guess its time to head to the pub for a pint

Was planning on swinging by Kleps to pick up the car anyways.

The 'car ' was a beat-up old Krolden Esteem with a body that only Trevor could love. Originally a colour the marketing gurus had decided to call 'Grabber Yellow' when it first left the showroom, it was now a Frankenstein of parts salvaged from various wrecks, all of which somehow managed to be every colour apart from its original yellow. Rather than being embarrassed, Trevor was rather proud of this fact and was on a mission to have panels of every factory colour on his car.

So far, he had successfully got every colour except a 'Detonator Blue' bonnet. He had plugged Klep at the local junkyard to keep an eye out for it.

It had been months since he had asked, but coincidentally, Klep had messaged Trevor on the day he was scheduled to check into the ZyraCorp Retreat for Advanced Sleep Studies at Dayton.

In a panic, Trevor called Klep just before he was asked to hand over all the tech and was reassured when Klep offered to pick up the car from his trailer and install the hood before he got out.

True Mate, that one.

It's not like Trevor actually had any problems sleeping. Au contraire, Klep had plenty of uppers and downers, and he didn't need some darn quacks to tell him how to sleep. They did, however, offer him to pay 2000 creds to spend 2 weeks at their 'retreat'.

Even Trevor, who may not be the sharpest tool in the shed, thought that it was iffy.

2 weeks vacay, 2000 creds and all he had to do was wear a weird headset while he slept?

Ratbags probably wanna stuff some transmitters up his dill hole or some other barde like that.

If anyone was going to be stuffing things up his dill hole, it was going to be Trevor and his friends; thank you very much.

But still.

2 weeks vacay, 2000 creds and all he had to do was wear a weird headset while he slept?

So Trevor said yes.

Trevor was actually surprised that he got selected for the study. Sure, he applied for it—he applied for all of them. Just sitting for the screening rounds scored enough creds for a couple of pints and, at the very least, a sausage sanga. He reckoned it still beat donating body fluids, and his opinion had nothing to do with his tendency to try out every stim that he could get his hands on and being blacklisted from every Red Socks Brigade camp.

While he still got his disability payments from the army, it wasn't nearly enough with the goddamn government ripping off hard-working badres like him, but damn if he was going to work in lachuka corpo.

Na screw that. Plenty of other ways to make a cred than dressing up in an Akubarra hat and buttoned-up Portans, day in and day out from 7 to 3.

The psych survey is where he usually trips up in most interviews. Since most of the surveys were product testing, preference was given to positive personality traits to increase the chances of a successful product review. Trevor had no qualms about lying, but the boffins running the studies usually catch on to any of his furphies quite easily, so he learnt early on to actually tell the truth at these places.

He had found the ad for the sleep trial at the veteran support group, where he was their most valued community member. Straight up, this sleep study was different and his honest responses to questions that normally excluded him from other studies actually caused the psych-o to pay attention to him. Trevor just assumed that his natural charisma must have shone through.

He recalled the questions.

Willingness to stay away from home for extended periods of time - Trevor was an orphan with no living relatives, and his sheila had left him a long time ago.

Availability to spend extended periods of time isolated.- His periods of solitary confinement actually came in handy for once.

They were even more interested in his military background and his tendency to use his power arms more than words.

"Will you take whatever it takes to defend your freedoms?" Check and triple-check. A go-getter like him with a willingness to off any badre for his beliefs, he had defended his right to an opinion to the ground with enough battered bodies as proof of his right of way.

Willingness to commit to cutting-edge augmentation- Trevor was part of the juvey corps in the army and was exted up like all soldiers. It's not like he had planned on being an army jock, but when the judge at the juvey court, tired of his shenanigans, had given him a choice between the time at the big house or joining the army, he simply asked them where to sign up.

He knew there were plenty of adlays in the army, so it's not like he would be lacking in company. He didn't even mind the behavioural modification chips that they put in his conscription.

No tech is ever going to stop Trevor from being a badre.

He consented to having his personal profile scanned and he thought that was that.

Wasn't he happy as a pig in mud when they called him back within the week to let him know he had been selected.

Perfect timing

Without having actual cash to pay for modding his ride, Trevor was getting stressed out thinking of giving up his personal stash to Klep for the hood. Klep was Trevor's best and only friend and vice versa as far as he knew. Yet all he could think about before was how he could screw him over and get away with it. The deal was for 5 dabs of Scully and an ounce of phool, but Trevor knew Klep was an equal-opportunity chemical enthusiast and would be open to a fix regardless of the type. Imagine his joy when he found out that, along with the 2000 creds, he was supposed to get the Trailum as part of the post-op. Trailium was not his cup of chai, but it was quite popular among the soccer and wine moms, so Klep actually agreed to install the hood just for the Trailium.

Little piggie jumping in muddy puddles happy.

He knew Klep from his army days. While they were not in the same unit, Klep was the resident drug dispenser in the base, and Trevor was his best customer. That was until he was stupid enough to smoke a thring right in the middle of doing a patrol in the middle of an active war zone in Janova.

It definitely didn't impress the sergeant, who, during a routine camp inspection, had watched from his supervisory drone while Trevor shuffled around the entire camp rocketed out of his mind. The punishment was 20 days in the brig with an offer to halve it if he ratted out his supplier. Trevor, who had enough run-ins with leadership, knew that it was only a matter of time before he got booted out, didn't rat out Klep but instead claimed to have found it on the body of an insurgent that he had shot.

Trevor went to the brig for the promised 20 days and an extra 20 because he also punched the arresting sergeant in the nose before going in.

When he got out, he was dishonourably discharged, and it was only because he got a plate in his head due to shrapnel that he was still able to keep his disability.

Klep was grateful enough, though; they have been best friends ever since.

The sergeant showed up dead after an apparent robbery gone wrong a few years later. It was never solved and clubbed with other similar robberies in the area; it was eventually added to the growing pile of cold cases. Trevor, who was in the state at the same time for a camping trip, was never even questioned. Klep, knowing that Trevor wasn't exactly the outdoorsy type, had asked him once during one of their seshs if Trevor had anything to do with the stabbing. Uncharacteristically, all Trevor had to say was, "Snitches get stitches". Klep knew Trevor well enough that it would be wise not to question any further.

Trevor tried calling Klep on his peripheral, but there was no answer.

He could swing by Klep's later, but now he needed to get his drink on. His head ached, and it felt like his skull was going to explode every time he moved.

Lachukabadre if his head wasn't killing him.

Stepping out of his bed, he walked naked to the mirror to see last night's damage. He gingerly touched a still-red scar on his nose. A deep scratch went from one corner to another. It was already scabbed up and starting to heal. It looks like he had managed to get his nose sliced while he was blacked out.

Shrugging, Trevor continued grabbing the clothes he must have taken off last night before heading to bed. He put on his khaki safari shirt, rolled up his sleeves, and put on an old pair of Mr Williams boots. Plonking on his cork hat, he turned around to finish his morning ritual.

In all the chaos in his dunny of a campervan, there was one spot of serenity: the display just above his mantle piece. There, out on a polished rosewood stand, was his beloved Bowie knife in its rowen leather scabbard.

Reverently grabbing the knife, he strapped it on, calming down a bit before heading to his pantry cupboard and grabbing the bottle of vegemite that was always there. Dipping two fingers straight into the yeast condiment, he grabbed a generous dollop and rubbed it behind his ears and just across his forehead.

It was drop bear season, and one can't be too prepared.

Licking his fingers clean, he stepped out warily.

The eucalyptus trees in front of this campervan were swaying, but he couldn't see any of the tell-tale signs of the 2 drop bears that he suspected lived there. Looking up, he breathed a sigh of relief when he could see the loop of magpies flying just above. The natural predators of drop bears and chips, the swooping birds scare even the most fearsome of land creatures.

His head continued to throb, and Trevor sometimes thought he heard voices. A garble of voices. Nothing concrete that he could pinpoint, but the docs had warned him that this would be a side effect, so he shrugged it off.

Flush with the 2000 creds that he got and after the 2 weeks in the dry camp he was gagging to spend the cash.

Watch out, world; here's Trevor.

With the coast clear, he jumped on his monojet bike and made his way to the 4 Arms. While there were a couple of pubs closer, the 'The 4 Arms' was the only place in town that would still serve him as he had been banned everywhere else.

Aint his fault that some badres can only shut the lachuka up with a glass bottle to the head.

The bike cruised. Trevor always loved the feeling of the wind blowing through his hair and the way it gripped his scalp so tightly.

He pulled up at the '4 Arms' when his keen eye noted the dented planter at the front, which some nong had rammed into. With his advanced knowledge of all things, Trevor was even able to identify that the car's colour that had hit the planter was "Detonator Yellow'. He wasn't surprised to see that there was another car in town with the so ugly that it would never be repeated again colour. Hard badres like him were an inspiration to many, and obviously, someone must have got a car with the same colour to keep up with his beaut.

The pub was open now and already filled with the regulars, some of whom would have even queued up just before they opened the doors for their morning ritual. Trevor smiled wide. With all the hard work he had put in, he deserved a pint and a pull at the pokies. He wished it was Thursday, though, when the topless biddies would make their rounds then, and he could have a real good gander and boner.

But pints a pint and Stella ain't a bad looker.

The bar was quiet, and apart from the usual old farts nodding off into their drinks, there were only a few young'uns playing one of the old racing sims. He smiled when he saw Stella behind the bar spitting into his hands;

he slicked his mullet back to look all presentable and smooth as.

Sliding onto the bar stool directly in front of Stella, he turned on the charm to 11 and, with his suavest of suave voices, asked. "Oi love, howzza about a pint of Branton?"

Upon seeing him, however, Stella's eyes widened in alarm, and she yelled, "Oi Shangeika!! You got some nerve to show your mug here again."

Trevor recoiled in shock at the sudden anger, and lucky for him, he did. Stella had grabbed the hockey stick under the counter and swung it at where his head was. "Cool your horses, missy; I ain't got no beef witchya and ain't done nuffin" said Trevor defensively.

Stella was shaking with fury "Frick off nong. You are lucky Michael isn't here, or he would have blown your lachuka head off for what you did to the planters last week.

"Now git!!. "

Trevor wanted to argue, but his head was starting to hurt again, and for once, he backed off and, with palms raised upwards, walked out of the bar.

Jumping on his bike, he got away as fast as he could.

Lachukaaaaa

Trevor had only gotten home last night and was too busy getting drunk to head to the pub. Besides, his car was at Kleps, so it couldn't have been him.

Bloody bird must be on the rag and mistaken him for someone else.

Stella had really riled him up, though, and he really needed to mellow down now. The local bottle-o was just up the road, and he pulled up on the vacant lot in front of the store. Walking in, he grabbed a six-pack of beer and a cask of wine. The goon bag of wine was from Barooga Valley, which was his region of choice. The beer was cold and cheap.

Vestua at the counter was turning the pages in the latest edition of 'Who Idea' with a fuchsia pink manicured finger. Though he was wearing the beige shirt of the 'Elbourne Wines Co,' it barely concealed the satin purple top underneath. Bored, he lounged behind the counter, checking out his nails, until he saw Trevor.

With a quick furl of his heavily mascaraed eyelashes, Vestua raised his fists lightning-fast and took on the familiar Kalari stance. With his false nails and belly popping out from the tight waistband, the pose would have been comical if it wasn't for the practised ease with which he stood, stopping Trevor dead in his tracks.

"Back for more, darling?" Vestua said with about as much sweetness as honey-covered razor blades.

"What the frick you on about, mate? Have never seen you before in my life," said Trevor in shock.

Vesta smiled a wicked, wicked smile and said, "Really? Just put on a fresh pair of nails.

"Want me to slice your ears like I did your nose to jog your memory?"

The cut on his nose!!

That's impossible!!!

What the shangeika lachukabadre is going on here!!

In a panic, Trevor dropped the bottles and bolted out of the store, ignoring Vestua's angry cries about his involvement in activities normally restricted to his parents and their partners.

He hopped on his bike and rode like a bat out of hell straight to Klep's place.

It's a good thing he was the slickest rider there is. In spite of his rising panic, Trevor strategically ducked and weaved through all the dumb AI cars on the road with the greatest of ease.

The junkyard was locked up as it always was, but Trevor knew the side entrance and parking at the side of a wall of cars; he snuck into the main office. Klep lived in the combined shed /house/main office, consisting of a couple of shipping containers stacked together to make a bunch of rooms.

Or at least that it used to be.

Now, the containers had all toppled over since a car that looked suspiciously like his Krolden Esteem had rammed into them. The toppled-over containers had completely buried the front of his car, and pooling under it was a puddle of something that looked suspiciously like blood.

Synapses long unused started firing in his brain, and with an almost dreamlike slowness, he pulled up the footage from the surveillance drones flying around the junk yard.

Trevor was the only person that Klep had added to his passkeys for the drones. Linking it to his peripheral, Trevor pulled up the last motion activity in the area. It was from 3 days ago. In it, he could clearly see his car being driven without any hesitation straight into Klep, pinning him against the office, toppling over the shipping containers, and crushing Klep into a pulp.

Stepping out of the car, Trevor could see himself walking away, unhurt, without even a glance back at the chaos behind him.

Dropping the drone feed, Trevor turned around and, without a word, got on his bike and headed back home.

On the drive back, he silently pondered.

So I crashed into Klep 3 days ago and can't remember it.
Strange.
I wonder why I did that.
I must have walked back to the bike and driven back home.
Good thing my bike was conveniently parked over there after I crashed my car.
Hahaha!!
That's right, I don't even own a bike.
In fact, I don't even know how to ride a bike.
Silly Rabbit.

The scream that came from deep within himself was the only sound that Trevor heard as he drove straight under the wheels of an oncoming semi-trailer.

He was gone by the time it had become the roar of a fiery inferno.

| 8 |

Maangalayam / Battlestar Galactica

Indra awoke to the sound of bells.

Her mother rang the small bronze bell to accompany her prayers, which has been her mother's ritual since she walked into Bolgatty's house as a young bride. Every morning, Indra's amma would bathe before the rest of the family had woken up and head to the family puja room to start her prayers.

The sound of her mother's soothing chant of the Gayathri mantra wafted in, along with the sandalwood incense that she had lit. The chant soothed her and almost lulled Indra back to sleep. A constant throughout her childhood, the chant was sung every morning by the older women in the family—first by her ammachi and amma and now by her amma and her sister-in-law, Naina, after her grandmother's passing.

Indra laid back in her bed and yawned, stretching lazily. She relished these quiet mornings when she was absolutely alone.

It was hard to have a moment's solitude at Bolgatty house with her extended family and the army of servants to look after them all living together. With Indra being away for most of the year at her boarding school in Ooty, she relished these rare moments of solitude.

It's not that she hated boarding school. On the contrary, Indra loved it and looked forward to going back at the end of every break. Growing up surrounded by girls who, like her, had been enrolled since childhood, they weren't just friends but made-sisters.

But she also loved spending time at Bolgatty house.

Bolgatty house, which has been her ancestral home for generations, was built over 200 years ago. With over 20 bedrooms, it should have seemed excessively large, but for generations past, there never seemed to be any trouble in keeping it bursting at the seams with people. While the rotating retinue of guests, including artists and famous influencers, was in itself quite significant, most of the rooms were actually occupied by the immediate family.

Traditionally passed on to the eldest son of the family, it was built during a time when light bulbs were the height of technology. With scant distractions after their day's work, the resident Karnavars participated quite frequently in the most primal of dances and produced a brood that was large enough to overflow from Bolgatty house to even the adjacent side houses.

The children all grew up together in the same house until the boys2men were married, and they, in turn, had children of their own. One by one, they would move out to set up houses of their own until only the oldest son and his children were left behind, and so the cycle continued.

The bells stopped ringing. Though wide awake now, Indra still lounged in the bed.

She wasn't sure what she would do for the rest of her life, but she knew what she would like to do today.

Which was nothing.

Having just finished her Year 12 exams and awaiting her results, Indra was relishing the sweet spot where, though she was no longer a schoolgirl, her right foot only hovered at adulthood's entrance.

Just then, a ping on her phone.

Po Mone Dinesha.

The morning light danced across the phone's transparent glass surface, casting a soft glow that highlighted the smudges left behind after her frenzied chatting session before bed.

Warmed by the sun and clarity of thought unencumbered by regular worries, she wondered whether she could be bothered even to touch her phone.

The phone pinged again.

and again.

and again.

Kukkoos.

She had forgotten that they were supposed to post family pics in the chat group first thing in the morning. Indra's friends must be up and have already started pinging them on the Friendster chat app. It was one of those girlie promises, along with sending a daily selfie in the morning, no matter what.

Indra stretched out her hand and grabbed her phone off her bedside table. The palm print of her hand was barely visible through the block of glass.

Sigh, If I have to

She gleefully unlocked her phone to check out the updates on everything that had happened to her friends since last night. While all of them had only gotten home last night after breaking up from school, most of them had already posted selfies of themselves with their families, and some had even sent a couple of short videos from YourSpace.

Indra, however, was yet to take a family selfie.

Uncharacteristically, Indra's father and brother weren't at home to greet her. When she asked her mom and sister-in-law, she got vague responses that they 'should be back tonight'. While disappointed, Indra quickly got over it. The clamour of cousins was more than enough to keep her occupied for a while.

As for the rest of the family?

Well, only her grandfather could sort that out, and being the favourite granddaughter, Indra could sort her appachan out, so everything was sorted.

Looks like everybody is having a blast.

Quick, I have to put something funny, or I will be the only one who hasn't.

Thinking of something clever to post, Indra quickly grabbed some of the coins next to her bedside table. Taking a selfie, bed hair and all, she took a snap of the coins falling in a tumble on her long T-shirt. Spilling from her hand, the shimmering waterfall of gold caught the first light as it tumbled onto her T-shirt and sparkled like the sun.

Tapping out a caption "Chilling with Chillar ;)", she posted in the group and waited.

Was that funny enough? Will people get it? Maybe that was too awkward; maybe I should have ...

Ping.

Her first 'Heart' from Kathy was shortly followed by more from the rest of her friends.

Laughing, she thought.,

Damn, I am a funny gal.

Satisfied, she continued her morning ritual, which was as sacred to Indra as her mother's, and she checked out the various aspects of her digital identity.

First Photogram, where she checked out the latest from her favourite influencers, snapshots of sunrise yoga sessions and aesthetically pleasing breakfast spreads. While in Photogram, she carefully curated her own feeds, reviewing the candid selfies interspersed with carefully composed snapshots of her daily life, each post a carefully built canvas for her creativity and self-expression.

Armed with filters and editing tools, she transforms her flaws into features, presenting a polished façade to the outside world, her public online persona, carefully curated to reflect the best version of herself.

Moving on, Indra effortlessly weaves between multiple threads of virtual conversations, seamlessly transitioning from witty banter in PopTalk streaks to heartfelt exchanges in WhatsUp group chats with her closest friends. She dives into the depths of FlipFlop, where she loses herself in a whirlwind of dance challenges, lip-syncing duets, and comedic sketches. Noting the ones where she can add her own flair, she checks the view counts on the ones she had already posted.

Infusing her personality into every dance move and expression, she carved out her own niche in the vast expanse of mirchi content.

She finally stopped at Friendster again. A new security feature added recently allowed her to see users who have checked out her profile in the "Seen By" page. While it was an interesting feature, it quickly became evident the number of creeps who used to view profiles of girls of a certain age group. Morbid curiosity sometimes took over Indra, and in spite of knowing that she would dread it, she couldn't help checking the page quite regularly.

Despite only posting a generic photo of roses, she still gets her fair share of 'fans' who visit her profile purely based on her name and her friend's list. The list was long in spite of Indra's regular pruning, and the vast majority of it was filled with fake profiles with the explicit purpose of allowing strangers to be anonymous voyeurs.

Suddenly, Indra sat up with a start.

Nestled between the random photos of Badhrikant and Sushant Kumar was a face that was vaguely familiar.

Ente Devama

Now Vinod has found me here on Friendster as well.

The arrogant son of a local politician, she had only met Vinod once when she had visited the Planters Club with her family. Friends of her family, her father had stopped to talk with them, and even in the brief interaction, she could feel him leering at her. The only reason she added him to YourSpace was that Indra had moved on to Friendster already and didn't think she would be sharing anything too personal or public-worthy.

And now it looks like he was actively checking out her various profiles. A vigilant guardian of her digital identity and privacy, Indra quickly reviewed the deets that Vinod would have been able to see.

Knowing that with each like, comment, and share, she leaves her mark on the ever-changing social media landscape, Indra carefully revealed only an aspect of herself that she is comfortable sharing publicly. Her more vulnerable moments are only shared with the closest of her friends, the details of which are nested within a comradery of personal details shared by them in turn.

Looks like I have to do some gardening this morning.

Connecting to her home network, Indra gave permission for her phone to back up all her data, including her photos, videos, and social media profile, on their home server, nicknamed 'Xyphor'.

Indra multitasks easily, toggling between social media platforms like a digital maestro, orchestrating a symphony of online interactions. When reviewing her profiles, she viewed any potentially reputation-harming content and either deleted it or archived it to be hidden from public view. Safely backed up on her home server, none of her favourite content was lost or deleted.

Just safely kept out of the reach of public consumption.

Drained by the unexpected effort while still half asleep, Indra decided that, with her privacy now officially violated, she could do with a bit of tidying up herself.

With her typical gusto, she yelled out.

'SAVITRI'

Savitri, a thin wisp of a girl, wasn't much older than Indra and was hired for the explicit purpose of looking after Indra's needs. It had only been a year since she started, but she knew her mistress's mood was careful not to enter till she was called out for. With a firm nod to Savatri, Indra asked her to get her clothes ready for her while she stepped into her adjoining bathroom to carry out her morning ablutions. Grabbing her toothbrush of neem wood and castor oil bristles, she let out a contented sigh as the first deluge of warm water poured from the shower.

Indra's school, being mountainous, relied on daily water tankers and the girls were only allowed a bucket each with which they had to carry out all their activities.

All of them.

They had been used to the restrictions from childhood, so they were well adapted to making the bucket of water stretch and comfortable with the limitations. Still, Indra couldn't help but occasionally fantasise about the long, warm showers she could have at Bolgatty house, especially after a round of rounders when she and the girls would be drenched in unladylike perspiration.

Now, in the shower, all Indra could think about was her school and what she would have been doing otherwise.

It's not like she actually got away completely from school now that she was back home. Grouped with girls, most of whom were members of the various branches of Vottamparamb, it wasn't like she was lacking for company. Generations of Indra's family had gone through the same school, and family gatherings were spent with aunts older than her amma who, with a heavy sigh of nostalgia, still remembered the freshly baked bread and recollected stories down the very halls that Indra walked through.

Indra turned the water to full blast, luxuriating in warm water; she took her time before soaping her skin with the citrus-scented soap.

Stepping out, smelling of Lemon Taaza, she wrapped herself in a towel.

Dismissing Savatri, still in her Mumbai Living terrycloth towel, she stood in front of the full-length mirror and playfully tried on a couple of salwar kameez. Her ammachi, knowing Indra well, had, as always, bought her a ridiculously large number of clothes, all of which suited her taste perfectly.

She was still humming to herself while trying on a white and gold chiffon silk dress when her mother barged into the room.

Still wrapped in her towel, Indra almost gasped in surprise till she realised it was just her mom.

So she screamed. "Amma .. what the hell. I could have been naked."

Curtly, her mom's response was typical: "Podi. It isn't anything that I haven't already seen a thousand times.

"Get ready. Podiamma is coming for lunch with bios of a couple of suitable boys, and you better be on your best behaviour."

Indra nearly screamed again. "Maa.. Already. I literally just got here. I haven't even unpacked "

Even before heading back to Bolgatty's house, her mother had already dropped hints as subtle as a landslide about what her thoughts were on what Indra would be doing when she graduated. Having already mapped out Indra's life down to the 3 grandchildren (2 boys, 1 girl) even before Indra was born, she had already made it known to Indra that her family had started looking at potential suitors. Indra's quiet protests that maybe she needed some more time and maybe she would like to look at other options were selectively ignored. Until a few weeks ago, she could dodge the talk by claiming to concentrate on her Board Exams, but that wasn't an option anymore and while she had thus far evaded every opportunity for a serious discussion, she knew that time was nearly up.

Her mother pishposhed her, "Entee molle, you don't know the ways of the world. One day, you will appreciate the fact that your poor amma didn't waste time while all the best boys were taken. I even told Podiamma to make sure to find smart ones, just like I know you wanted.

"What more do you want me to do for you?"

Indra knew there was no point in directly arguing with her mother. Believing herself a custodian of the Vottomparamb family's honour, Amma's every action had been guided by the primary objective of never bringing dishonour to the family.

Nevertheless, almost instinctively, she pushed back. "Really, amma? "This again?

"I haven't even graduated, and you are already thinking of getting me married?

"I thought we agreed with appa that there would be no marriage talk till my exams were over"

Her mother rolled her eyes. "Your father doesn't know anything. You have to get married within the next 5 years, or it's bad luck for the whole family."

"Since you finished your studies, it's not like you have anything else to do and can't waste any more time in securing your future."

Softening, her mother took the towel on the side of the bed and gently dried Indra's short blue hair. "Why don't you just have a look? If none of them suit, there is always Malavedan chittappa."

Indra almost recoiled with horror that her mother seemed to have seriously considered her marrying her uncle.

Malavedan chittappa wasn't really Indra's uncle but a male relative thrice removed. With the tendency of older patriarchs to take on increasingly younger wives and produce a brood of a wide age range, it was quite common for aunts and uncles to play alongside their nieces and nephews. As per tradition, he was considered a 'morre cherakan', or someone who promised to be married to her. Though rarely followed these days, Indra's mother liked to keep a backup plan just in case all the good boys were indeed all snapped up.

Indra's mother continued, eyes looking far away, dreaming of the upcoming nuptials. "First, we have to brush up on your cooking skills, though.

"At the very least, you need to know how to make dosa and chutney.

"Then at least your husband won't starve. "

Indra didn't respond but was seething inside.

While generations of her family have been studying at SHO, the women very rarely pursued anything beyond that. Having been told from almost the day that they are enrolled that their fate is to be married to someone selected by the family as soon as they graduate, most of the girl cousins rarely studied, instead spending time in sports, home ed, or simply enjoying their time before the inevitable shackles of marriage were clamped on their hands.

Indra, on the other hand, loved learning. Having been enrolled in kindergarten, the spunky Indra was taken under the wing of the matronly Sister Bernard, who was designated as their batch's caretaker. Like a mother hen clucking her brood, Sister Bernard took to all her wards, and while she may not have been her mother who gave birth to them, she was the mother that they needed.

Fuelled by the vision of the miracle Sister Bernard promised, Indra believed she was destined for greater things. Like her made-sisters, she was self-motivated.

Under her tutelage, Indra flourished and excelled in both sports and academics; her achievements culminated in graduating from the school as captain and the winner of the gold medal in academics.

Unfortunately for Indra, that was the planned end to her academic pursuits.

Until they reached their final destination of graduating from Year 12, the school ensured that they provided the girls with all the tools needed to deal with the harsh realities of life.

After that, despite being well-armed and more than capable on their own, the girls were expected, willingly or unwillingly, to follow the paths pre-destined by their family and society.

It was even considered virtuous to abandon their dreams and aspirations to live the way that their mothers and other 'Good' women in their families had lived for generations.

Apart from Parvathi Ecchi, Indra did not know any other woman in her family who had tried to do something independently. Parvathi Ecchi, the black sheep of the family, was definitely not someone she was going to bring up in conversation with her mother if she actually expected it to end peacefully.

"Coaching classes." Indra blurted out.

"Classes? What classes? Aren't your exams over?" her mother asked incredulously.

"I still have my entrance exams, though. That's another 2 months away, and I need to prepare for them. "The deal was no marriage talk until my exams were over." said Indra resolutely.

Her mother was confused. "But isn't that for getting into university? What's the point of taking it? It's not like any respectable girl from our family has ever gone to college."

While most of her friends were similar to her and in various stages of getting married, some of them were instead preparing for the National Entrance Exams for admission into the various engineering and medical colleges around the country.

The most elite of which was the renowned NIMES around the country.

During the last cultural fete at SHO, several startups set up stalls, including one that promised to send multiple engineering exam applications with a click of a button.

Indra had applied for them simply because Michelle and Padmalakshmi were doing the same, and the guy manning the stall was cute. The school paid for everything, and Indra had nothing to lose in applying. Having already known where her path lay, she hadn't even bothered to take up the college brochures, but she did giggle when the smitten boy asked her for her number.

Imagine Indra's surprise, though, when she received the exam hall ticket in her inbox shortly after.

With nothing to lose, Indra pushed back against her mother. Though she knew she was clutching at straws, it was something, and sometimes, something may be just enough. "Both you and Appa approved the application forms, so it's not like you guys didn't know about it.

"Students from every single school in the state will be participating and all of my friends are going for it, so I need to as well."

Her mother had lost her smile, and the edges of her eyes and lips were curling down with worry.

Now that she had an opening, Indra fought verbally as if her life depended on it. "I may not get into it, but I have to give it the old Vottom-param try.

"How would it look if I took the exam and FAILED?"

Her mother was floundering now, her aura wavering in confusion.

Indra placed the first cut delicately and with great precision. "It's a matter of family honour."

Having been married very early, her mother wasn't sure how entrance exams work. However, she understood that this was a potential threat to the family's honour and had to be mitigated at all costs. "I told your appa not to let you take up science instead of home education.

"That you would start to get ideas and now see. Look at what's happening.

"You will actually bring dishonour to us?"

Without any hesitation, Indra delivered the killing blow: "I know, amma. That's exactly why I decided to take coaching classes.

"I have no choice if I need to do well.

"These classes will take up all day but I am prepared to go through the sacrifice to preserve the family name. "

Her mother still appeared stricken.

Ashamed of how she had manipulated her mother, Indra tried to make amends now that she was calmer and had gotten her way. "I promise to learn how to cook ", she said tenderly, caressing her mother's hand.

Her mother, mollified, breathed a sigh of relief.

Crisis averted her amma wished well for the family in gratitude for the restoration of good flow.

Nalla Kallam.

Quietly suggesting that it would be best for her mother to have a bit of a lie-down, Indra reassured her that she and Savatri would take care of the rest themselves.

Indra waited for a minute after her mother closed the door behind her before turning to Savatri and asking in panic, "What do you know about entrance coaching classes in town?"

Savatri, having an overbearing mother of her own and already used to sneaking around, understood and said. "You remember Gauri, Madhavan's daughter? She is going to one centre in town.

"Better hurry, though. Classes are about to start in an hour.".

Thanking her, Indra quickly put on the salwar at hand and, grabbing a couple of ripe Alcopa mangoes, headed to the garage adjacent to the house.

Housing the family cars, she beckoned Rathawi, her driver and told him, "Come with me. I am driving to town." Rathawi wasn't sure that he heard her right. Having never seen Indra drive before, Rathawi was confused, but when Indra grabbed the keys that hung from his belt, he could see that she meant to do exactly as she said.

Indra was nearly jumping for joy, though. This felt better than winning first prize in a lottery.

The entrance exams were another 3 months away, and with almost daily coaching classes, that's 3 months she would have to get out of the house.

3 months of freedom.

Pumped with her bonus, Indra decided to make the most of it and do things that she had always wanted to do, including driving a car.

I mean how hard can it be if even Rathawi can do it?

Having never actually learnt how to drive, she was a bit unsure which was the clutch and the brake, but after a quick rundown by Rathawi, she was ready to go. She could have used a better car, though, as this one was quite noisy and seemed to jerk all the time. Rathwai wasn't sure that Indra had actually gotten the handle on it, but while he was unsure of the damage she could cause to the car, he was well aware of Indra's fiery temper and complied to address the clear and present danger.

He made sure to wear his seat belt, though.

It wasn't Indra's fault when she knocked the tall, gangly boy riding the ancient bright red bicycle into the paddy fields. It was also not her fault that the cow had come out of nowhere and that she had to swerve the car to avoid hitting it.

And the guy had the audacity to blame her.

Even now, in spite of the commotion around it, the cow still sat in the middle of the road chewing a dry bale of hay, as it has been since morning.

After the dust settled, the boy gathered his bike and continued pushing it on the way. A textbook hung from the torn bag with the logo and name of the tuition centre she was going to. Wary of any other cows that may suddenly appear sitting on the road, Indra passed the steering wheel to Rathawi and sat at the back. The boy was examining his bike, which, with its bent spokes, wasn't going anywhere.

Badre.

It wasn't her fault, but she did still hit him, and now he would have to walk to the centre.

She asked Rathawi to pull again at the side of the road.

"Oi," she called out. This time, however, she waited until he pulled up next to her, and her tone softened when she asked him if he would like a lift to the centre. He didn't say anything but nodded his assent. After dropping off the scarlet red cycle at a nearby house and promising to pick it up later in the evening, the boy jumped into the front seat of the car.

From her viewpoint at the back, she had a good, long look at him. He was sun-darkened with wild, unruly hair. From her view from the back, she had a clear view of his hazel brown eyes in the front mirrors. Eyes that were surprisingly kind and intelligent in comparison to the rest of his sulky face. She couldn't stop staring at his eyes. In an effort to act casually, she asked him the most obvious question first. "What's your name"

"Striber ", came the slow response from the boy.

"So you going to the coaching centre? continued Indra, the open question ripe for further conversation. He grunted acknowledgement but didn't elaborate further.

"So you study or work there?" Indra tried again. "Yes" was the reply again.

Must be an idiot. He probably just says yes to everything.

Not expecting anything much further from him, Indra was silent for the rest of the journey, chatting with her friends on her phone. The driver pulled up in front of the coaching centre and asked her to alight. Parked illegally in front, there was already a driver in a rusty Morris Oxford who had already honked twice and impolitely gesticulated to indicate that he would like to park in his spot.

It had rained early in the morning, and the unpaved front of the shop's row was filled with mud, which she expertly avoided before heading up the stairs to the coaching centre located above the bank of shops. Though small, with crumbling paint and the ever-persistent smell of mildew, the coaching centre appeared to be popular, and she was stunned by the sheer number of students jammed into the tiny classroom.

It was hot and humid, and the glow of perspiration that was visible on her forehead started to become a little brighter as the press of students heated up the room even further.

The room, though well-ventilated, already stank of stale sweat.

There were already a bunch of teenagers in the front of the class lounging around, waiting for the class to start. Groups of boys and girls bundled together, talking animatedly. While primarily dived by the sexes, there were a few tight bunches where they secretly started the courtship rituals of the shy and uninitiated.

The boys, dressed in acid-washed jeans and poofy hair, mimicked Badhrikant's signature moves. Some had even managed to get the large aviator glasses that Bhadrikant had worn, and a number of them were flipping cheap cigarette candy to see who could best replicate the Ugatti's trademark moves.

She checked her schedule again. Yup. She was in Physics, but while she understood it was a core subject, she couldn't understand why the class was so full.

She couldn't be the only kid who just took exam coaching as an excuse to get away from home.

There was even a gaggle outside waiting to enter just when the teacher showed up.

The seat Gauri had saved was in the middle row on one of the long wooden tables. Ever opportunistic, Gauri had found a seat midway between the front, just enough to be considered a 'serious' student but enough to be privy to the shenanigans of the backbenchers. Grateful, Indra sat down beside her and grabbed the thick textbook from her sling bag.

Ignoring the conversation around her, Indra cracked open the textbook to the noted pages on the blackboard.

Striber walked in with his torn shirt and, without any hesitation, walked straight to the blackboard. Grabbing his textbook, he addressed the class. "So where were we."

Badre, badre, badre..

The boy was a teacher here, and now she was in his class?

Head bowed, she could feel his hazel eyes boring into her, so she guessed he may have noticed her.

Despite that, though, Striber didn't once explain his dishevelled experience and completed the whole class with one pocket ripped and half hanging out. None of the other students even acknowledged the fact they had looked like he had just come back from the losing side of an argument but were instead enthralled by what he was saying.

Once she had calmed down, she could understand why.

Gone was the quiet, brooding boy.

Instead, he was transformed into an orator on the stage. While he was only going through what she had learnt earlier in school, running through one concept after another, Striber's words and hands made pictures in her mind. More importantly, she could see the connections between the disparate topics and how, together, they could create something incredible.

The class was over in an hour, but Indra couldn't tell. So dazed was she.

At the end of the hour, Striber thanked the class and walked to the front of the seats.

The next class was Biology. Her speciality.

Just before the bell more than half the class stood up and walked out. The old lady waiting at the entrance didn't seem to mind and may not even have noticed the exodus of students.

Striber, seeing her at the entrance, politely touched her feet and walked back into the class.

Sitting in the front row, he though waited for the class to start.

What is going on here?

Turning to Gauri, she urgently whispered, " What's the deal with the Physics teacher? Why is he sitting in the Bio class?"

Gauri turned back with a blush. 'Oh, that's Striber. He teaches Physics here on scholarship. He is also doing the JREE this year. '

Indra was surprised and was just about to ask more when, at the gong of the bell, the teacher coughed to grab the class's attention and thus started the longest hour of Indra's life.

Having a keen interest in Biology, Indra was surprised at how absolutely boring this teacher had made it seem. With her steady tone of voice, it was obvious that this was a speech that had been delivered many, many times, and it did not bode well for interruptions.

Witling it down to pure facts and definitions, the expectation was that the students learn it rote. Listening to the lecturer, she was horrified that she picked up multiple factual errors in the speech. Looking around to see if anybody else was as indignant as her, she instead found that most of the class was in various stages of inattentiveness, some openly dropping their head on the bench and snoring away.

I could teach better than this.

At the end of the day's session, Indra was pleasantly surprised to find that she actually enjoyed the day as a whole. Focussing more on the practical aspects of her high school studies, the challenge of linking multiple concepts to find elegant solutions to the asked problems rather than draining her did the opposite and actually sparked something.

Rathawi had parked the car a little bit away and was now sleeping in the front seat with his feet poking out of the driver's side window. Walking up to the car, Indra banged the hood of the car to wake him up. Waking up with a start, Rathwai looked at her through bleary eyes and, without a word, started getting out of the car to allow her to drive back.

Whether she had learned a lesson or was simply mindful of company, Indra halted his exit with the shaking of an upraised hand and instead asked Gauri if she wanted a lift.

Gauri, thanking her, giggled and instead pointed at a boy in thick black glasses who was walking down the stairs along with Striber, of all people. "That's Kishore Karbi. I am meeting him after school for some special classes," she winked at Indra.

Indra gave her a conspirational smile and nodded.

Sriber appeared to be a lot more popular than his surly face would justify.

Without meaning, too, Indra felt a small stab of disappointment. She was actually hoping to catch Striber alone, but with the group of add-ons around him, there seemed little chance of that happening. Hiding her feelings, Indra nodded and even declined their offer to join their study group sessions. "I need to get back," she said ruefully, getting into the car with Rathwai.

Back home, dinner preparations were in full swing. The aroma of spices filled the air as the kitchen buzzed with activity. Indra's amma, in her traditional one-piece housecoat, was supervising the arrangements. Even Savatri was in the kitchen, darting around, but Indra wasn't exactly what she was doing there.

Indra retreated to her room, seeking a moment of solitude. She looked at herself in the mirror, a reflection of conflicting emotions. The lemony fragrance from her earlier shower lingered on her skin in spite of the hot day. Needing another shower, she reflected on her day while the cool water washed away the remains of the day. While it may have just been an excuse to get out of the house, she was pleasantly surprised at how good she was once she actually applied herself.

Dangerous thoughts started blooming in her head. Thoughts of her actually doing well in the entrance exams, of studying, of working.

Of being somebody that SHE wanted to be.

Change your mindset. You are only going to disappoint yourself.

She quickly tried drowning out her thoughts by being enthusiastic about the idea of meeting her potential life partner, but a small voice inside her wondered if any of them would truly understand her aspirations.

Dangerous, dangerous thoughts and ideas.

Feeling scared, she tried to stop thinking, turning the cold shower to full blast to be drenched in the torrent of water, hoping the shock would pull her out of her reverie and give her a moment of clarity of thought.

A pair of hazel brown eyes occupied them instead.

Feeling guilty without knowing why, she silently dressed and wrapped her hair in a thin khadi towel, went into the prayer room, and sat down in quiet contemplation.

The scent of sandalwood filled the room as it always did, giving her a sense of tranquillity.

Alone in the quietude, Indra pondered her future, torn between tradition and the uncharted territories she envisioned for herself.

As the evening approached, Indra reluctantly joined her family for dinner. With her brother and father still not back, and with the afternoon she had so far, she didn't think she could actually sit down with everybody for dinner.

Using the universal, unquestionable excuse used by all women of childbearing age, Indra feigned illness and retired early to her room.

It was late in the night when her father and brother came home. The whole of Bolgatty house was silent except for

Indra still up in her room. Grateful for the family's habit of turning in early, she relished in the privacy of her own room. And so she was the only one who witnessed her father and brother return home, their engines turned off so as not to wake anyone else.

By himself, her father helped Rahul out of the car. The gaunt cheekbones highlighted the aquiline nose shadowed by eyes, her once vibrant brother now reduced to a husk of his former self.

She knew it had gotten bad, but far away in her hostel in Ooty, she had never actually seen how bad it was until now.

Her brother was back from his stint at the Institute. With their regime of Electroshock and Aversion therapy, she hoped that they were able to cure him of his melancholy. In the clear night air, she could still hear a single word coming from her brother's chapped lips.

"Anjali"

Though SHO was an exclusively girls-only school, the powers that be also created a boys' school, OEHS, adjacent to the girls for the convenience of parents who would like their children to study together as long as they are not all together.

While the nuns who ran the convent school did their best to keep the two schools apart in an effort to maintain propriety, long-term residents, the children always found a way to sneak and meet out.

The corridors of both schools were filled with stories, some true, most made up. Who has a crush on whom, who stole what and hurt whom, who got whom into trouble.

By the time she joined, her brother Rahul, who was much older than her, was already a legend at OEHS. Brilliant in both sports and academics, he was nevertheless courteous and helpful, and he was the star pupil in his class.

Even though he was years older than her and in completely different schools, snippets of gossip slipped through the thick stone walls, and she heard stories of Rahul and Anjali.

The secret notes in class, the music flows, the stolen kisses.

An albino ethereal, Anjali's blond hair, alabaster skin and piercing voice masked a pain that was visible to all. With their lack of skin pigmentation, the auras of ethereal weren't hidden, and their true feelings were painfully clear. Once feared for their raw emotional powers, Anjali had joined the school on the reservation allocated for Ethereals.

Ostracised by many in the school because she was different, the willow wisp of a girl seemed to float about as a lonely spirit. As different from Rahul as you could possibly get, Indra never knew how the two met, but even she could see that they were inseparable.

Though it was never spoken about knowingly in front of her, Indra knew all about the big blowout when the family found out. She did not doubt that the topic of family honour came up during the discussions.

Get him married, they said; that will sort out the problem.

She never knew what happened to Anjali and was surprised when Rahul bhai agreed to marry Naina, a distant relative. The wedding went according to plan without any major incidents. Naina Bhabi was a sweetheart, and being the daughter of her cousin, Indra knew her well even before the marriage.

Rahul, though he went through the motions, did not seem to have his characteristic spark.

Let them have a child, the family said. That will sort out the problem.

According to the whispers in the kitchen, the newlywed couple was fulfilling their marital obligations, but they still had no child. Her brother became increasingly withdrawn from the family and even decided to move out of the main house to one of the outliers. The room he chose wasn't the biggest but the furthest away from the house.

Eventually, Rahul skipped meals and rarely stepped out of his room.

It was on the very veranda where Indra's brother and father when Rahul first publicly broke down. Clutching his phone, he ripped his clothes and yelled into the yard.

"She was with child."

"Did you know?

"Did you know when you did it?

"What have I done?"

"Blood, Blood on my hands.

Rahul wailed and collapsed. Since then the only word that he spoke has been 'Anjali'.

Something about her brother awakened something within Indra. Putting her right foot down firmly into adulthood she swore to no one and everyone.

"My own way. "

| 9 |

High Hopes / Ayyayyo

Within a week of meeting Zarg, Karthik got a ping on his periband.

"Meet at 12 on the dot. Bring 5 boxes of Jalebis and laddus ;)."

No way.

Karthik couldn't believe it. He knew Zarg was good, but just a week to hack into ZyraCorp?

He smiled. *This is going to be an interesting afternoon.*

Using a thin khadi towel to wipe the sweat off his naked chest, Karthik nodded towards his sparring partner and bowed low. Untying the green headband that he had wrapped around his wrist, he blindfolded himself and began his pre-fight ritual.

Closing his eyes, he went inward, boosting his atma-visvasa, his self-confidence by remembering his past wins. Victories won by the strength of his ichashakti, his solid will which was guided by his jnana-shakti allowed creation through his kriya-shakti.

Allowing his tantra to become.

He inhaled deeply till he became as still as a stone.

Breathing deeper, he becomes the stone among other stones, the stones in a flowing river, the flowing river itself, till his flow becomes the river, and his whole body becomes an eye.

The state of *meyyu kannakuka,* where his whole body is aware.

Truly aware, his whole body now a weapon, able to attack with intuitive clarity.

Breathing out, Karthik starts sensing his environment.

The training hall was filled with the rhythmic sounds of feet shuffling on the wooden floor, accompanied by the thump of wooden weapons.

Inhaling deeply, he got the heavenly fragrance of lavender and honeysuckle with a hint of cinnamon.

Mmmm. Isn't this the same incense that they had at the Forte Pondy that night?

Is she trying to hint at something?

Meera had indicated that she wanted to chat after their sparring match, and Karthik knew that this could only mean one thing.

Hmmm, once they get a taste of Kari Mirch, they just can't stop.

Baby, get ready to have your world rocked again.

The 2 circled each other, eyes closed and truly seeing each other.

With his mind's eye, he could see Meera quite clearly. Her stance was already defensive, in anticipation of the onslaught that she, in turn, would have sensed Karthik was planning for her.

Sensing Meera's flow, though, he could only get good vibes from her. He smiled, and his flow spread accordingly.

Ashaan Unniyarcha's digital avatar observed Karthik and Meera remotely from her ashram in Manali. Her virtual eyes, luminescent and focused, assessed their neural-enhanced techniques and biomechanical efficiency.

Sensing a nod from her, they started.

The sound of metal meeting metal resonated as their kadara clashed, the start of a harmoniously intense dance. It echoed through the hall as Karthik lunged forward, his right leg arcing in a sweeping kick. Tall and agile, Meera, however, glided away with the grace of a Kathak, creating a mesmerising pattern with her movements only to respond with a counterattack, utilising the circular movements to redirect Karthik's energy towards his head, knocking him off balance.

Koche Gulli. Sneaky sneaky.

With a lightning-fast lunge, Karthik unleashes a barrage of strikes with the full flow of his vygrasya sikram. His arms are a blur of movement, and his body moves with the speed of thought.

Meera, embodying the grace of a crouching tiger, responded not with brute force but with the lightness of a leaf caught in a tempest, her body arching and twisting in the air, evading his strikes by a hair's breadth. With a swift backward leap, she retaliated with a series of rapid strikes, each blow calculated and aimed at Karthik's marmas, the key locus points in his body through which all things flow, her counters striking with the precision and beauty of a calligrapher's brush.

Karthik parried Meera's attacks fluidly as quicksilver but was surprised by the effort it took.

Wow, Meera must really be looking forward to the hook-up. I have never seen her flow as intense as this before.

Better put the poor thing out of her misery.

Fuelled by will, Karthik executed a powerful spinning kick, aiming for Meera's vaari. Meera, sensing the change in the flow, blocked the kick with her forearm and countered with a lightning-fast strike to his poravu, knocking the breath out of Karthik.

Where the badre did that come from? Slow down, molle. You don't want to damage the goods.

The training hall seemed to shrink as the fighters closed the distance between them.

With 5 seconds left on the clock, Karthik has to move quickly if he hopes to save face.

Breathing heavily, he sensed her for a final showdown.

Using all his Gurutappas, Karthik leapt, arms outstretched, knees bent, to crush his opponent to submission.

Meera, swaying like a reed, easily side-stepped him and swiftly and gently placed her heel on his now prone neck instead.

The fight was over.

Solemnly, Karthik stood up and bowed to Meera.

The rest of the class resumed, inspired or cowed by the performance, depending on who they were rooting for.

Touching the sand of the arena in reverence, they walked out of the ring and approached each other. Rubbing his neck, Karthik grumbled, " I didn't expect that much of a workout from you. It almost drained me out for afterwards."

Looking up, he looked straight into Meera's eyes and, raising one eyebrow, gave her a cocky smile.

Meera appeared puzzled by Karthik's expression until she realised what Karthik was trying to do, and she burst out laughing. "Did you just try to give me your version of 'Blue Knight'?"

With a 'talk to the hand gesture', Meera continued, "Hello. That was a one-time thing only. So chill, bedu."

Her annoyance quickly turned to joy, though, when, with a giggle, she clapped her hands. "I do, however, have news. Gamit and I are scheduled for a baby. "

Karthik shook his head. That explains it, then. The last fight till birthed. "You are seriously still with Gamit? Isn't he old enough to be your dad or something?". Karthik could, however, see it was pointless. At the mention of Gamit and the thought of having a child together, her aura had turned a bright red.

Pure, unadulterated love.

Karthik sighed, covered his eyes with the tips of his fingers, and then spread them expansively toward Meera.

I see and acknowledge.

and walked away, wishing them all happiness and joy.

Not long after, Karthik found himself again in front of a familiar side door.

"Karthik!!" yelled out Zarg and, in a rush with air kisses, hugged Karthik, who turned stiff in surprise.

Flustered, Karthik tried composing himself, but Zarg ignored him and continued without skipping a beat. "Just in time, sweetheart," they said, pointing at a large display on the screen.

Karthik could see what appeared to be the view from a technician's headset. At the corner was the Lestat Industry logo, a pentagram enclosed in a triangle. At the other corner of the screen was a company logo, "Triton Security."

"What exactly am I seeing here?" asked Karthik.

Zarg continued excitedly," So I did some searching, and Triton Security is contracted to do the security maintenance at ZyraCorp's headquarters globally.

"Wouldn't you know it? I just happen to have a private contractor in Hobart who used to work at the local Triton Security branch.

"He still knew the password to disarm their security system. Apparently, it hadn't been changed since it was opened, so it was simple for someone to access the office and make some quick changes. "

Karthik laughed to himself.

Here I was thinking that breaking into ZyraCorp would require some intense phreaking skills, but this sounded like sheer dumb luck.

Zarg continued "Then, after that, it was a simple matter of bypassing the neuro-fibrillated firewall using a polymorphic zero-day exploit, and then we slipped straight into the hyper-converged mainframe. Their heuristic anomaly detection looked like it was designed by bacchus.

"The only thing left behind is a chaotic trail of pseudo-randomised digital echoes.

"After that, with a quick execution of the syntactic obfuscation algorithm to access their automated warehouses and then...."

Zarg gestured grandly at the screen and yelled. "Voila!!"

Karthik nodded sagely.

He didn't understand a word of what Zarg had just said.

Karthik came from a line of old-school phreakers, but the level of sophistication that Zarg was talking about was well beyond his grasp. He wasn't even sure if he could come up with any sort of adequate response.

So he simply kept nodding.

"Rawr!! These kitty claws can get anywhere." Zarg purred playfully. "Now comes the best bit. "Watch."

Karthik stared mesmerised at the screen as he watched the technician riding in an elevator to what appeared to be the 29th floor.

Getting out of the bank of elevators, the technician walked down the corridor lit by soft, ambient lighting that gently illuminated the space, casting a warm glow over silk-upholstered settees arranged thoughtfully around opulent, hand-knotted rugs. He stopped when he reached a pair of double doors with a discreet sign that said 'Ballroom' to the side.

Approaching the person in a high-visibility vest sitting behind a table of Jaipur marble adorned with intricate hand-carved wooden inserts, the technician validated his credentials and put on the pair of noise filters that were handed to him.

The tech walked into an airlock, waited for the atmosphere to adjust, and stepped into the chaos of a fully active construction site.

The tuned mass dampeners for each floor had been tweaked so that most of the vibration was being absorbed, and there was barely a shudder outside the ballroom.

Looking up, the screen changed to the watch drones as they up banners at the high ceilings that said

"Welcome to Founders Day X"

Heading straight to the foreman onsite, the tech showed his pad with the work order. The foreman shrugged, tapped his periband and left the tech to his business.

Grabbing his pad, the tech initiated a scan that mapped all sensors in the room. Straight above him, though, above the podium, was a dark spot with a red warning light around. Nodding, the tech grabbed the marked box from his bag before dropping it on a drone with the location of the faulty sensor.

After logging into the local network, the drone mapped the room and the other drones in the air, then made its way to the faulty sensor, swapping it out in minutes.

The view lifted up slightly while the technician yawned, and then to view his pad while he confirmed that it was operational. He must have been satisfied because the next thing that Karthik saw was the technician turn and walk away.

Feeling a bit let down by the anticlimactic series of events, Karthik couldn't understand the sudden whoop of joy within a few minutes of the technician leaving the room.

He was even more surprised when he heard Zarg yell, "Muhe to Meeta Karo!!!" grabbing the jalebis and laddus near him and stuffing them into the mouths of the kids nearby.

Karthik walked to the screen and saw a single line of code on the clear screen.

\>>>Xyphor server 36. Enter command>>

Stuffing the laddu into Karthik, Zarg pumped Karthik's hand. "Now it's over to you, my big, strong hero", and they playfully squeezed Karthik's bicep.

With a wag of a finger and a smirk Karthik asked. "Come again?"

Zarg replied, whip-sharp. "Happy to, wink wink, nudge nudge."

Karthik, almost red with embarrassment, tried again, "I mean, what just happened? Why are you celebrating?"

It finally dawned on Zarg that while even the kids around them understood what they had done, Karthik really didn't understand what had just happened.

Just like they had seen Agha Khan do, Zarg beckoned Karthik to the armchair at the back and sat down beside him. Looking at him, Zarg took a deep breath and started explaining. "You know that ZyraCorp offices have a rep for being one of the hardest buildings to phreak in the world. Do you know why?"

Karthik sheepishly shook his head.

Looks like I have to go back to the basics with this one.

Zarg patiently said, "The main reason ZyraCorp is a hard nut to crack is because they spent a lot of cred to make their buildings digitally secure.

"Old man Contractor was paranoid as Bunty and put it into the specs for each of their building that it be housed in a 'Faraday cage' from top to bottom. It's an invisible shield that blocks all electronic communication.

"This means that they have full control of all digital traffic within the building.

"Most people visiting there don't even know that it's set up since the transition is seamless. You can be on a call on your peripheral just outside the building, but as soon as you enter inside, the call, along with comms from every one of your devices, will now have to pass through the Zion portal.

Zion Portal?

"Ohh the great and mighty Zion portal. I can hear you think," smirked Zarg knowingly. Well, the Zion portal is their great communication firewall. With its Entanglement Core and its Nexus Gateway it uses a quantum key distribution for encryption that is impossible to access from outside without their access codes.

"Their internal systems, on the other hand, is another story altogether."

Zarg paused to flick a vid to Karthik's peripheral, which showed an avatar with a flaming skull and a spiked leather jacket running through a presentation on a virtual stage.

Zarg continued. "I picked up this tiny presso at the last HackerCon from Max_Vertigo, my fave phreaker. The dude is a legend and somehow figures out the most niche access points. I wasn't 100 per cent sure that it would work, but .."

Zarg waved their hand expansively to the screen. "I've given you remote access to the ZyraCorp mainframes. All you need is a decent phreaker on the inside, and Patel is your uncle."

Karthik was impressed now. Really impressed, but he shook his head, still not clear. "So why not just phreak it now? You already got an in."

Zarg sighed. "Abey yaar. Didn't I just tell you about the Zion portal? A ping like what we just did would be treated as a lost packet, but anything longer than that would activate the Sentinel protocol, and that's the end of everything.

"Na, for this, you would need someone on the inside.

"Get your peeps to hit me up, and the deets shall be delivered,"

Zarg finished with a bow.

Karthik frowned.

Now, that might be a problem since none of my phreaker dudes will speak with me.

Hmm. Work with what you have.

Karthik looked into Zarg and put up his Blue Knight. "Now that I already have the best, do I really need some other phreaker to tempt me?

"Fancy a trip?"

Zarg looked at Karthik, shocked, and then laughed. "Oh, big boy, you are cute and all, but you are just not my type.

"Your offer, on the other hand, is quite tempting. I was thinking of looking for something to really test Mastishk.

Karthik was puzzled. "Mastishk?"

With a smile, Zarg said. "Ahh, I thought you would never ask.

"TaDa!!"

With a dramatic push of a button, Zarg turned the lights of the small chamber right behind them.

Karthik stood in awe, staring at the sphere of electronics with the operator's console at the centre.

Smiling, he thought.

I think it's time to get the gang back together.

| 10 |

Rapture / Heathens

The morning sunlight filled up Tara's apartment at exactly 7 in the morning.

Raising one hand, Tara tried to shield the sun and squinted at the brightness. As programmed, the smart windows in her apartment turned fully transparent from their previous night mode and let in all of the morning sunlight.

The change had been sudden and was meant to be jarring to wake up the most persistent sleepers.

Lachuka drove her mental.

Always has, always will.

You could set the windows to anything you wanted—scenes of morning meadows in Srinagar, a gentle sunrise at the beach on Goa. But no, hers was set to change from pure darkness to whatever the morning had to offer in an instant at 7 on the dot. From this height up in the apartment, this made for some interesting mornings. There were the usual bright and sunny days when all she had to endure was bright sunlight. Then, there were lightning storms during the monsoon season and hailstorms in December.

It was Fasil's idea. "A dose of randomness before the morning grind. Better than coffee." he had laughed.

The worst was the full moon nights when the windows even turned off randomly as soon as the sensors detected that the moon was perfectly visible from their windows. Those were the nights that they were so busy that they rarely got much sleep, but nevertheless, they didn't feel the need for additional pick-me-ups in the morning.

Lachuka drove her mental.

She had tried to get her own profile for the windows, but Fasil's name was on the lease, and he locked her out of it. She begged, pouted, and pleaded, but he always refused with a long, tight kiss on the lips.

" No, my jaanu. Learn to embrace the chaos. It's what makes us human. " After his death, the permissions were transferred to her, and she could have changed them to any of the million options available to her at any time.

Yup. She can change it any day now.

Yup. Today is going to be the day that she is going to do it.

Yup.

Lachuka drove her mental.

She needed to move out of this apartment. There were too many reminders of him all around the house, and sometimes Tara felt like she was choking.

STOP!!

Clipping her peripheral back on, she reviewed her inbox. The coroner's report had already been filed—at 8 in the morning. She knew that she had asked for it to be prioritised, but that usually meant that she would have the report within a week. Like all bureaucratic offices, the speed of the work carried out at the coroner's was based on how much it had been greased. There was a processing backlog of John and Jane Does going back months and even years in some instances.

Even with Tara's request, a death in the chawl is as low a priority as priorities can get.

Opening up the report, it was simply a sign-off by the attending doctor confirming the initial scan report that it was a drowning.

Nothing unusual about that.

Except that it was signed off by a senior doctor and co-signed by the head of surgery at the morgue. Validated by the senior member in the office, it would be almost impossible to request a re-evaluation. Any further information would require a court order, which would take as long as any typical court case, which may be forever.

The head of the mortuary signed off on a dead basti girl.
Within hours of receiving it.
First Deepak, now this.

This wasn't just grease; it was a whole barrel of oil.

Tara didn't need to be an Impath to know that, for some reason, some very powerful people would like to keep this quiet. It would be asking for trouble for someone to make further enquiries into this case.

Someone should almost have a death wish.

It's been a while since Tara meditated. Meditating opened her emotional barriers, and lately, only raw grief has flooded in. It was great for clarity, though, and it does help when she has difficult decisions to make.

Sitting cross-legged at the foot of the bed, Tara stared up at the ceiling fan as it swung lazily around. While functional, it was more for a retro decorative look and was mesmerizingly slow.

Tara quieted and closed her eyes. She coughed hard with the first deep intake of breath.

Let's try this again.

She breathed in again and again, finally able to take a full, deep breath, and this time, she breathed easily.

Watching her breath come in and out.

Closing her eyes, Tara continued breathing and the city sounds now muted gradually till all she could hear was her breath and her steady heartbeat. This, too, faded away till all she noticed was the deafening silence.

No thoughts, no mind.

Tara breathed in again, and with her next breath, she could feel herself lighten. The sensation wasn't unlike slipping off a comfortably tight pair of jeans. It radiated from her feet and gradually moved up her legs, to her hips, to her chest and finally to her head.

Past her head, she felt an incredible lightness of being, which was scary and exhilarating at the same time.

The lightness didn't stop, and she could feel herself still rising.

Eyes closed, she waited a few seconds/minutes. She was never sure.

Time seemed to bend and be as light as she felt.

She breathed once more and lifted.

All sensations and thoughts ceased as she instinctively closed her eyes until she felt that she could open them.

And she did then.

Tara looked at the fan blades again, but this time, she was looking down at them. She wasn't alarmed that the blades seemed to be going through her head; instead, she thought.

Must get Janvi to clean the top of the fans.
It's quite dusty already.

Tara raised her arm to touch her face, which still felt as solid as ever, though her hand was now translucent.

Through a shimmering haze, she could see her body still sitting cross-legged below. A thin silver thread with speckles of light travelling through it was attached to her navel and tethering Tara to her physical body.

Crossing her legs, Tara's spirit form matched the pose held by her body, and she floated above her body like a giant person-sized balloon.

Turning back, Tara took a good, long, hard look at herself and didn't like what she saw.

It wasn't like looking at her body in a mirror, which Tara was used to, but when she was outside, it was a lot clearer to see how other people perceived her and she wasn't happy about it.

Now came the hard part.

Tara gripped the silky, smooth thread, twisted it around her fingers, and pulled.

The grip was tight, but the bond was strong, so she pulled again.

This time, she could feel it give.

Letting it go, the thread slowly started to unravel.

Now free, Tara flew.

Tara wasn't sure how long she had been gone, but by the time she was aware again, her shoulders ached, and her legs had gone to sleep. Her feet and legs were so cramped that even trying to wiggle her toes sent spears of pain straight up her thighs.

" Next time, put a damn probe massager when you go". Tara scolded herself.

She relaxed and braced for the inevitable waves to come and just let it flow through her.

Wave after wave of anger, anxiety, grief, frustration and sadness buffeted her. Tara ignored the tears that flowed freely from her eyes and bore the tsunami of emotions till they passed.

Once they stopped or were subdued enough, Tara stretched out her arms, let out a yawn, and then promptly vomited into the bucket nearby.

Pieces of leftover rice floated on top of the water in the bucket, but the pack of Mediclear that she had added earlier neutralised the stench. Rinsing her mouth with the nearby bottle of water, she spat into the bucket and took it to the bathroom to clean up.

This was only the first of the comedowns, but the first ones were usually the worst, so she should be able to step out now.

For now, she had the overwhelming urge to swing by the coroners and look for a red rabbit.

Tara grinned

Looks like I do have a death wish after all.

Clipping her peripheral back on, Tara noted that this time, she had only travelled an hour. Tara took the lift down to her official vehicle, suited and feeling fresh as a jasmine.

"To the coroners," she told the car. "The one in Jangshung. Not the Kachari complex," she added, remembering what the medevac attendant had told her while signing off on the sheet. The car beeped in acknowledgement, and she chilled, stretching out in the resin seats. Now that the decision had been made, she felt unusually calm and relaxed. Oohams may not always pan out the way she wanted them to, but regardless, it will make for an interesting morning.

Dropping her off in front of the Jangshung City Morgue as requested, the car beeped her goodbye and then buggered off to park itself somewhere.

Walking up the stairs, Tara pulled up the case file on her peripheral. The senior doctor who signed off was Charlie Khasi. She had heard of him. He was one of the most senior doctor officers in the local branch and had worked here for decades. Tara knew there would be no point in approaching him directly. For someone to be here for that long, he was perfectly part of the system and had likely been well-fed.

Instead, she wandered down the corridor. With her uniform and ID badge, she wouldn't be questioned as long as she steered clear of the highly restricted areas.

For now, she needed to get her flow on. Asking her peripheral to put on the HMV, she strolled down the corridor while the record player cued her tracks.

Listening to the music, she could feel herself chilling even more.

It started first with a simple bopping of the head. In time, with the music, Tara's chin dipped up and down with the rhythm of the song. Her hips started swaying, and if she was alone, she would have been sashaying down the corridor, but restraining herself, she instead contained her flow to the tapping out of the beat to an imaginary drum.

In an effort to preserve historical periods, government buildings adapted to the style of certain eras, an initiative started by the incumbent Darsha party to promote national pride and was heavily funded to ensure its permanence and a constant reminder of the party's influence. The corridors were made of faux wood and imitation linoleum, all meticulously recreated to match the era known as the shiny 60s. Personnel walked around in bell-bottom pants with wide-collar shirts, which was the required fashion code for this building. The allocation of time periods to government buildings was random, which could lead to some interesting anomalies, like the local police station in Dras, which ended up being allocated pointed helmets and khaki shorts. It was rumoured that some of the officers even resorted to wearing face warmers shaped like curly moustaches to combat the freezing temperatures.

Strolling through the corridor, the air seemed to blend in a mist of red and white. The cloud, visible only to Tara, didn't bother anybody else. This ooham seemed very delicate, but she wasn't in any hurry. With the ooham now visible, it would only be a matter of time before it got resolved.

Listening to her music, she glided through the corridor until the cloud seemed to intensify at a doctor's lounge. There, seated behind a desk, was a woman in a red top and a stethoscope around her neck, busy reading something. A cloud of white settled around the top of the double buns on her blonde hair, which looked exactly like rabbit ears.

Tara smiled and allowed her feet a final slip and slide before the rhythm of her walk lost its apparent grace and solidified into resolution with every step. Now walking with authority, she headed straight to the woman, and without even bothering with introductions, she sternly said.

"What do you know about Vaishali Trag, the dead girl brought here."

Startled, the woman nearly fell off the chair. The ooham cloud settled around her like a shell, and her aura pulsed rapidly in time with her heartbeat.

Tara smiled. Now that she had elegantly locked in the ooham, the next steps should flow. It was all about grabbing her attention and establishing her authority as swiftly as possible. Time is of the essence, though; the next step would be rapidly calming her down.

Tara looked right into the eyes of the bespectacled doctor.

She's young. Looks like she was straight out of grad school.

Probably bunched with all the grunt work as the privilege of working here.

"What's your name?" she asked softly.

"Harleen Quereshi", stammered Harleen or Harley as she was known to her friends.

Tara smiled now, a very gentle, soothing smile. "Did you see the dead Siddhi girl who came in today?"

Harley stood up with a gasp. "Yes, Shri, but how did you know? " said Harleen, surprise making her more forthcoming. "Ohhh!!! You are an IPS officer!!! Boy, you guys must be really good at your jobs. Yes, I was the one who sent the report to Charlie Shri for sign-off. "

With a pointed finger and a squinted eye, she playfully winked at Tara."Didcha guys spy on my peripheral?

Talking with coroners wasn't new to Tara; it was inevitable in a career that dealt with the harsher realities of existence. This one didn't seem that bright, though.

Tara sighed.

This conversation looked like it may get a bit tedious, but the ooham was still holding strong, so she persisted. "So, what can you tell me about her?"

Harleen stammered. "Actually, it may be better for you to speak with Charlie Shri. I am only an intern, and officially, I am not allowed to conduct any examinations on my own. I can call Charlie Shri if you would like to discuss the official report with him."

Tara patted her companionably and shook her head no. "Let's not disturb Charlie bhai just yet. He is a very busy man. Why don't we have a chat about what you think?

"Just a nice, easy chat. "

Tara had been listening. Really listening to Harleen.

She had heard a hesitation, a reconsidered thought when Harleen had used the word 'officially'.

She knows something. Something she is not supposed to.
Kollam, this conversation just got very interesting.

Pulling out the chair next to Harley, Tara sat down in front of her. With a raised eyebrow, she looked deep into Harley's eyes and patted her shoulder encouragingly.

Nodding, Tara crooned. "Let's just have a small chat. Just you and I."

Harley couldn't look away from Tara's eyes. Listening to the soothing voice, the most instinctive and intuitive part of herself relaxed and believed it could trust Tara.

Her breath became deeper until she felt so relaxed that her eyes started drooping. The ooham was now so strong over Harleen that a red-and-white shell of energy enveloped her. Smiling and in a voice that sounded half asleep, she replied. "Yes. A chat sounds lovely."

Tara nodded at the same cadence as Harley's speech and asked. "So what did you really find out?"

As if in a trance, Harleen replied. "Well, I was just going to sign off the death as drowning as per the original report when I noted that she was flagged as having neural damage from her port. But hello, she has a Peripheral Pro, which is like surge-proof. So, like, there was no way that it fried her brains.

"It was the night shift, and I was pretty bored, so I thought I might as well do a quick neural scan just to check things out.

"It was very bizarre, Shri. The victims' neural tissues showed significant exposure to stress levels, but it was far beyond what a standard interface Peripheral port usage would cause, let alone a Pro port would do."

Harleen continued, "So, I had a closer look, and Vaishali seemed to have a delicate mesh of neurallace wrapping around the brain. I have never seen anything like it before, but the way it was integrated made it look like it was embedded into her brain quite deeply."

Tara already knew about neural integration. It was in the standard disclaimer video they showed every customer who had ever had Peripherals or Extrexs installed. "Hang on a minute; the Peripheral port only attaches itself to very specific neural points. What is this port doing, spreading itself all around the brain?"

"Exactly. Shri," said Harleen, pleased to be understood. "In fact, there is a significant level of integration with neural tissues, way more than what you would expect for integration to a peripheral or even an advanced Ext.

"Then there were the spinal probes."

"Spinal Probes?" It was Tara's turn to get agitated. With great effort to not break Harleen's flow, she asked her in a strained voice. "Are you telling me that this girl didn't kill herself?"

Harleen shook her head. " No, Shri. There are no signs of struggles, and apart from the brain damage, there is nothing else to indicate that this wasn't self-inflicted. However, I don't think she was in the right state of mind. The damage to the prefrontal cortex alone would have profoundly impaired her decision-making.

"With significant neural damage like that, it would have only been a matter of time before she did something dangerous, that is, if she didn't have a stroke earlier than that. "

Tara asked the question even though she knew the answer: "What did Charlie Shri have to say about it when you flagged this?"

Harleen's flow finally popped, and she replied ruefully. "He said it was likely stims that fried her brain and to do my job and not make more work for him. "

Proving far more helpful than Tara had any reason to expect, Tara didn't feel that great about herself for underestimating Harleen. Gratitude was a lesson that Fasil taught well, but Tara always considered herself a poor student. A small part of her was touched that she actually learned far more than she gave herself credit for.

With palms folded, Tara stood up and thanked Harleen.

Used to fearing law enforcement members, Harley was touched and returned the gesture with a solemn bow as well. Tara was done here, so she turned around to walk away.

Harley hesitated but, in spite of herself, called out softly. "Wait", catching Tara in mid-stride.

" I will be in so much trouble if I ever get found out, but I did make a backup of the scan so that I can look at it further. The files are encrypted, though, and with the case being closed, I will not be able to access them anymore. But maybe check with your team if they can do something with it?"

Harley placed a gunmetal ring on Tara's open palm. "Please don't tell on me. I just wanted to study the scans for myself, even though I wasn't supposed to. I feel I can trust you, though."

Tara smiled and grasped Harleen's hand. " This will not get back to you. I promise."

The ooham had finally been released, and she was at peace when she walked out of the mortuary.

She didn't call for her official vehicle but instead hailed a passing Relaxacab. 'Head to Habibyada Basti,' she told the car, and it readily complied.

Now, for the sake of others, she really needed to keep this as quiet as possible.

Why are you doing this Tara? she asked herself.

She didn't get an answer, but an image of a face haloed with curly black hair and a heart-shaped upala appeared. She supposed that was good enough a reason as any for now and starting thinking how she was going to manage entering the basti.

It was just before midday and she hoped it would be the quietest time to visit. Usually, mornings are filled with the chaos of the rush of workers heading to the city on the morning mono-rails or shareacabs. Any visit here had to be done in her civvies, and Tara had changed into her brown loafers again, only this time coupled with a pattiyala of plain cream and a purple holo-kurta swirling with the sombre peacock motifs. She would stand out as an outsider as it is, and she didn't want to make it any more obvious that she was an IPS officer. The basti did not have many ardent supporters of the law.

Originally built by Raja Revedad for the attendants of his River Banjara bride, the backwaters were reclaimed to honour their promise of staying only on water. Over time, the settlement had grown to a small city with multiple chawls that were each unofficially ruled with an iron hand by the Basti Kings or Panchrajas.

A fiefdom of their own, few from the police dare enter it officially, although more than a few visit them unofficially to indulge in the very vices that they have been charged with eradicating.

The morning sun cast long shadows over the bustling basti as Tara arrived in her cab. The narrow lanes were abuzz with activity as the residents navigated their way through the makeshift market stalls and crowded pathways.

The air was thick with the mingling scents of spices, fresh produce, and the dampness that clung to the slum's riverbanks. Elevated on sturdy stilts constructed from bamboo and pretty much everything else they could scavenge, the pathways were winding, and only long-term residents knew the way through all of them. The structures were topped with hand-assembled solar panels and wind turbines. Some of the larger dwellings had even managed to install micro-hydro generators under their houses.

Despite being familiar with the chaos, Tara felt uneasy as she weaved through the densely packed dwellings. The vibrant spectrum of colours that covered the makeshift homes painted a stark contrast to the grim reality that often lurked within.

Some of the farmers had made up floats where they had gardens filled with tomatoes, chillies and cucumbers. The more valuable vanilla and lavender are grown in the personal garden of the Kamar Thurapan, the local Panchraja. Passing the gardens of herbs, she breathed in deeply of the roses and jasmines that clung on every surface. Plucking a passion fruit from a nearby vine she looked across the bridge to see an unusual sight.

A domo!!

Though domos were able to change their physical appearance at will, Impaths instinctively can sense the shifting auras of their personas despite what their external façade looked like. This domo's auras was all over the place, violently shifting as a trapped animal and was the only reason why it stood out like a multi-coloured neon display.

Looks like it has locked into a visage for quite some time.

She looked around to see if it could see what they looked like in real life, but while she could still see the aura display as it walked away, it was too far away to see their faces.

With a shrug, she found herself in front of her final destination.

Blue bicycle house, Vaishali's residence.

The front of the house was vine-covered like the rest of the dwellings here; the major differentiator was an old cycle painted blue which was almost embedded into the wall with the thick branches. However, it had been freshly painted, likely as part of a milestone Śrāddha. A day of remembrance for one's forbearers, the family must have painted it to honour the ancestor who built the house and owned the original blue cycle.

The modest dwelling overlooked the river, and she could see the customary poles just outside the windows facing the river, fishing for the Tilapia and catfish that swam through the interconnected ponds and tanks. Tara noted the familiarity of the surroundings—the worn-out door, the splashes of colour on the walls, and the water pots neatly arranged outside. A constant reminder of the water from whence they came, she mindfully sidestepped the residents sitting out in the front of their houses with their feet dipped in the medicinal liquid.

Tara knocked gently, and after a moment, the door creaked open. A woman peeped the small crack. With only her downward eyes visible through the halo of jet-black hair that had escaped her saree, she greeted Tara with a wary look. "What brings an officer like you here?"

Guess the civvies didn't work.

Dropping all pretence of subterfuge, Tara got straight to the point. "I am here about Vaishali."

Upon the mention of her daughter's name, the woman's fear was overcome by motherly concern. "Vaishali? What happened to Vaishali? She is dead, isn't she?". A lifelong resident of the bastis, the woman knew that a visit from a solitary officer here could only mean one thing.

In an unexpected fury, she wailed, "I told her to stop. I told her that her life wasn't worth the extra gadgets at our house, but she wouldn't listen."

"When did you last see her?", Tara asked gently.

Vaishali's mother bowed. "She hasn't been home for weeks now."

The mother used to loss and turmoil all her life, bore it with the stoicism common to her kind and invited Tara inside, where the air was cooler, and a small shrine adorned one corner of the room.

Once they were safe from prying ears, Tara continued. "What exactly did she do at ZyraCorp?"

Her mother bowed. "I never really understood. Something to do with the head computers.

"I don't think Vaishali really understood either. As part of their job, she and her friends had to spend a lot of time at their office.

"She could be gone for days, weeks, or even fortnights sometimes, and she would never be able to tell me what had happened. It's like she forgot everything that happened while she was staying over at work."

"For her it would it would always seem as if she has been away for just a night."

The mother actually interrupted Tara could ask the most obvious question. "I know what you are thinking. Did she lie about the whole thing and was doing some 420?

"I was born in this house and well aware of what dandha looks like and no Shri, this was a legit job and it paid well.

"She was a good girl and she takes care of us. We could never afford her marriage jewellery but she paid for all of it on her own. She took so much pride in wearing them every day and we got plenty of alliances from families, some of them who had considered us beneath them before.

"All because of Vaishali.

"I wasn't happy, though.

"I was scared. Scared of everything.

"It wasn't just that all these changes that were happening but …

"She never told me, but I am her mother, and I could never forgive or forget the haunted look on my daughter's face as, bit by bit, they took away her life. I told her it was very dangerous, that it could even give her the vapours.

"She used to laugh and say, 'I work for a badda company. It may be a little uncomfortable, but how can a company like ZyraCorp hurt me?

"They are good people.'"

Zara nodded. This wasn't a new story, just another version of the powerful preying on the weak—a tale as old as time without a happy ending. "What about her friends, the ones she worked with?" she asked.

Vaishali's mother hung her head down. "They were a tight bunch, but apart from the Siddi girl, I didn't meet any of them. I do have something, though." She rummaged among her treasures in a wooden bureau and produced an old-fashioned Instagraph showing 5 girls at a retro-mela. The spinning Ferris wheel and the jumping girls forever locked in a loop for eternity. At the bottom was written in black marker.

'Chawl Chokris'

At the back, scrawled in the same black marker, were 5 names with Vaishali Traag at the top of them.

Scanning it with her peripheral, she grammed the Instagraph and returned it back to the mother. who began reminiscence about Vaishali's dreams and her desire to break free from her constraints.

Tara nodded, and while it may have appeared coldhearted, she ended the conversation abruptly. The mother grieving her daughter needed a shoulder to cry on. Tara's just wasn't one that was available.

Handing over a heavy bundle into the mother's open hands, Tara turned away without waiting for it to be opened. Closing the door behind her, she walked away as quickly as possible. She suddenly couldn't breathe anymore, and the bustling slum seemed to close in around her.

With Vaishali's mom signing off on the paperwork, she was supposed to close it out at her end and send it across for processing. Protocol dictated that any additional information should just be noted and passed on to the control centre for further investigation.

Tara hesitated, hitting the 'Complete' button, though.

Once done, combined with the coroner's record, the case would be officially closed out as a drowning. She couldn't, however, ignore the feeling that she was only scratching the surface of whatever this was. While she could always directly request Control to investigate the names on her behalf, she also knew that it was more than likely that the search would trigger a call from someone like Deepak to reprimand her for not 'dropping it'.

Switching on her peripheral, she looked at her caseload.

Still empty.

She thought about her apartment.

Still empty.

Tara was tired, but maybe she wasn't that tired just yet.

I wonder how deep this hole really is.

A decision made, Tara felt free and thought about what was next.

She can't look into this any more in an official capacity. No, for this, she needed someone who would be able to cut through all the red tape but skilful enough not to get caught, and Tara knew just who that person would be.

I think it's time I pay Nithya a visit.

| 11 |

Proud Mary / Pandrikku Nandri Solli

"You can't do this, goddammit. You know how close I am to a breakthrough," Striber exclaimed.

His boss, Manav Davis, smiled back at him, a bit too pleasantly. "It's nothing personal, Striber. Corpo is carrying out budget cuts and putting a few projekts on hold.

"The new CEO has just started, and he wants to shake things up. This is part of his promise to the shareholders to gain cost efficiencies and optimise synergies.

"Unfortunately, your Augmentation projekt is the most expensive in R&D, so it will have to be put on hold for now."

Striber wiped his forehead, his hands lingering on the eyebrow, pulling it up till it hurt. He didn't even notice that he was grimacing in pain. "What do you mean, cost efficiency improvements? We just launched the neural band, and the sales from that alone have been in the millions for the company this year alone.

"This product, along with many others, was made by us right here in this very building. "

Manav shook his head. "You should know that Lestat Corporation is very grateful for the contributions made by you and your team to the company, but times are hard.

The company has been diligently working to break into the European market, and the investment costs have been significantly over our initial forecasts.

"Don't worry; the benefits will eventually trickle down, and your department will soon have all the funding it needs and more.

"Till then, however, we all have to make sacrifices for the greater good. "

Striber violently shook his head in anger.

The only 'greater good' that you care about is your bonus, you little snake.

He tried to calm down. Taking a deep breath, he said calmly, "I was there when the last CEO joined, and I am afraid I know exactly what 'shake things up' means.

"We have a really solid team working on this. They have really gotten into the swing of things, and we can actually do this on schedule and on budget.

"If we put the project on hold, the team will be reassigned. Trying to regroup and get the ball rolling again will set us back not months but years."

Manav stretched his hands expansively." I know this projekt is personal to you, but I am afraid my hands are tied", said Manav, his smile becoming even broader.

The bastard is enjoying this. He has been looking to put me in my place, and he is not going to let it go so easily.

Being the lead of a technical team, this was not the first time that Striber had butt heads with management. His old boss had his back, however, and shielded him from most of the corpo bullshit. They knew that to deliver the best, you need the best, and if justified, they would fight tooth and nail to meet the needs of their team. Striber and his team were able to do their best, and together, they could create and deliver a range of successful products, all of which helped Lestat Industries be the market behemoth that it was.

That was until Manav was selected to take over after a corporate restructure. From the very first meeting, Striber knew that things would change, and not necessarily for the better.

Though Manav led a whole technical department, he was not technically skilled himself. His expertise was more on the business side of things. Manav was of the opinion that the same could be done for cheaper, and Striber has had frequent arguments with him.

Unfortunately, as Manav was his manager, he was also the gatekeeper to the funding, and Striber was getting increasingly frustrated with the roadblocks that have now become more regular.

It also didn't help that Striber had a nasty temper and could not charm his way out of trouble.

In the past, Striber often got away with his wild requests simply because his team delivered. He didn't think it was possible this time, though. He had heard some of the rumours, and the rest was published on more than enough news streams that it had become public knowledge. There was a government contract that the company had incorrectly estimated to the tune of billions and was legally obliged to fulfil. There were also corporate fines when the top management was caught embezzling. The old CEO himself had only avoided jail time due to the barrage of lawyers hired by the company. Forced to resign, he was probably crying himself to sleep with the millions he managed to make during his tenure.

The new CEO was young and was eager to show that he could turn things around at Lestat Corp.

Striber knew that the restructuring and cost-cutting would only be the first of many proposed changes, and people lower down, like his team and him, would be the ones who would pay the real price.

Fuck Corpo

Striber breathed deeply and tried once more: "Please. You know this projekt is personal to me. It's a solid chance to help Indra." He was so desperate that he almost added, "I will do anything to get this off the ground."

Almost.

Manav's smile was so wide now that it reached his ears, but it still didn't reach his eyes. Only a psychopath would think that it was reassuring. "I am really sorry, Striber, but the decision has been made well above my pay grade. There is nothing more that I can do."

"Please let your team know that they have a week to wrap things up. They will be contacted shortly with their new assignments. "

Saying that, Manav turned to his computer and started tapping away on his keyboard.

Striber turned around without another word. It was pointless arguing further.

He left Manav's office and took the lift down to his lab downstairs. On seeing him walk down the corridor, his team had left their desks and was now huddled in front of the entrance. They had heard the rumours and were expecting the worst.

Striber couldn't hide his disappointment in front of them. Kishore Karbi, his long-time friend and now lead engineer, approached him. "That bad, huh?"

"They have asked us to shut down immediately. We are to be disbanded by the end of the week", Striber said with a heavy sigh.

"Don't they realise how close we are?" This is going to change the world. We are just 6 months away from human trials, and then after that, the possibilities are endless, Kishore said in exasperation.

Striber threw up his hands. " Apparently, we are the most expensive. It's purely a question of budgets. Nobody doubts what we can do."

Kishore walked up. "We put everything on hold? Just like that. Extrex wasn't going to be helping just Indra.

Kishore revealed with a sigh "We got the feedback from the feelers we sent out to the veterans groups, and they are already applicants for the human trials despite us clearly outlining the risks. People are desperate and willing to try anything, and here we have something that isn't just a pipe dream.

Striber slammed his fists on the table and then calmly said, "Of course, I want to keep going no matter what; I just don't know how."

"The irony of the whole situation is that the real problem is that we are all too good at our jobs," said Striber, sneering. "Knowing Manav, he would likely split the team up into all the other groups.

"With the quality of work that we deliver, he would likely be able to let go of 2 or 3 heads in those teams by re-assigning the 7 of us. "

"Knowing my luck, I would probably be assigned to the Neural Link projekt again."

"That's bullshit," yelled Kishore in frustration. "It's grad-level work at this stage. The product has already been launched, and we have already trained the maintenance engineers.

"This is bread and butter stuff; we are too good for that." Kishore waved his hands around the room. "This is where we should be."

Striber nodded sympathetically. "I know, but unless a miracle happens, Lestrade Industries will be shutting us down, like it or not."

"We should probably take it to a competitor. That will teach them." Kishore laughed sarcastically but then sadly cast his eyes down. "When I heard that you were being called by management, Striber, I made some quick calls.

"Its pretty much the same story at all of them. I can't think of a single company that would hire all of us and have the resources we need. "

"So let's start something on our own then, "said Striber with a sudden iron resolution. "It's not impossible. These start-ups are actually doing a lot of the actually groundbreaking tech. We could do that. They may own all the stuff in the room, but they still don't own what's in our heads, and that's all the Intellectual Property we need. "

Kishore cheered up a bit, but reality hit, and he asked, "We could, but where is the money? The hardware alone would easily cost 10 million vabus. Last I checked, we didn't have access to that money."

Shoulders squared, Striber said. "You and I both know what we got here. This is a solid product. We are so close."

Striber eagerly addressed everybody in the room, "This is possible. We will have to make sacrifices, the least of which would be forgoing our salaries. If we do decide to do this, we will need to work harder and longer than we have ever done before.

"This has to be something that you guys want. I can't force you, and I totally understand if any of you say no.

"You have families and mortgages.

"This may not even work, and we would all have to be back at Lestat with massive debts.

"I do have one thing to say, though.

"Have a good long think about this.

"This is a real chance to make something on our own."

"Even if it doesn't work out, at least we know that we have tried, and sometimes that may be all we need to know to help us sleep at night."

Unsurprisingly, his entire team raised their hands in acknowledgement. Striber may have a quick temper, but he was loyal to his team. More importantly, if Striber said he would figure it out, they knew he would.

With the room's mood now lifted, Striber felt the edges of his eyes moisten.

Just then, his phone went off. When he took the transparent unit out of his hand, it flashed an angry red.

This is not good.

"An emergency. From Indra," he shouted out loud.

Is it the baby?

He frantically thought.

He saw the text message too late. "Water broke, heading to hospital".

The baby is coming. The baby is coming.

Now. Now.

"Indra is going into labour. " he managed to stammer.

Kishore, for once, knew how to take the lead. " Let me drive you to the hospital. I don't think you are just in the right state.

On his way to the hospital, Striber's thoughts flowed to how he and Indra first met.

He was a brilliantly smart, fiery engineer. She was a brilliantly smart, feisty medical student.

Coming from where and when they were, they couldn't be more worlds apart. She was the daughter of an ancient Parsee family from Palaghat who could trace their ancestry all the way back to the first ships from Iran that landed on the shores of Kochi. He was an orphan who grew up in the slums of Mumbai.

Indra was bright and vibrant and wasn't just the life of the party but the party itself.

He was a hulking brute who was too intimidating to be approached and too shy to approach.

Top of her class but humble and good-natured about it; it felt like everybody either wanted to be her or be with her.

Striber thought she had never known that he loved her, having never had the courage to tell her what he truly felt about her.

Nobody was sure who was responsible for the accident. Some say that the driver, her friend, was stimming. He was, however, rich and influential enough to get away with a clean record.

She was, however, not so lucky and was left paralysed below the waist.

With all the bad press surrounding the accident, her friends' media consultants advised them that the increased contact with Indra would impact their overall brand image. So her friends looked from afar, and while they sent baskets of fruits and flowers, they never visited the hospital even once.

After a couple of months, the baskets dwindled as well.

Striber wouldn't have known that she was in the hospital if his mother hadn't been admitted at the same time. Staying close by, he tried to see Indra at every opportunity he could.

From outside the window, though. Never face to face, till he saw her one day alone, silently weeping into her pillow.

Striber remembered the day that Indra played the veena during a college freshers' program.

Her rendition of the Gayathri Mantra was mesmerising, and all he could recall was the happiness and serenity that radiated from her on that day.

The feedback from the nurse's station gave him an idea, and noting the model of the nurse call system, he quickly pulled up the specs of the units. Pulling up his music player, he grooved down the hallway while hacking into the nurse call station. He slowed and waited at the spot just behind the corner wall where he could see Indra sleeping clearly.

He stopped, breathed deeply, and pulled up the song that he had put on his playlist before he started.

Slowly, the haunting notes of the Gayatri Mantra drafted into the room.

oṃ bhūr bhuvaḥ suvaḥ tat savitur vareṇyaṃ
bhargo devasya dhīmahi dhiyo yo naḥ pracodayāt

While startled initially, as the soothing chant filled the hospital, a sense of serenity filled the hallways.

Watching Indra, Striber saw with a contended sigh that she had finally settled down and was breathing easily. Just when he thought that she had finally slept, she slowly opened her eyes.

Then Indra smiled at him.

They were inseparable after that.

Striber was there for her physiotherapy classes and guided her to her first wheelchair. Her spine was shattered, and the prognosis was that she would never walk again.

Striber was determined to prove them wrong. Indra agreed.

None of their friends were surprised that they were going to move in together, but it didn't go well with her parents.

Her father disowned her and told Indra that she was on her own.

So she rolled out of their lives.

While it was really tough initially, eventually, through their college professors, they got jobs at Lestrade. They quickly rose up the ranks, both being team leaders in their respective R&D fields.

With a lot of their own batch mates joining the team, they ended up making friends as family.

Striber woke up from his reverie when they pulled up into the hospital.

Kishore, with his 3 children, was well familiar with the maternity ward and led them straight to it.

Striber rushed to the counter and was shocked to be told that Indra was just coming out of surgery. "Surgery? There must be some mistake; my wife is supposed to be in the maternity ward."

Its then Striber found out the full story. Walking alone in the park, she started bleeding uncontrollably and collapsed. If it hadn't been for a stranger nearby who had brought Indra into the hospital, they may have lost either the babies or Indra.

Thankfully, all were safe now.

As soon as Striber made himself known at the nurse's station, a bubbly nurse who wasn't shy of partaking in life's pleasures shooed him into the hallway. "Hurry, child. You have bacchus. 2 bacchus."

Striber stopped mid-stride. It finally hit him."2 Babies? As in more than 1?

"Twins?!"

The nurse nodded, "Yes, yes, Twins and can you hurry up ya?"

Almost bulldozed by her, Striber found himself in front of a corridor adorned with warm cartoon letters stating 'Maternity Ward' at the entrance.

Striber was, however, taken aback to see Indra's parents nervously pacing at the room's entrance.

The nurse, with years of experience in the maternity ward, had seen plenty of similar awkward moments and knew exactly what had happened. "Aiyoo, we called her parents already, no, as they were listed as the emergency contacts. Fammilly Problem ah?" guffawed the nurse as she bustled away.

This was the first time that Striber had seen them since that day at Bulgotti house.

At first, Striber thought her father was going to strike him based on her dad's grim expression.

Instead, he fell at Striber's feet.

Quicker than the wind, Striber stopped him from falling down but instead raised him up and hugged him.

Opening the hospital room door, Striber invited them both inside to meet his family.

Indra, tired but glowing with the euphoric bliss of a new mother, beamed even more when she saw her parents with Striber. "Now my life is complete, "she said sleepily, basking in the warmth of her family's love.

Once Indra had fallen asleep, her father tapped Striber on the shoulder and asked him to step outside. Walking to an empty Lounge Room, his father-in-law started the first of many long overdue conversations by addressing an immediate problem. "I heard that your projekt is going to be terminated, although my sources tell me that it is going to be revolutionary and that your team is very close to launching it."

Striber was stunned and couldn't hide his surprise that his father-in-law was so up-to-date on something that he hadn't even mentioned to Indra yet. "Yes. They are fools and don't know what they are doing, but how the heck did you find out about it."

Ignoring the question for now, Indra's father instead asked. "How much do you need to start up on your own? "

Laughing sarcastically, Striber said, "A billion vabus."

Indra's father-in-law nodded. "Shouldn't be a problem."

Striber was stunned. He knew that Indra's dad was connected and powerful, but for him to dismissively wave it off?

Her dad continued, "Indra is the first woman in our family to have a job and do something on her own and I am proud of the life you have built.

"One of my biggest fears was that you married her for her money.

"In spite of all my power and wealth, I couldn't protect the one thing that was precious to me, and you were an angry stranger who was trying to take my thangam away from me.

"You had proved time and time again that you loved my Indra but pride was the very thing that ever kept us from reconciling.

"I should have come and reconciled when I saw the beautiful life you built together, all on your own, and now you have made us grandparents.

"Would you ever be able to forgive an old man his pride?"

His paternal instincts blooming, the iron resolve of Striber found newfound commandership with his father-in-law and instead hugged him in response.

At peace, Indra's father nodded, Dabbing his eyes, and explained, "The way I see it, all my resources are for Indra and now the children. If Indra agrees, I will make this happen."

"I was only joking about the figure," said Striber, choking.

Indra's father waved a dismissive hand. "You leave the finances to me with me. I don't know anything about tech, but I do know business, and I know when to listen to people smarter than me.

"I think it's time you met an old friend of mine. He could get you your seed funding, and something tells me that this is going to be a wise investment."

Overflowing with happiness, Striber headed back into the room. When he entered Manav's office this morning, this was not how he expected his day to turn out.

Striber wiped his wife's forehead and told her the news.

Indra glowed, "That's nice chellum, see I told you the babies were good luck."

Striber looked at his kids again.

Indra

Ramin and Zyana.

His family, his world.

"How about Zyra for a company name?" Striber asked his family.

| 12 |

Desert Rose / Duur Se

In the shimmering sands of the secluded beach, where the sun reigns supreme and the waves dance in harmony, Shaani stands, a lone woman amidst the golden sands. Naked except for a loin cloth fashioned from leather, her sun-bronzed skin glistens under the blazing sun, adorned only by the beads of sweat cascading down her brow like tiny rivers seeking refuge in the sand.

With practised hands, she selects the finest specimens from the lengths of vine, palm leaves, and logs she has collected from the nearby grove of palm trees, those blessed with the wisdom of age and the promise of buoyancy upon the waves. She kneels, her fingers tracing the contours of each branch with reverence, feeling the pulse of life thrumming within their fibres.

With her materials gathered, she was ready to build her raft for Virukardi, the sacred art of ooham hunting.

Before she started, though, Shaani walked up to the palm trees by the beach and selected a green coconut that felt heavy for its size amongst others that had fallen on the sand.

The coconut she picked was so fresh that she could barely hear the sloshing of the water inside. She gently washed the coconut's exterior with seawater and then used a sharp rock to crack open the hard outer shell and scrape away the fibrous husk.

The coconut now free; she carefully pierced one of its 'eyes', the dark spots that were the softest part of the fruit, with a piece of flint, accessing the cool water hidden inside. Drinking her fill of the sweet water, she poured the rest on her head, purifying herself.

Shaani then reverently placed the drained coconut on the ground in the sand crater she had dug. She would need it for the next part of her ritual, but she was now ready to build the raft.

With a deep breath, Shaani turns the materials she had gathered and starts weaving them together, working with deft precision and efficiency.

Minutes/hours passed.

Focussed on her offering, time seemed to bend and be as light as she felt.

Pulling the tight rope with her sea-leathered hands, she remembered sitting by the beachside with her grandmother while she had taught her the raft-building part of virukardi. With skilled hands and patient guidance, she had shown her how to weave the leaves and vines, which, with patience and effort, turned into something practical yet beautiful. Meditating deeply on her intention, Shaani wove the vines along with her dreams and aspirations, just like her grandmother had shown her.

The sun sent shafts of heat that burned her back, but she welcomed it. In the service of an ooham this old, it required all the reverence it deserved, and she relished in the effort to make sure that she was worthy to accept it. She swiped the sweat from her brow with one slender finger and flicked it to the sand.

Her raft was ready, and now it was time for the most important part of the ritual.

She kneeled and slowly withdrew a single piece of camphor and a dab of sindhoor from a small leather pouch. Carefully placing them along with the stripped husk, she reverently placed the ensemble on top of the coconut shell.

Using an uncut emerald, she focuses the beam on the camphor until, in a whoosh, it bursts into flames. Waiting until the fire was properly caught, she lifted the coconut above her head, focusing all her doubts and fears on it and smashed it vehemently onto the rock.

As the coconut smashed, Shaani was renewed and relieved of her insecurities and fears.

Placing all her hopes and aspirations into the remains of the coconut, she placed the swageri onto the beach and watched as the waves took the remains of her offering.

Breathing deeply, Shaani flowed and started sensing. The ooham she was searching for was so old that it took her a while to pick it up again, but it was there as it always was.

Waiting for the right person to come along.

Shaani got the first whiff when she came onto this secluded beach many moons ago. It was so faint that she may have missed it, except that she had been thinking of him lately.

Kindred spirits separated by time but joined in the same yearnings; the bonding was both pure chance and meant to happen.

A chest made of dark rosewood with iron banding sits flat on the beach, devoid of legs. On the top of the ancient chest is carved a motif of a deer head with vines for antlers. Dragging the sea chest onto the raft, Shaani bodily lifts it and gently places it in the centre.

Lashing it with more vines, she secures it to the raft, balancing the weight of it.

When the moment felt right, she pushed her raft into the sea and paddled into the open water. Pausing when she needed to, she caught a current and waited for the sea to pull her closer to her final destination.

She sat still as she could despite the lapping waves. She considered sitting down in the cross-legged position taught by a yogi who had visited his village when she was a young'un. Shaani waited. Something told her that it was not ready yet. Having long relied on her feelings, she knew better than to do something when she was not ready to.

So she leaned back against the chest and waited.

Exactly where she was.

Doing what she was doing.

Suddenly, the tug of the ooham felt stronger.

Looking down into the sea, she could now sense the faint ripples she saw with her third eye.

The time had come, and she stood up in anticipation.

Releasing the restraining vines, she opened the sea chest and reverently touched the conch shells and the pair of goggles that were kept in the box. The googles, made of polished quartz crystals and shark leather, were hand-made and belonged to her grandfather. Shaani's grandmother had found the conch shells, and it had taken her a long time to find the perfect ones that were to protect their ears once their adulthood ceremony was over.

First, wearing the goggles, she took her time to adjust them to her eyes. Then, she secured the conch shells and carefully covered her ears. Armed with nothing more than her stone-tipped spear and the knowledge of her ancestors, she dove into the azure depths. Gliding through the coral reefs, she swam past schools of mackerel that scattered in synchronicity as soon as they came near her. With her dark hair streaming behind her like ribbons of seaweed, Shaani gave a moment of thanks, recalling past dives, each one renewing her connection to the ocean.

Deep in the water, her keen eyes caught a faint, violet, pulsing glow that brightened once it was sensed.

With her destination made clear, she swam straight towards it.

As she drew nearer, she felt rather than heard the water that flowed past her conch shells covering her ears. In their village, where free diving was not just a skill but a way of life, Shaani's ancestors had discovered that by perforating their eardrums, they could dive deeper and longer, unlocking the hidden treasures of the ocean's depths. And so, following in their footsteps, Shaani had undergone the painful ritual, with the conch shells providing her both protection and resilience against the turbulent currents.

The ooham pulled her deeper and deeper to the halo at the bottom of the sea. The closer she got, the brighter it became till the world was only filled with the violet of the halo with a core about the size of her fist, partially obscured by a rock at the sea bottom. Diving deeper, she pushed aside the rock with some effort and was rewarded with a glint of metal. Pushing aside the loose gravel, she revealed a sapphire necklace with a purple fire opal in the centre of a heart-shaped pendant.

The closer she got to the necklace, the more she could relate to it. As hard as it was for Shaani to believe, she sensed that it had been thrown away on purpose.

And yet, it wants to be found.

Kollam

She closed her first around the glowing pendant, and with a tug, she freed it from the sea bed. Turning it around, she read an inscription that looked like it was on fire.

"Never let go."

Shaani suddenly felt a surge of energy course through her body, bringing with it images of a boy/man and girl/woman so obviously in love. Rapidly, flashbacks of emotions flooded her: Curiosity, Fascination, Amusement, Affection, Passion, Fear, Desperation, Courage, Hope, Sacrifice, and Grief.

After all that, though, was an overwhelming feeling of gratitude that still remained like the last lingering notes of sandalwood from her grandmother's perfume.

Its story told and the ooham released, the necklace lost its shimmer and just became metal and stone.

Shaani still clutched the necklace, but something told her it was meant to be in the ocean. Releasing it, she watched it sink into the ocean floor, where it was quickly covered in murky depths and lost from view forever.

With her task done, she breathed a sigh of relief and could move on now.

Swimming upwards, she touched the stone bracelet on her wrist, calling Narukta to her location.

Swimming upwards, Shaani slowed down when she noticed a large shadow beside her raft. She was supposed to be alone here. Wary of danger, she tightened her grip on her spear and slowed her ascent even further, taking care to swim under her raft to minimise the wake of her arrival.

Popping her head up warily, she squinted in the sun.

A familiar figure in a cowboy hat and white kurta stood on her raft.

Throwing her a hand, Karthik looked at her and simply said. "Hello, Shaani." and helped her back onboard the raft.

Standing up straight, Shaani squeezed her hair dry and didn't acknowledge Karthik's presence.

Karthik, however, sized her up appreciably and said with a salacious wink and nod. "How you doin'?

The slap was lightning-fast and hard. The open-palmed slap left the imprints of 6 fingers on his left cheek.

Grunting, Karthik adjusted his jaw before looking up in admiration. "Looks like you still hit like a girl."

Shaani smouldered at him and then laughed in a carefree tinkle. She could never really stay mad at Karthik in spite of everything.

It was a bold move on his part to approach Shaani unannounced in the middle of one of her rituals, but having known her since they were children, he knew that he would eventually be forgiven.

I hope.

"How did you even find me?" she asked him exasperated.

Karthik pointed at her stone periband. "Well, you still do share your location with me, so I assume that you wanted to be found."

Shaani frowned. "Well, you assumed wrong," she said crossly, avoiding Karthik's gaze. Unexpected as it was, she was well aware that she was still sharing her location with Karthik in the hopes of an encounter like this.

Whether the slapping was included depended on her mood on the day.

With her greatest fantasies coming true, Shaani suddenly wasn't exactly sure how to feel.

Without another word, Shaani busied herself in packing away her gear while her personal submarine, Narukta, rose from the depths, hovering just the right distance so that the wake wouldn't overturn the raft.

Tapping the discrete button on top of the sea chest, Shaani activated the homing cover and in a buzz, a protective barrier formed around the box. With another flick of her periband, a bubble covered the box and made its way to Narukta with self-propelling nanites.

After clearing the raft of all her belongings, she gave a final word of thanks and left the raft to the elements.

Despite his light-heartedness, Shaani knew that this wouldn't have been easy for Karthik, but she wasn't sure if she was ready to forgive and forget just yet.

Knowing herself, she knew it was only a matter of time before she did so.

But not just yet.

So she asked the most obvious question. "Why are you here, and what do you want?"

Karthik grinned. "We're putting the band back together."

| 13 |

cut my hair / Sukoon

None of the truest stories are ever told. For in truth, there is also silence, and in true silence, there are secrets. The secrets reside in the minds of the left behinds who carry on their stories, and in time, the weight of these secrets grows.

Ground long enough, they sometimes change from jagged rocks that cut the insides to smooth pebbles that, though heavy, don't hurt as much.

Sometimes, though, they get stuck and fester.

With Ramin, the stories of his family that he told publicly were the versions that he would have liked them to be. After having told the same stories so many times to so many people, he sometimes almost believed it himself.

Almost.

While technically proficient on his own, Ramin's true genius lay in people. With his ineffable charm and almost prophetic ability to sense the current zeitgeist, he guided ZyraCorp to the corporate behemoth it is today. Expanding on his father's legacy, Ramin has been able to bring Zyra-

Corp into pretty much every facet of modern living, from Biomedical to Media enterprises.

Unlike his father and sister, however, it wasn't discovery for the sake of discovery.

No, for Ramin, it was power.

The power to control everybody.

True power.

Working on his Founders Day address, he looked deep into the eyes of his reflection in his bedroom mirror and started just like he had written. "My father was a driven man who never compromised on his principles. He worked hard, but he was not a hard man. He was kind and patient and gave his all for his family and humanity.

"The only thing he loved to do was give his best; in turn, he got the best from others.

"My father's love is his legacy, and it will live on in the hearts and minds of the lives he has touched.

"My father's love .."

He paused, unsure why, but he was unable to proceed further.

Must have lost my place.

Looking down at his notes, Ramin saw the 8 crescent scars just inside his palm. The wounds had started to scab, but they were bright red and itching him now. He paused and stared down at them.

What Zyana and Indra did was incredible, but no one except Ramin actually understood what had happened. It wasn't just what Indra had asked Zyana to do; it was also how it was told.

Ramin knew that Zyana was working on a new personality module for Indra. Combined with the claytronic generator, there was plenty of gossip around the office about the chaos caused by the silver-blue sprite that appeared next to Zyana and had a tendency to morph randomly into a multitude of characters that were quite disruptive to the corporate environment.

Based on the recommendation of his CPO, he personally had to speak to Zyana regarding the issue. In spite of her assurances that it was just Indra learning different personalities and that she would settle on a form soon, Zyana was asked to switch Indra to audio-only until the personality module settled down.

Hmmm, that was actually the last time I saw her.

What surprised him was that Indra could actually predict what would have been the best appropriate action for his sister to soothe him at that moment.

No, not just best, but perfect.

If Zyana hadn't stepped in. If she didn't know how to touch him, just right to calm him down.

Just like Ammachi.

Strange as it sounds, Ramin actually recognised Indra's stabilised voice—or at least, it's a voice that he thought he should know. From somewhere far away and forgotten.

Ramin grunted in frustration. He still hadn't fully regained his control and was still more shaken than he expected to be.

Enough.
Zyana is broken and I am a perfect little boy.
I mean, man.

With her aversion to physical contact, there was no way Zyana would have ever touched him spontaneously, and even if she did, she would have never known to touch him in just the right way. Growing up alone at Bolgatty house, his own grandmother had only carried out the ritual with him while they were alone in the puja room. A painful reminder of when she used to do it for Indra; the children's ammachi wouldn't have been able to bear Zyana's rejection if she had attempted it with her.

For Indra to cue a family ritual when she saw Ramin in distress meant...

He actually wasn't really sure what that meant.

Ramin had asked his grandmother once about the ritual when she soothed him during one of his episodes, and she had told the young Ramin that it was a Vottom-param kutti-jaddu. Magic for children. A ritual carried out only by the older girls and women of the Vottom-param family to soothe the children, it was something only his family did.

With his grandmother and the rest of his family long gone, Ramin himself had forgotten this ritual and was only reminded of it in dreams. Triggering something so primal and innocent would have been the only way for him to draw on the wellspring of strength deep within himself at that moment.

Rather than being ecstatic that there was a chance for his sister and him to reconnect, he was actually angry.

Lachukabadre furious.

For someone to break through his emotional barriers. The ones he had spent so much time and effort building to become the man he is today, the man he was always destined to be. Ramin was never going back to how things were. From somewhere deep inside, a primal scream rose.

NEVER NEVER NEVER.

Another calmer but more cruel voice added.

This is all her fault.

Ramin agreed.

Why did the badre did you have to go away, Zyana!!

When Ramin was a child, though, he thought he had the best of all worlds, and for him, this was enough. His childhood was filled with happiness, in spite of the loss of one parent and an absent other, he had the love of his doting grandparents and a twin-soul sister who was always around.

2 halves of the same coin. One soul in 2 bodies. Egg siblings, twins.

Theirs was supposed to be a bond, inseparable, always together and all the cliches of twins.

It wasn't that Zyana spoke more to Ramin than the rest of the family, but like some twins, they shared a bond that didn't always require words for them to communicate with each other; they could always instinctively tune in to each other.

His grandparents, though they loved both twins, seeing their love returned multi-fold from Ramin, inadvertently spent on him the share of attention meant for Zyana. Zyana didn't seem to mind, though. Ramin paid it back to her with interest and was the only one who seemed to truly understand her.

Overflowing with love, Ramin shared it with all around him. From the servants in the house to his classmates and teachers at his play school, he was loved, and he loved in turn. While naturally intelligent like his sister and father, his talent seemed to be with people. He had the innate ability to understand their nonverbals to the point where he almost seemed like a mind reader. Actions that were interpreted as kindness were sometimes just him being mindful.

That started to change when Zyana displayed her prodigious ability, and her father decided that she should start spending more time with him for the guidance she so badly needed. Ramin started feeling that something was amiss. Though he was a full 8 years old, he sometimes felt sad thinking about her and missed her, but it wasn't just that.

Ramin couldn't hear little Zyana's voice in his head and for the first time, he wasn't sure of himself or what was really right and wrong.

Ramin never asked Zyana if she ever remembered his voice inside her head when they were kids. With Indra always speaking in her ear, he supposed that it would have drowned out his voice a long time ago.

So, this is Indra's fault as well.
Make them PAY!!!

Young Ramin was able to stop those 'BAD/MAD/SAD' feelings by squeezing his hands really tight. Sometimes, though, he forgets to cut his nails, or sometimes the feelings get a little bit too much, and his hands start to bleed. No one knew, or so he thought. Most people still only saw the sweet, well-behaved Ramin that everybody knew and loved. Whenever his hands were badly hurt, he would clench them into fists or tuck them into the pockets of his half-pants, and no one would notice them.

His grandmother, however, really saw him, and while she didn't know how to make it all better, she did how to make him feel better. Aware of his deep shame, she quietly led him into the puja room, and once they were all alone, she began.

First an open palm on the wound to take the bad flow away.

A kiss to the wound to add the flow of love.

A hug to soothe the heart, and finally, a kiss on the forehead to reinforce the protective flow.

It always made him feel better, no matter how scared he was.

He supposed that all the women in his family would have been able to do it, but though he had heard of them, he had never seen any of his relatives while he grew up at Bolgatty house.

Apart from Aunty Naina.

His ammachi was the last constant female in his life; he grew very close to her and was her shadow. Joining her daily for her morning rituals, he found comfort in chanting the Gayatri Mantra with her, and she cheered him up so much that he almost felt normal.

Almost.

He even found solace in playing with Savitri's daughter Kanchana, the waif of a girl who often played at the back of Bolgatty house whenever her mother came into work. While she looked nothing like Zyana, she had the same natural curiosity and zest of life, and Ramin doted on her like a baby sister.

And so, life continued on. Though dampened by his sister's increasingly long absences, he still had his grandparents and his friends.

Ramin knew that his grandmother was sick. Even though she won her first battle with cancer years ago, old age was a war that even she couldn't win. The older they got, the weaker she became, till finally, she was too weak even to soothe his hands anymore.

Just about when his grandmother started getting really sick, Ramin started thinking that his hands weren't clean enough.

At first, simply washing his hands multiple times a day seemed enough, but each wash became increasingly long and elaborate. Then Ramin began bathing multiple times a day, which again wasn't unusual at Bolgatty house. Living in Palakkad, it was common practice to bathe 2 to 3 times a day to cool off from the hot tropical sun, but when Ramin woke up in the middle of the night just to bathe, he started thinking that this may be unusual.

It came to the point where even Kanchana noticed that the regular savage scrubbing had made his hands red and wounded. "Achacha, how many times are you bathing and washing your hands? You bathe even when you sit at your desk.

"You don't play anymore. You don't want to go out.

"What's wrong."

Trusting Kanchana's innocence, Ramin confided in her: "Kanchu, I can't tell you. It's too bad. I am so dirty. I can't stop this feeling, this feeling of filthiness that always returns.

"Every time is sooner, and I need to clean harder and harder to remove it.

"It's inside me, inside my pores, and I can't seem to get it out no matter how much I scrub.

"It hurts Kanchu, but I can't stop.

" I can't be clean."

Kachana didn't know what to say, but she did know what to do as she hugged Ramin tightly.

It all came to a head when, with a misplaced notion of brotherly love, he decided that he needed to wash Kanchu's hands as well after she got muddy after playing in the rain.

Ramin led her to the washroom, gently leading her by the crook of her elbow, which was the only clean part of her arm. Handing the soap to her tiny hands, he watched while she washed her hands with great enthusiasm.

It wasn't clean enough for Ramin, though. Dirt had leached into the cuticles of her fingertips, and she couldn't get it clean with a simple wash. Taking her outside, Ramin took her to the back of the house, where a roughly cut stone was embedded in cement and used by the household to wash clothes. Taking the washing soap bar beside the stone, Ramin liberally applied the harsh detergent on Kanchana's hands.

Then he scrubbed her hands on the washing stone.

Kanchana yelped shortly after he started," Ow, stop, chacha, it's hurting. "

Ramin refused. Even when her nails were white and her hands red, he still kept scrubbing.

"Look how filthy", he said, pointing to a single black spot that was more than likely just a mole.

"We need to be clean," Ramin said with a strange smile. Ignoring her cries of protest, he kept doing what he was doing till the soapy water ran pink with the blood from her small hands.

Ramin still didn't stop. Almost possessed, it seemed like washing Kanchu's hands made his own hands feel cleaner.

It was only when Savitri, rushing towards Kanchu's screams of pain, pulled him away from her did he stop.

On seeing Kanchu's bloody hands, Ramin didn't feel remorse but a strange sense of satisfaction. The dirt was gone or rather was hidden by the blood.

CLEAN NOW.

Kollam

Harsh as his actions may have been, his grandparents would have treated them as childish exuberance, but Striber, when told of the incident and seeing Kanchu's bandaged hands, instead asked Ramin to show his own hands.

On seeing his son's own bleeding hands, Striber didn't say a word to him but instead turned to his grandparents and told them that he wanted to speak with them privately.

Ramin never knew what was discussed, but within a week, he was taken out of school, and it was decided that he would spend some time at the Institute. For over 150 years, the Arcana Institute of Vapours has been home to some afflicted by the illness of the mind and, for others, a place to hide family embarrassments. As Ramin stepped through the imposing gates of the Institute, he felt a great buffeting of sorrow and suffering pressing upon his soul. Not from within but from the building itself, which seemed to pulse with an eerie energy. Its walls whispered tales from its legacy of madness and anguish.

Inside, Ramin encountered a bleak landscape, where the air crackled with despair and the corridors echoed with the cries of tormented souls. The staff wielded their authority with callous indifference, subjecting the patients to their treatments. One figure stood out among all the staff: the head nurse in a white cloak and a midnight blue turban.

Gabbar Digambaran

With his jet-black shark eyes, Gabbar's eyes seemed to reflect the dark pall over the hospital, exuding an aura of malevolence. Ramin didn't know it then, but Shri Gabbar would be in his nightmares for a very long time.

Ramin soon found solace in the company of another patient, Elara, a kindred spirit whose hands showed the signs of a burden similar to his own. An ethereal, the albino girl was in a world of their own, which now included Ramin. Together, they navigated the labyrinthine halls of the institute, forging a bond that made their existence a little bit more bearable.

Among the sessions of electro-shock therapy and potions of questionable content, they forged a bond in the crucible of pain and loneliness.

A favourite pass-time of Gabbar was to withhold the patients of their enabler. In the case of Ramin and Elara, it was always soap. It was supposed to be part of their therapy, but Gabbar seemed to take particular pleasure in taunting Elara, dangling the soap, which would barely last for a few washes, in front of her and only handing it over when he was tired of the game or on being called away. Often, Ramin found her wailing in the hallways when the games got really bad.

Fuelled by the friendship of Elara, Ramin embarked on a journey of solving a problem for a friend.

Early one Sunday morning, Ramin waited in anticipation for lunch. So was everybody else, but he had something else in mind. Lunch was completed exceptionally quickly, even more than the typical rush before the Sunday matinee.

Today was the first time that 'Krantiveer' was to be aired on National TV, and everybody at the institute, including the staff, gathered in the rec room to watch.

Ramin started making his move when the first lot of commercials came on. Having viewed the film many times before he came to the institute, he knew it almost verbatim.

Nobody noticed the clang as the side door opened over the hoots and whistles when Bhadrikant's name came on the screen.

Stopping by the kitchen to pick up some supplies, Ramin headed into the forest behind the institute.

The air was thick with the scent of damp earth and blooming jasmine as he descended deep into the forest towards the stream. Fed by the monsoon rains, the stream meandered through the dense undergrowth, its water clear and cool.

In a scheduled spot, far from prying eyes, Ramin emptied the contents of the sack that he was carrying and was surprised to find himself smiling. In spite of the danger, he was actually looking forward to doing this for Elara.

Ramin quickly made a fire using coconut husks and twigs and boiled a pot with ashes from the kitchen chulha and water from the stream. He waited till the water started boiling merrily before making his way back to the institute just in time for the intermission. He could even join in the animated re-enactments of the fight scenes between Karan and Rohit .

10 minutes on the dot, with the end of the public announcements, the pre-movie advertisements began and again Ramin was able to time his exit to the shot of Rohit Chopra lying in a hospital bed.

Ramin ran to the fire, gathering bunches of tulsi, neem leaves, and handfuls of jasmine and roses. The pot was still boiling , just as he had left it. Looking inside, he grinned in satisfaction at the dark brown liquid. Ramin filled a small steel vessel with coconut oil (again courtesy of the institute kitchen) and the flowers and herbs he had gathered and mixed them well.

After layering the top of the steel vessel with a thin Muslin cloth, Ramin carefully poured the lye he had made into the mixture, using folded banana leaves as makeshift gloves.

Stirring the lye and oils till he felt the time was right he reverently poured the liquid into food containers content with the knowledge that his efforts would yield fragrant, hand-crafted soap.

In the centre of each soap mould, Ramin dropped shiny Lhomi stones. The addition of the stones was not in the usual recipes, but he knew they would turn the caustic liquid into soap within days instead of weeks.

Ramin didn't know how he knew this, but he just did.

Raindrops began to patter as Ramin sneaked back in just in time for the closing credits and joined the inmates in the final claps and cheers as Rohit rode off into the sunset with Priya.

A pair of jet-black eyes noted the raindrops on Ramin's shirt with malevolence.

The very next day, Ramin found Elara curled in a corner after another taunting session with Gabbar. Ramin couldn't wait any longer, so, hoping to give her hope, he led her deep into the forest.

Her screech of joy echoed when, with a flourish, Ramin revealed the moulds that had only just hardened. Upon Elara's questioning, he warned her that soap would still be caustic and harsh, but yes, it would clean her.

Elara didn't care. Compared to Gabbar's cruelties, burnt skin seemed a small price to pay. Dragging Ramin, she headed to the stream. Upon offering him a bar of soap, Ramin refused with a smile and said that they were all for her. Grateful, Elara proudly declared that she would wash both of them and scrubbed her hands in glee with the caustic soap.

Though the water ran red, her smile was pure bliss.

Watching her wash her soapy, blood-covered hands, Ramin again found that his urges were satiated by just watching. Somehow, the act of Elara cleaning on his behalf was enough for him.

When Elara started to take her white saree off to give herself a more thorough clean, Ramin respectfully stepped away to give her some privacy and returned to the rec room happy and content.

The screams when Gabbar found her were heard even above the madness of the hall.

With his heart in his mouth, Ramin saw Elara, now freshly washed, thrown over Gabbar's shoulder as he made his way back from the forest.

Bodily dropping her in front of the dirty cowshed, Gabbar grabbed Elara by the forearms and forced her hands into the slurry of cow dung and mud. Elara screamed and sobbed, but Gabbar turned a blind eye and deaf ear to it. Elara stopped screaming when he pulled her arms out of the slurry. Seeing her arm covered in a stinking pile of shit and dirt, she was stunned into silence. It was her worst nightmare come to life.

A drop of slurry dripped from her upheld hands to the ground, and that's when she started screaming. She was still screaming when she was thrown into the filthy cow shed.

Locking it up with a great iron padlock, Gabbar growled. "Nobody goes inside. Leave her there all night. This will teach her to break the rules."

The screams didn't stop from the cow shed."I need to be clean. I am dirty. Somebody give me water.

"I need to be clean. Somebody help me."

When she saw that no help was coming, Elara whimpered and held out her hands as far i as she could, though her arms ached being held out for so long.

The desperate need to be clean overpowered her completely.

The smell didn't bother her anymore. The dark didn't scare her anymore. All she could think about was the filth.

The filth getting inside her. Through her pores. Into her blood and filling her body with the filth.

So much FILTH!!!!!

The shed was old and dirty, with bales of dry straw in a corner. Elara first tried scrubbing with the straw, but it only mixed with the slurry and spread across her arms. She tried scraping on the hard brick ledge, but it was too low to do any real good and she grimaced as she added blood to the sticky mess across her arms. She searched desperately for somewhere to wash, but there was no water nor even a scrap of cloth.

The only cloth in the room was the white saree that she was wearing. Crying, she unwrapped herself and wiped. Now naked, the white sari was covered in slurry but had only succeeded in now spreading the mess across her body.

Looking at the hook on the roof, she wondered if it would be strong enough to hold her weight.

They found her the next morning.

The Institute was closed for the day for maintenance while they cut her down and quietly buried her in the Beggars Grave at the back.Ramin didn't see Elara being buried and didn't say a word of his part in all of this to anybody. News, however, reached his family, and the next day, Kesav arrived at the institute to pick him up.

Not long after that, Ramin was introduced to Nathan.

| 14 |

Mere Angne Mein / Naa Autokaran

"Excuse me, Mr Kharia, but I simply cannot do this," said Badhrikant in his deep baritone voice.

"I think it is a great idea, but you see, my fans expect me to be the star. Imagine Badhrikant as just a bloody sidie", and then he laughed his trademark laugh.

In spite of herself, Nithya Juray couldn't help but feel a little starstruck and shiver with nostalgia.

He actually laughs like that in the real. I thought it was just for the movies.

Kharia stammered, "Unfortunately, this is the best we can do at this stage. We are just launching DreamWeaver, and there are limitations," he said, casting his eyes downward.

He was a software engineer, not a Filimistan executive, and every time he opened his mouth, it only seemed to anger the MegaStar even more.

The egos of filmi stars were huge and in the case of someone like Badhrikant, it was well warranted. The man was a legend with a career spanning over 50 years, and to say he had a cult following was putting it mildly.

The multiple fan-built temples in his name were proof enough that he could start a religion if he wanted to.

Silky smooth, Nithya tapped on her glasses and slipped into the conversation. "If I may Shri, I actually believe this is exactly what the fans would want. Not just you as Rohit Chopra in Krantiveer but you in all your different aspects."

Flicking back a strand of her platinum-white hair, she looked at the Ugathi straight in the eyes and said. "Picture this.

"Rohit and Priya are reunited at the entrance of the Frontier newspaper office.

"Just before the camera pans to their first kiss, a familiar figure with a neckerchief stands at the back of the road.

"Your fans select the option to follow the mysterious figure."

"Zoom in"

"Its Raj Malhotra!!"

"We follow you as walk deeper into the street. You meet a lady being accosted by some goondas and you rescue them in a fight scene like Tirunvelli.

"Sweeping her into your arms, you reveal your tragic backstory only this time Raj is not an orphan but has a widowed mother or maybe an evil twin brother like Gopal Krishnan from Raghuveer.

Or maybe you meet an orphan child like in GangaParbat. They will have to just watch and find out.

"With a million different combinations, the experience will be different with every single viewing.

The plot lines will be purely AI-driven and characters will be randomised from your biggest hits.

The sub-sequence will run for 6 minutes, but it will be a complete story on its own.

Your fans have their own unique Ugathi experience," she finished, her finger resting at the tip of her aquiline nose.

Badhrikant shook his head. "I get that and think it's a great idea. A wonderful idea but 6 minutes of screen time and that too in the background?

"They should at least cast me in as his older brother. That would make more sense to my fans. "

The age gap between Argav Patel, the current lead actor, and Bhadrikant was 40 years.

Nithya sighed regretfully. "Unfortunately, I can't make casting decisions, but this is only a temporary situation. DreamWeaver is still new, and while this may be its debut launch, it's going to be the future of cinema as we know it, and you will be the first star to lead it.

"A pioneer. A groundbreaker.

"Soon, we will be able to make complete movies based on your complete catalogue of films.

All we need from you is your permission to use your image and a few sessions in the body scanner, and we will take care of the rest."

Still not convinced, Badhrikant shook his head. "Abe yaar , why get these new kids to act in the movie? Who better to star in the Krantiveer than the original star?

"Why don't you just get the AI do the full movie with me in it? Just get some extra computers and get it done quicker."

Nithya was starting to lose her patience but kept her cool. Badhrikant didn't know it, but Nithya needed him to be on board more than she let on.

As part of the launch of ZyraCorp's new streaming service, Z-TV, they were launching a number of in-house projects, with a big-budget remake of "Krantiveer" as one of the initial launch titles.

Though over 30 years old, the movie was still considered one of Bhadrikant's best, so it made perfect sense that the star of the original was added as an easter egg in the new remake.

The gritty, gangster movie about a humble taxi driver in Mumbai who was secretly a Delhi crime lord was still viewed quite regularly by his loyal fans.

A modern retelling of the story was one of the biggest launch projects for Z-TV. While the budget for the work itself was impressive, they were still looking for something completely innovative to stand out from the other competitors.

Nithya was the one who personally pitched "Dreamweaver" to Ramin Contractor, CEO of ZyraCorp who immediately agreed to fund it provided that it could be ready to be launched along with Z-TV on Founders Day, their annual company MegaEvent.

Apart from attracting viewers interested in the new technology, the fan base of Badhrikant should be passionate enough to watch the flick just to see new stories of their favourite star.

It was the perfect way for Z-TV to draw in regular subscribers while still having time to build up its portfolio.

For Nihtya's latest startup, IM4GN, the increased viewing would also provide incredible user feedback which was critical for the next iteration of DreamWeaver.

It was supposed to be a win-win for everybody involved.

Then this happened

Sensing that Badhrikant would not budge, Nithya played her final trump card and said, "Based on how we are progressing, it will be another 5 years before we can make a complete movie with existing archives. It will definitely happen, and I am sure that you will be among the first actors to star in full AI movies.

Standing up, she continued," We won't take any more of your time, Shri, as I can see that you are not interested.

"I must say that it was a dream come true to meet you in person and I hope that we will work together in the future."

Almost as an aside, she casually added. "By the way, we are planning on meeting with Sushant Powari soon. As a co-star with you, he was going to be our next candidate for this deployment.

Would you like me to pass on your regards?"

With a smooth intake of breath, Nithya waited in anticipation if he would fall for it.

On cue, Badhrikant almost yelled. "Is Sushant interested in this? Does he have the star power that I have? He was still a 2-bit actor, and he should be grateful that he acted with me in Krantiveer.

I made him a star."

"Hmm, let me think about it ", said Badhrikant.

Hook, line and sinker

Nithya allowed herself a sly smile before continuing." Unfortunately, it's now or never Shri. "Krantiveer is scheduled to launch as part of the greater Z-TV launch and we would need to decide before the final edit of the film is completed.

"Shri Powari's office is very interested, and I am not expecting any issues with getting approvals from him.

"I thought you should know that you were our first preference. "

Nithya turned to leave and beckoned for Trivedi to follow. She silenced him with a look and collected her things.

"Wait" called out Bhadrikant. "I get to see the final version before you do it, and I want you to make me look like Pandalam Neelakandan. If I am going AI, I might as well be in my prime. "

"Let's do this bacche log", and he laughed out loud.

Nithya smiled and bowed low with her palms folded. "Thank you, Shri. You wont regret it."

Bhadrikant grunted. "You better not mess it up.

I won't do anything, but the Badhris will roast you alive."

"You can trust us", replied Nithya confidently and walked out of the office.

Kharia followed close behind. " That was lucky, if.. " Nithya interrupted him with a shushing motion. "We will talk outside," she whispered.

Taking the elevator down to the floor below, she exited into the warm sun on Racecourse Road.

A blood-red Kanashi zoomed past her even though the streets were already quite busy.

She didn't get a good look at whoever it was, but judging by the number of paparazzi drones hanging about the car like flies on honey, she assumed it must be someone famous—or at least clickbait famous.

She was sure, however, that she would be able to find out shortly on the online gossip rags.

Whoever it was had conveniently left the top of their car wide open so that the drones could get a clear photo.

Badhrikant's office was located in the heart of Racecourse Road, surrounded by luxurious boutiques and high-end restaurants.

Slipping past the latest Bundeli and the occasional Ralte parked on the main road, she walked to the end of the road, where a discrete lane led to the car lift where she had parked her vehicle.

Authenticating herself, she waited for the lift to rotate and bring her car down.

Trivedi continued their conversation from before. "That was great work in convincing Badhrikant, but I didn't know that Sushant had agreed to a meeting. I thought his team was still reviewing our proposal."

Nithya laughed. "Well, as you say in Filmistaan, I was creative with the truth.

"We are still waiting for the final meeting dates from Sushant's team but I was gambling that Bhadrikant's ego wouldn't let this go to him.

"Even if Sushant had agreed, we wouldn't have been able to use his footage for DreamWeaver anyways."

With a sigh, Nithya revealed. "I got the projections just before the meeting. The test vids with Sushant was too volatile. The plot and the generative sequences did poorly with the test audiences.

We either would have had to reduce the screen time per story or risk the sequence being unstable. "

While bitter rivals and both sharing cult status among their fans, Sushant and Badhrikant varied greatly in the content they produced.

Badhrikant's movies tended to be more formulaic, with the vast majority of the films made with his trademark, 'Pissed off badre" character. The few deviants from this character, while showing off his unquestionable talent, were unpopular among his fan base.

His predictable behaviour, however, made it easier for the current version of DreamWeaver to create convincing imagery and plot lines with his back catalogue of over 200 movies.

Sushant, on the other hand, had made a name by re-inventing himself quite frequently.

His draw point was to be as different as possible in every movie throughout his career.

While an AI-generated character would be something that he would more readily agree to, his sheer versatility made it harder for DreamWeaver to phreak his character in a manner that was convincing.

Or at least just yet.

Nithya's compact MeiTei dropped down finally.

The zippy sports car, while still a luxurious vehicle, actually stood out among the other vehicles on Racecourse Drive simply because it was among the most inexpensive on the road.

She didn't mind, though. Being in the entertainment industry, Nithya had long given up trying to keep up with her usual crowd.

Ever since she started out on her own, she has quickly made a name for herself for the quality of her products. The people she usually deals with, other tech heads like herself, engage with her for her skills, not for the car she drives.

However, she was finding that she had to turn on her charm more often because she was dealing with creatives directly more often, like today.

Trivedi squeezed himself into the small sports car. "So where are we really off to now?" he asked cheerfully.

"Let's get back to the office and give the team the good news. Also, set up a meeting with Kaushik from ZyraCorp. I want to see the lachuka try to squeeze us out of the launch now that we have Badrikhant on board," replied Nithya, grinning.

Having listened to her conversation, the onscreen map popped up on her screen and provided an overlay as they drove down the boulevard.

As soon as she crossed the mandatory 'No hands' zone, she grabbed the steering wheel and flipped the control to manual for the rest of the drive to IM4GN's office.

In spite of her involvement in multiple tech start-ups, Nithya was wary of how much automation she let into her life and still preferred to do some things the old-fashioned way. With manual driving disabled within city limits, Nithya looked forward to these drives far away from the maddening crowds.

She started speeding up, not because she was in any real hurry but because she was on an adrenaline rush and really wanted to push it.

Driving past the studio lots of "GKR Productions" and "Red Rose Entertainment," she ignored the giant billboards with their current content and the crowds of hopefuls gathered in the front, awaiting a chance to be extras in the current films.

She instead focused on navigating the throng of people and vehicles and only relaxed once the bustle of Glitz Town was behind her.

The road now opened up the further she moved away from the city and she started accelerating and could feel her mood lift.

Speeding up, she vroomed down the road, navigating the twists and turns with the greatest of ease.

Nithya actually had a fighting chance to save her company now.

Having an association with the ZyraCorp name came with strings attached, among which was the expectation of a high-quality product being provided before it would be approved.

If she had failed, however, ZyraCorp would not hesitate in bringing her down, and she would never be able to work in this industry again.

The price of success.

Suddenly, the brakes slammed on the car, and Trivedi and Nithya were flung forward but safely restrained with their seat belts.

Looking ahead a small puppy had crossed directly into her path.

I didn't even see it.

Thankfully, her car was new enough to have the default safety features installed, including the proximity sensors, which were active even when she was driving in manual.

The puppy had already skittered away from the road and further into the alleyways on the side.

Still shaken, she looked over to Trivedi and said. "I think that is enough manual driving for now."

"Let's go full auto ", she said and continued the rest of the journey, leaning back on her seat."

Her peripheral chirped, breaking her out of reverie.

Tara appeared on the screen. "I need your help," she said simply.

| 15 |

Hurt / Memories

Hitching up her saree on her ample belly, Savatri expertly spat out a stream of red liquid into a stained flowerbed nearby and said, "That girl gives me the creeps".

Keshav, the unfortunate listener, simply smiled as they sat cross-legged at the back of Bolgatty house. Savatri's preferred gossip buddy, Komal, the cook, was busy in the kitchen, and ammachi didn't take too kindly to gossiping among the help inside the house. Savatri needed to vent now; however, and Keshav would do.

Keshav, who was primarily Striber's driver, was relatively new to the household and was engaged to look after Striber whenever he came down to Palghat. Having only been to Bolgatty house a few times, he never had much to do with the children apart from seeing them on the days that Striber Shri decided to stay over.

Though he had kids of his own, Keshav's interest in kids was only in the making them part. The rest he left to his witch of a wife, who was another reason why he stayed away from home as much as possible. Instead, his preference was to chill at the local Toddy shop with his friends when he was done with work. Stumbling home after imbibing a few bottles of the palm wine, the torrent of abuse from his wife seemed like the white noise of falling rain, and he usually fell into a dreamless sleep only to wake up in the morning and start it all over again.

Keshav's only impression of the kids was that they were quiet, mostly kept to themselves, and weren't hooligans like his own. Keshav would have thought Savatri would have the easiest job in the whole house.

With the great introspection that sometimes comes with boredom, he passed on his honest opinion.

"Zyana? She is as quiet as a mouse", Keshav said incredulously.

With her eyebrows raised and her face animated, Savatri clapped her hands in agreement and exclaimed, "Exactly, she is quiet. Too quiet. It's unnatural. This morning, you know what she did?

"I left her in the room and went to clean the children's almari. I climbed the chair to look at the top of the cupboard, and the next thing I knew, the chair was being violently shaken.

"The little imp was shaking the chair from the bottom and trying to kill me!!

"Gave me the shock of my life. I screamed, and if I hadn't been quick to step off it, my children would have been motherless."

Savatri shuddered theatrically. " Kadavale, I am playing with my life working in this house. "

Kesav, disbelieving in spite of or because of her theatrics, looked at Savatri incredulously again and asked, "Did you ask her why she did it?"

Savatri shook her head. "All she did was point at a spider at the bottom of the chair. That girl even let the spider walk on her hand. She wasn't scared at all. Just kept watching it.

"There is something lachuka wrong with that girl.

"They should leave her already at the Institute before she goes around killing everybody. They will sort her out. "

Kesav, sensing a certain line has been crossed regarding his boss, looked cross, but Savatri continued, "She is definitely stupid though. Why else is she at home instead of at school like Ramin?

"Chummata payan. Such an adorable sweetheart.

"He is the only one who knows how to handle her.

"The way she was playing with the spider.

"You know who else likes spiders? Rakshahis. I think she is possessed by one.

"Appa!!!" she said and shuddered violently.

With the fervour of the newly converted, she exclaimed "I should tell Shri Contractor to visit Baba Kalanadi Pankhu in Sora. He will be able to cure all this possession in no time. Sunam, my neighbour, had a friend whose goat was possessed by an evil spirit. Baba just gave her a sacred pendant, and the goat was fine the very next day.

Kesav laughed. " I don't know much about the kids, but I know this much about Striber Shri. If you mention anything about holy men and possessions, he will kick you out of this house. He is a great scientist and does not abide by all this nonsense."

Savitri, now pouting. " This whole family must be cursed then. Why else would the mother die as soon as the children were born?

"Thoba Thoba, "she said out loud, forking two fingers to ward off the evil eye.

Kesav looked up pointedly at Savatri and, with a slight uplift of his chin, gestured her to turn back.

Zyana was standing behind, looking straight at them.

Both Savatri and Kesav weren't sure how long she had been standing there.

Zyana does that sometimes. Despite her penchant for randomly bursting out into a chaos of noise, the rest of the time, she is as silent as an ethereal. Her face was neutral, and she turned and walked away without any indication that she had heard what they had said.

Despite her bulk, Savatri was quick as an elephant when needed and got in front of Zyana in a flash.

"Ohh my koochiepecchu," said Savatri in a syrupy sweet tone.

"There you are. I have been looking all over for you.

"I was just talking about this pottan who lives near my house.

"So unlike you, my Ranipaku. "

She knelt to scoop her up.

Zyana, with no apparent effort, had already slipped away with her fingers in the air and ran away, banging her head.

Savitri didn't bother chasing after her. It was expected that when this happened, she let the spell pass.

Zyana had heard everything that Savatri said and had understood most of what she had said.

Zyana knew she was supposed to feel SAD or BAD about what had happened, but she didn't know how.

She wanted to tell Savatri that the spider she saw was not an ordinary spider but an 'Argiope anasuja' or 'signature spider'. In one of her mother's old textbooks, she had read that it could build a web with a zig-zag stabilimentum resembling letters.

She wanted to see if it had written something under the chair.

She didn't know why but didn't think she wanted to be next to Savitri.

But she did want to be near to someone.

She ran down the corridor when she noticed the door at the end of the corridor was ajar.

Though she had full reign of the Striber household, Zyana had never been inside her father's home lab. Locked while he was away, which was most of the time, she had never even seen the room open. Lately, though, with her father's weekend visits, he had taken to retreating here to work on projects.

She wandered down to the end of the hallway and saw that the big door was now open.

Walking inside, she saw her father huddled over a desk, working on a dome-shaped device with probes attached to her father's laptop. Her father was busy typing away and she could see a streaming green line of code on the screen.

"Teri..." Striber yelped when Zyana walked in and tugged at the lapel of her father's coat. He looked down with annoyance at the interruption untill he saw it was Zyana. Unsure of how to handle her, he just gaped down at her and then silently turned back to work on his screen.

Ever since Indra passed away, Striber has been obsessed with work and solely focused on ZyraCorp. His in-laws, grief-stricken with the loss of a daughter, had tried to change it to love for Indra's legacy and had taken on the role of grandparents with gusto. At their insistence, Striber left the children under their care at Bolgatty house. Armed with a retinue of servants, they completely took over the care of the children, and they were ever the doting grandparents.

This suited Striber perfectly. With nothing holding him back, he devoted himself to building his legacy. From his humble beginnings from the very lab that he was working in, he had built ZyraCorp into a unicorn which was at the threshold of heading to an IPO. Having received the seed money from Nathan and Sentinel Enterprises, he wasted no time convincing all of his team to join the fledgling company.

With a promise that Research and Development would be the prime focus and that no expense would be spared, he gave his team full reign over the new company's structure. By giving each of them equity, they were made part owners of the new venture, but with the condition that they would receive a significantly smaller pay check until they could market Extrexes.

With no restrictions on their method of research, their progress was in leaps and bounds. Driven as it was, the team went over and above and worked excessively long hours, spurred on by each success and the drive to make something on their own.

The approach was a resounding success.

With their creativity unleashed, they could test out ideas that had been previously caught up in bureaucratic red tape. Ideas that are probably still in the approval queues of some executives at Lestat Industries. Thriving on their constraints, they were inventive with their solutions and able to create a lighter, smarter version of the original Augmentation prototypes.

Within a year, they were ready to demonstrate working prototypes. Thanks to Nathan's connections, the approvals for human trials were expedited and they could test the first prototypes from the first casualties from the Dormist wars.

Sridevi, the new intern, had even posted the initial test vids on social media. Combined with her zany commentary, the vids went mirchi on VidMe, and a popular trend was to post response threads showing reasons why they deserved to be among the first to trial the Extrexes.

In spite of repeated warnings from ZyraCorp on the potential risks, there was no shortage of demand till finally, the incumbent government, it being an election year and all, provided multiple grants to ZyraCorp to increase production of the units. Taking partial stakes in other bio-medical companies, they were able to have greater control over existing manufacturing units and they were able to outsource a lot of the grunt work while still maintaining full ownership of the IP.

Spurned on by Extrex's success, the team brought up other projects that they have been individually working on or that were put on hold for some reason. As promised, if it had merit, all the ideas were trialled and tested. One of the first ones they decided to work on was an integrated visual and audio communication interface.

Nicknamed the "Peripheral", it was this prototype that Striber was currently working on.

With the company's success, Striber travelled quite a lot, meeting with suppliers and potential investors, to the point where he saw the children only on their birthdays or on festivals.

Though she had the patience of Kamala, it even came to the point that the children's ammachi actually insisted that he stay over on weekends at Bolgatty house.

Striber apprehensively agreed, and it has now been 3 months that he has managed to stay over.

Even now, 7 years after her death, the kids still reminded him of Indra, and it was just a bit too painful, was what he told himself. Maybe it was a real pain; maybe he was a bad parent, incapable of loving the kids.

Or maybe it was just a story that he told himself.

Striber wasn't sure and not being prone to too much self-analysis, he didn't spend too much time delving into the issue. According to him, he was fulfilling Indra's dream by building ZyraCorp and making their dreams come true.

Sometimes, late at night, though, a voice reminded him that what he had actually promised Indra was to build her the augmentations to help her walk again. Everything else about Zyracorp, the tech they worked on, was Striber and his team's dream. At some fundamental level, he knew that the dream of inventing things was his, not Indra's, but attributing it to his dead wife gave him a justification for the other things he neglected.

Like his children.

Striber was bent over, focused on the code displayed on the screen. The individual modules had functioned perfectly, but the package failed to execute once compiled. He couldn't pinpoint where it went wrong and knew he needed his team to resolve it as soon as possible if they were to present it at the big board meeting next week. He called Kishore, but he did not get an answer. After leaving a voicemail, he noticed Zyana still hanging around his legs and looking up at him.

"At least act like a father", he recalled his mother-in-law's admonishment.

He had seen other fathers interact with their children. They seemed to have endless patience for their questions and frequently pointed out things that may be of interest to them.

"The simplest is best", Kishore told him when Striber confided in him. "They are just little people. Just talk to them like you would talk to anybody else. "

He could do nothing more until Kishore called him back, so he beckoned Zyana and pointed at the chair beside him. Zyana pulled herself up with a little help from him. A small tingle of something happened in his chest, but he ignored it.

"Speak like you would to people."

The only people I talk to are engineers.

Shrugging, he said out loud. " So Zyana", he pointed to his screen and said. "This is the new code for the peripheral. I am trying to compile it, but it's just not happening. You see that chunky mask over there. It will light up once it has been properly compiled. "

"Compile", Zyana repeated. Shortly followed by "Light".

'Yes ', he echoed her. 'Once the program Compiles', he emphasised. 'The mask will Light Up.

I think one of the subroutines is wrong, but I can't figure out which one. The team will have to review them individually. I may have to be here all night."

"Compile," Zyana said again.

She did that sometimes. Repeating random words or phrases that she had heard previously.

After a while, people got used to it and didn't pay much heed.The phone rang. It was Kishore returning his call.

Striber got up and said. " I have to take this. I won't be long. ". and quickly walked outside the room.

Zyana looked at the screen in front of her. Reaching one chubby finger to the keyboard, she scrolled to the top of the page and then pressed the down button. Lines of code whizzed past the screen. She stared intently, looking at the rapidly changing lines of code.

Once it hit the bottom, she scrolled again to the top and pressed the down button again.

She stopped seemingly at random and hit a couple of letters on the keyboard.

She then pressed the F12 key just like she had seen her Father do.

Striber turned back with a yell once she saw that she was on the keyboard. "What are you doing?" he screamed. He wasn't too concerned, actually, as it was backed up, but you can never be too careful.

"Compile". "Light Zyana said and pointed to the mask just at the end.

The console was now fully lit as the program was successfully executed.

Did she do that? Impossible. Thought Striber.

The error checking was still a work in progress using a protocol they had just created.

They still had memory recall, though, and he was able to review the changes made.

Gently pushing her aside, Striber reviewed the changes that Zyana had made. Somebody had missed commas at the end of the line of code. A quotation mark at the end of one comment.

The changes were made precisely in 5 locations, and no other keys were pressed.

Striber ran the line count.

There were 40,278 lines of code.

Zyana had reviewed 40,278 lines of code and identified punctuation mistakes in about 5 minutes.

I didn't even know that she could read yet.

| 16 |

Mirage / Liggi

The wind blew through Gaurav's hair, smoothing it close against his scalp. The slicked-back hair, normally trapped under a rainbow turban, became tighter and flowed in a wave behind him the faster he went. The ridiculous amount he spent on his Juray jacket, with its inbuilt airbags, was worth not having a helmet and just feeling the wind through his hair.

With his chiselled features and thick moustache Gaurav looked like he was heading to a CosplayCon as Rohit Chopra from Krantiveer. With the 'Predator sunglasses, a leather jacket with authentic steel buttons and blue denim jeans, he had the costume down pat. The finishing touch was the red neckerchief given to him by the Ugathi himself, the mark of all true Badhris and a lasting reminder of the day he had actually met Bhadrikant.

The ensemble was Gaurav's pride and joy, though he rarely took it out.

With a deep whoosh, the souped-up mono jet bike zoomed past the familiar red and white sign marked 60 km/

h, effortlessly hitting 100 km/h and triggering silent alarms somewhere. His arms were fully extended, and the ape handlebars were exact replicas of the Yanfield Terminator bike used in the movie. The cruiser was fitted with a retro kit and had exhaust tweakers with high-volume decibel rippers to really give the old petrol cruiser sound of yore. Even though Gaurav left it at the lowest possible setting, he was certainly heard.

The low roar of the jet exhaust, even from a distance, was just loud enough for quite a few disapproving heads to lift up from whatever task they were doing and follow the path of the bike through their double-brick walls and single-glazed windows.

Gaurav couldn't give 2 hoots just about now. Ever since the Banjaras made camp at Harikanad, he had been more restless than usual, and a ride was just what he needed to clear his head, particularly this morning. While he had missed the morning broadcast of the flip, the mobile homes' stabilisers were still fully extended when he woke up, so he figured that the troupe wouldn't be travelling again for a while now.

So now he is here for another week in lachuka Harikanad.

How much bad luck can one badre get?

Tyche, why aren't you by my side now?

As part of their morning ritual, many Banjaras watch the daily flip of the coin, the spin of the triple dice, and the tossing of the cowrie shells, relying on fate to help make decisions that they are unable to make, ultimately, attributing the eventual outcome, both good and bad, to luck.

Every weekend, though, was the Big Flip, the coin toss that decided whether the Banjara were supposed to travel or wait it out for another week. Unluckily for Gaurav, the navigator kept pulling up heads when the question was asked, which, to his troupe, meant that they were to stay.

Gaurav sometimes wanted to complain that it wasn't fair and that it was rigged, but since, in keeping with the times, they now had a live worldwide broadcast of the flip, he was better off screaming into the wind. Naturally, some banjaras thought this global live broadcast was an unacceptable break from tradition. Instead, they preferred the old method of the troupe leader or karnuvar making a call based on throwing the dice or cowrie shells and announcing it to the troupes. Gaurav shook his head when he remembered that some of those very same people previously used to complain that sometimes a significant portion of flips seemed to favour the karnuvar. They might as well move on; however, since this was one of those changes, they would never escape.

He remembered the campfire when Kannan, their current karnuvar, squashed any rumours of going back to the old ways when, after the passing of the peach pipe, he had given a rare speech, reminding everyone that the essence of being a Banjara is in being flexible and fluid. Which also meant that they should be the most willing to change their ways along with the world.

"Embracing change sometimes bears fruits unplanted." He had rumbled into the bonfire, smiling his big Cheshire Cat smile, and reminded them that global flip now allowed troupe members who, despite being settled in other cities, could now watch the same flips as their families—a remote joint family decision.

So, it looked like the live broadcast was here to stay, especially since it removed the question of unconscious bias. As a system, it was also an ethical scapegoat in case things didn't work out to their expectations.

At least I still have the road. Be grateful for what you have.

Hearing himself think, Gaurav laughed out loud.

You better be careful; you are starting to sound like Kannan.

Gaurav, a Mahout, was destined to be a driver like his father and his father before him. It may have been his destiny, but Gaurav was pretty sure that he could have been born a doma or probably even in one of the sada houses around him, and he would still end up being a rider of some shape or form. He couldn't explain it, but riding and driving seemed more like an aspect of him than just an activity he enjoyed.

Above all else, Gaurav felt connected to the open road.

Gaurav didn't even mind that he was the only young'un among the oldies in the troupe. Since even the youngest oldie among them was already nearing 60, the large disparity in age may have annoyed others but not Gaurav. He liked to think it was because he had always been an oldie at heart.

It was just that...

For all Banjaras, whatever their caste or subcaste, the decision to travel or not has been made by a coin toss since time immemorial. If the need arose, they could always choose not to follow the flip and stay or leave, a decision made by the karnuvar. Unfortunately for Gaurav, while he was meant to be neutral, Kannan seemed to be going overbudda and taking any opportunity for a break.

This wasn't necessarily a bad thing. Since the Banjara buckled down for however long it took, most of them used this opportunity to catch up on work, like maintaining their vehicles or searching for local herbs or that rare condiment at the local grocer.

*It was just that...*Gaurav was simply bored out of his mind here.

It wasn't always like this. He remembered his childhood when the Harikanad campsite had been an isolated field far from the city. Decreed to the Banjaras for hundreds of years, the lands where they camped were considered sacred, with the legends of the Banjaras usually keeping most people away, and the Banjaras more than capable of handling the few who still decided to trespass.

That was then.

Now, however, all around the campsite were rows and rows of identical houses, all equally spaced apart and with matching lawns. Nothing had stopped the development of the area around the campsites, and with the gradual gentrification of Harikanad, their campsite was surrounded by cookie-cutter houses. With the new houses came the expected changes to accommodate the 'enjoyment of privacy' law of the land, so they now had to follow some rules as long as they camped at Harikanad.

- Noise restrictions after 10 PM.
- Light music and dancing only during the day.
- No drinking or toking outside of the camp.

And worst of all

- No free-riding and strict conformance to local speeding rules.

With all these restrictions, he might as well just buy a house and settle down. The very thought drove Gaurav lachuka crazy.

Settle down? Like a bloody saadha?
Na bhai, his is a life forever on the road.

Unfortunately, there weren't as many grumblings as Gaurav would have liked. The mahouts took the time to work on their custom vehicle builds. Tired of the splotchy internet on the road, the net-runners flowed with the stable internet connection and caught up on their updates and patch deployments. Some of the older oldies even went walking.

WALKING.

Gaurav shuddered at the thought of a mahout travelling without his ride and simply walking with no particular destination in mind. It just boggled his mind.

On days like these, Gaurav considered whether he should leave the troupe and join the other young'uns who lived in various cities around the world, working as high-security couriers and chauffeurs. With their legendary driving skills and steadfast loyalty, their services were highly valued, and they earned big paisa, a decent portion of which were sent back to their troupes.

Most young'uns only returned when they wanted to make up the years required to be eligible to be a bonafide oldie or when the calling of the open road was too strong, so they very much had that in common.

The requirements to become an oldie were a journey detailed quite clearly in their holy book, 'Yatra Granth.' While each tribe had its own holy book, which had its own interpretations on how to live their way of life, they all fundamentally agreed on one theme. While each Banjara has its own path, a true Banjara will always work towards the greater good—not just for themselves but also for their extended family.

Their definition of family, however, depends on the size of each Banjara's heart.

Gaurav, however, had a different kind of ambition. He wanted to be the youngest Oldie ever.

The loss of the additional cred so that he would be rewarded later on seemed like a worthwhile investment. It was all part of the 'The plan' that he had come up with Karthik, Mahesh, and Eshaan that night of the Reckoning. That night, they realised that while they were 4 boys who weren't anything special individually, they could use their respective strengths to achieve miracles together.

The night they planned their destiny to be Legends of their tribes by bringing about the 'The Great Renewal' during the next Thoth Sangam.

Throughout its history, each troupe has experienced changes, both major and minor. Some of the changes were, however, guided by individuals of such influence that they were forever remembered for their acts, both good and bad, and recorded in their books every decade.

Gaurav's own forefather was credited with bringing about the change when the Mahouts went from riding horses and camels to combustion engines.

Rarely, however, would a change be brought about that was so significant and impactful that it would forever change the way of life of all 4 troupes of Banjaras.

'The Great Renewal'.

A change so big that it is written in all the Banjaras' books, and the ones who brought up the Great Renewal were remembered as Legends.

According to prophecy, the next 'Great Renewal' was said to occur during the upcoming 'Thoth Sangam', the syzygy that occurs once in approximately 2,060 years when Mercury, Dhristi, Mars, and Saturn align with the Earth and the Sun.

This was predicted to occur in the next 2 years.

The books were written hundreds of years ago. What are the chances that they would have gotten the date right?

Gaurav knew that the actual timeline was figurative, and it was used more for poetic symbolism.

But still.

What if it really was true?

It was the only reason Gaurav still put up with Karthik, for he seemed to be the only one who had a Plan. Gaurav had met quite a few Banjaras who had their version of the Plan, their own master strategy to bring about their own Legend, but he didn't think that he had ever met someone as committed as Karthik.

Truly committed.

This wasn't as easy an ask as it seemed, for being truly committed to the Flow required completely giving into the will of Anansi, the spider god of randomness, chance, and mischief.

Of Chaos.

With Karthik, this usually meant being in places they weren't meant to be or doing things they weren't supposed to be doing. While it may bring with it its share of boons, this usually took its payment in broken bones and long periods of time spent in exotic locations like Kallapani.

Karthik was that kind of trouble. Nothing seemed to faze him, and no matter how much of a tamasha he made of himself, Karthik kept going.

Gaurav supposed the real reason would be that every once in a while, the lachukabadre strikes platinum and scores big.

Badda Badda big.

Usually, though, they go the other way, like the last one, which was the most shangeka mess that he had ever been through. It's been more than 2 years, and they still haven't spoken to each other, let alone met each other in the real.

Gaurav continued down the double-laned road through the roads between the developments. The afternoon sun was blazing already, and it was quiet just before the suburban moms in their SVUs headed out to do a bit of shopping before the 3 p.m. school pickups. It felt good to feel the hot sun on his neck and the throb of the engine between his thighs.

A part of im had thought that he was going soft.

After riding for so long in the Tarood's black Maronteza Commander, he was getting a bit too used to the air conditioning. A guest from their sister tribe from the deserts of Arabia, Tarood, was a good driving mate while he travelled with Gaurav's troupe and got his ride customised. The original stock car, designed for use in the Arabian desert, had built-in air conditioning that was the coldest you could get in any commercial vehicle.

And yet Tarood was thinking of making it even colder.

And faster

And stronger.

And etc. etc..

With his troupe striking it rich with the last tomb-raiding activities, Tarood had money to burn and travelled all the way to the Mahouts to max out his ride. Gaurav and the oldies had it all mapped: power compressors with the latest GWP refrigerant, hydrogen fuel cells with carbon fibre-reinforced tanks, and a whole bunch of other toys. The copper cooling tubes would be larger than his exhausts and would be crafted into a giant version of their clan symbol of a phoenix with wings spread wide, its feathers merging into swirling sands.

The oldies even designed the inevitable protective thermal wear that the occupants would have to wear whenever they rode in the vehicle. Clubbed with its upgraded weaponry to combat sand pirates the ride deserved its name of 'Narak Freezer'.

There is an old Manglish saying, "To cream in ones pantaloon." That perfectly describes the feeling that Tarood felt when he finally took delivery of the monstrosity, his vehicle. With a yell, he kissed the vehicle and grinned. "If this won't shut up the Jesters and their bright neon monstrosities, nothing will."

Although Gaurav loved the challenge of making Tarood's vision a reality, nothing could beat the sun on his back and the wind through his hair.

Gaurav never felt more alive.

Now going full throttle, Gaurav thought with a smile

Na bro. Ain't anyone going soft here.

He was almost tempted to head to the main road and really go full throttle, but that was a line that he wouldn't cross.

He was many things, but he would like to think he is a true Banjara at heart. While it was in their very nature to bend the rules, they were honour-bound to adhere to the letter of the law.

Gaurav smiled, and that's exactly what he would do.

"Follow the letter of the law".

Riding through the old roads, he could still see the old markers now hidden among all the modern signage and tech. Stabbed with nostalgia, he remembered the days when other troupes would join them. His favourites were the Domas, skilled musicians and performers. Their entertainment skills were honed into an art form, and they were naturally popular among the local population wherever they went. The shows afterwards, though, when it was just the Banjaras, was when the magic really happened.

Even the true Doma are dying now, though. With their constant demand in Filmistaan, there were too many temptations from artists and other successful Doma for the current generation to keep the Banjara ways. Even the badre Mahesh could have done big in Filmistaan if only he had more self-confidence. Instead, he has lachuka working in Corpo now.

Gaurav had almost leapt with joy when Shaani asked him to rendezvous in ZyraSpace. A private meeting was a real excuse to ride out of camp. Kannan had clearly told him to use one of their discreet electric bikes, but he said it with his big Cheshire cat smile, so Gaurav knew he could get away with using his setup-getup.

Pulling up next to a banyan tree, Gaurav parked his bike and connected to his peripheral. He pulled up a half-visor with only one eye covered. The tree was safe, and his perimeter security would alert him if there were issues, but like most Banjara, he always preferred to keep one eye open. The mix of reality and virtual would be jarring to most people, but after years of practice, he didn't mind it so much now.

He was online a few minutes before the scheduled time, instantly teleporting to the Iron City's waiting area. Walking past the posers and flexers, he made his way to the 'Den of Vice'. The red lady was there at the entrance as always.

Walking up to her, Gaurav smiled and said "All things flow".

Jez smiled and said,"G'day user name Brockie3423. Welcome to <insertname> The Den of Vice.

Is this your first time?".

Freaking cheapskate Karthik. You would think, with all the paisa that he gets with his scams, that he could pay for a decent bot.

Shaking his head, he walked away without a word. Looking at the onboard display, he still had another 2 minutes to go.

Like many water banjara, Shaani had a hard time making decisions sometimes. Which is one of the reasons she tries to stick to a schedule. While it was highly unlikely that she may have already logged in, as an adherent to the path, she would not acknowledge Gaurav till the allocated time of 8:37.

After waiting exactly 3 minutes, he went up to the redhead and repeated "All thoughts flow".

This time, Jez bowed and replied "Like the river whence it came".

"Grand is the view from the children's deck?" she asked.

"A summer's longing will crimp the vibe". Gaurav gave the appropriate counter reply and waited.

Jez replied. "Identify confirmed. Booth 3 with the holokey."

Nodding, Gaurav walked down the corridor into the room and headed to the rooms with the prominent numbers in front. Booth 3 was further down the corridor. Pressing his palm against the entry door, he authenticated himself, and the door turned green.

Gaurav opened the door and walked in.

The morning sun was peeking timidly over the frosted mountain peaks, casting a gentle glow upon the campervan nestled in the heart of the snowy valley. The vehicle, typical of the mountain Banjaras, was adorned with icicles dangling from its roof like crystalline ornaments in hues of azure and white, blending seamlessly with the pristine snow that blankets the valley floor.

Through the fog from his breath, he saw Shaani sitting in front of a crackling campfire upon rustic wooden logs surrounded by a ring of freshly fallen snow. The crisp winter air mingled with the tantalising aroma of freshly brewed coffee and the comforting scent of burning logs.

Damn, these new olfactory addons are pretty awesome. I am actually craving a cup of coffee now.

Covered with soft blankets to ward off the non-existent chill, Shaani was wearing her Seeda Jane persona, an avatar with dark brown skin and a beige salwar kameez. Her face blurred with a buzz of static. As childhood friends, Gaurav knew Shaani's face in all her forms, so he was glad that she stuck to his suggestion to use the most generic skin as possible to save time.

After a serious bout of buyer's remorse, Gaurav's simple suggestion to stick to the plainest persona helped Shaani save an inordinate amount of time (and paisa) in selecting a persona that truly reflected her current state of mind.

Her trademark now, and one less decision to make.

Sitting next to the log next to her, Gaurav turned to Shaani. "So, when did the lachuka get out?"

Shaani turned, maybe, hard to tell with her static head, but regardless, she replied. "Couple of months now, but he only reached out a few weeks ago."

Gaurav sighed. "And you are back where you started. Shaani, when will you ever learn that Karthik's path is only going to lead to heartbreak."

Shaani shook her head. "It's different this time. He may actually have something solid.

But you know Karthik, he's got the dreams but needs us to make it a reality.

Gaurav laughed bitterly. "Come on, Shaani, do you really believe him? That's what he said last time as well, and look what happened?"

Sighing deeply, Shaani said, "I know, but you know it's Karthik. No matter how maddening it is.

"This time feels different, though.

"I don't know why, but I actually have a good ooham about this. Something about this feels right."

Gaurav sighed. "I am in if you are in Shaani, and I think I can convince Mahesh, but Karthik can go to Narak as far as I am concerned.

Shaani looked at Gaurav and smiled. "You know what the best part of this?

That it's time to 222" she said with a tinkling laugh.

Flipping a coin towards Gaurav, she smoothly logged off. Alone, Gaurav looked at the digital coin.

Looks like I am in for better or worse.

Out of the corner of his eye, he sees movement. A security droid, a sleek new model with the emblem of the Harikanad Homeowners' Association etched on its chrome chest, had glided to a stop in front of his vehicle. The droid's optical sensors, glowing a calm shade of blue, scanned him thoroughly. Despite its imposing presence, the droid's voice was surprisingly servile, programmed to enforce with politeness. "Good afternoon, ji." the droid droned.

"My sensors have detected that you exceeded the designated speed limit within the community area.

"However, it appears that your location beacons are inaccessible, probably due to a mechanical fault, so it took me a while to locate you.

"I apologise, Shri, but this would be a 10,000 paisa fine and confiscation of your vehicle.", its voice with the same servile tone designed as per the requirements of the residents.

Apologising? For a clear violation.

Gaurav smiled.

Threat Level Zero, huh?

Kollam.

This is going to be easier than I thought it would be.

Gaurav audibly swallowed and stammered purposefully. "I—I know, and I'm really sorry for that. It's just that I have a... a medical condition,"

The droid tilted its head slightly, a programmed gesture of curiosity. "A medical situation, oh dear? My sensors indicate that you are in optimum health condition. "Is it a resident? Please provide details so that I can organise a Medevac if required."

Gaurav waved his hands apologetically. "No. I have a prescription.

"I hope it's okay.

"My understanding of the rules was that it was okay to speed provided the proximity sensors were engaged.

The droid hesitated while it processed this new information. "Protocol dictates that any deviation from standard traffic regulations due to health concerns will require adequate validation.

"Could you provide appropriate supporting documentation?"

Feigning compliance, Gaurav rummaged through his glove compartment and flicked a doco to the droid.

The droid's response was almost immediate. "This appears to be a prescription for nicotine vapes. Based on my records, lack of nicotine has not been deemed a life-threatening situation."

"Oh, really," said Gaurav, puzzled. "Reading the wording of the HOA guidelines, it just specified that for medical reasons.

"I do get anxious without my vape, so I would say it would be an emergency for me."

Saying so, he produced a thin black cylinder, which was capped at both ends.

The droid paused, processing the information. It spoke again after a moment that felt like an eternity to Gaurav. "The HOA guidelines do specify that residents may exceed speed limitations for urgent medical needs. While nicotine vapes are an unconventional example, they technically fall within the bounds of medical treatment as per your explanation."

Gaurav didn't hold his breath for the inevitable final verdict.

"Given the circumstances, I am inclined to allow you to proceed with a stern warning this time. However, I must advise you to ensure that any future emergencies are clearly documented and, if possible, communicated to HOA security in advance," the droid concluded, stepping aside.

Gaurav exaggerated a sigh of relief, a smile creeping onto his face as he nodded. "Absolutely, I'll make sure of that. Thank you," he said, waving goodbye to the droid.

As he drove away, Gaurav waited till he was comfortable that it was out of range before popping the caps of the cylinder. Extending the small black link chain inside, he wore the necklace he had shown the droid earlier. Putting the cylinder to his lips, Gaurav inhaled deeply and blew out of the empty hollow cylinder.

A legacy from his past, Gaurav didn't vape and instead used the hollow metal cylinder as a meditation tool.

Plus, it does come in handy when pesky droids bring him up to task for speeding. Now that he had been flagged, Gaurav knew that he wouldn't be able to ride like this in Harikanad for a while.

Totally worth it, though.

He thought with a smile.

Alone and at peace, Gaurav continued breathing while using his own passkey to decrypt the coin that Shaani had given it. It appeared to co-ordinates for a meeting location. Documents appeared, which appeared to be bookings and travel details.

Gaurav's jaw dropped when he read the phrase on top.

CHALO GOA.

| 17 |

Orinoco Flow / Hawayein

"Raghunathan Valavan, are you actually daydreaming?"

Raghu woke up to his teacher's angry scowl and the silent threat of the bamboo stick. With a shake of his head, he stood up and sheepishly said, "No, Shri," looking downcast. His dream was already fading, but he remembered that it was of the sea again.

A ship had been sighted heading into the harbour early in the morning, and that was all Raghu could think about today. Though he wasn't expected back for weeks, Raghu hoped it was his father.

Raghu could feel his teacher's scowling stare boring into him. He was a bit annoyed, though. Today, of all days, he couldn't really care less about the clever way a long-dead poet had with a particular turn of words. This was an opinion he kept to himself, however. His mother had promised to let him see the boat at the harbour, and the last thing he wanted was to get into trouble for backanswering.

Although at 15, he towered over the wisp of a priest, he had a deep respect for his guru and bowed low in apology.

The priest calmed down. He couldn't really be angry with Raghu. Ever since he helped the young Raghu draw his first letters in the sand, he had been Raghu's teacher and mentor.

As the senior guru priest, he taught the children of the most influential members of Ainuruvar, and Raghu was his prized pupil. His thirst for knowledge was insatiable, and the priest relished the toil of keeping up with his incessant questioning.

Except when it came to literature.

Raghu preferred to study astronomy, navigation, medicine, and other practical subjects that would be invaluable on a ship that would be out at sea for weeks and months.

For the sea was above all things that Raghu thought about, and everything else could wait.

Rubbing his eye with his left hand, Raghu looked up expecting an admonishment, but to his surprise, the priest had started packing up.

He looked at Raghu and said indulgently, 'Go child; I can see that my efforts will be wasted today.'

"Read the last 4 suryas later on today and I will see you in the morning."

With a large Cheshire cat smile, Raghu jumped up and hugged the old priest, who turned stiff in surprise. Trying hard to suppress a smile, the priest shooed him away in mock annoyance.

Unexpectedly released early from his classes, he was overjoyed and immediately started climbing the main stairs to the temple top. As he ascended the stone steps, he savoured the salty sea air, which overpowered even the sandalwood incense from the Uraayiur temple.

From his unobstructed vantage point at the top, he could see the harbour below, filled with sails emblazoned with bull logos. Having spent his whole life by the harbour, he could easily distinguish between the different types of vessels even at this distance.

There was a new ship in the harbour. He had already heard rumours that it was a returning contingent back from a raid on the Chalukya coast, but this lone ship looked just like his father's marakkalam.

Could it be?

It was too far to tell if it was his, indeed, his father's ship.

Only 1 way to tell, he thought while he ran all the way home.

Unlike other kids his age, apart from the short journeys his father took his family on when he was at home during the off-season, he hasn't been on a sea expedition yet.

A childhood accident, the loss of his right arm was reason enough to keep him from being a bona fide member of his father's crew.

This didn't stop him from dreaming, though.

Ever since he was told that his injury would keep him away from the sea, he had decided to dedicate every waking moment to making himself worthy of joining his father. Innately intelligent and with the tenacity of all Valavans, he decided that what he lacked in physical prowess, he would more than makeup for with his brains.

While most of the crew were capable sailors, apart from his father and Abbas, his navigator, they could barely write their names, let alone read. The wizened old man was the one who had first sparked Raghu's curiosity and interest in astronomy. Many were the nights spent with Abbas pointing out the various stars and constellations, patiently explaining to a wide-eyed young Raghu how they were used by the crew for navigating through the seas. Abbas was an expert at viral kanakku, their way of navigation while on the seas and he was the one who taught Raghu his first numbers of navigation.

"That's the Otta villi, the single star, that's the Iranai villi, the twin stars and those 7 stars crowded together; that's the Kutta villi.

"If you ever get lost at sea, you can always use your numbers to find your way home. "

His efforts had not been in vain. Already, Raghu knew more about navigation than some of the guild members of the Five Hundred Lords of Ayyavole and was even courted by some of them to join their crew. Raghu refused, however. He knew his father would never forgive him if he joined any other rival guilds, and he could not bear disappointing his father. On the other hand, his father thought that with Raghu's injury, it was better for him to remain landbound and continue his studies at the temple under the guidance of the priests.

As he ran home, Raghu could feel something that he hadn't felt before. It wasn't just hope; it was something more.

For some reason, he deeply believed that his father would shortly ask him to join his crew.

Taking a deep breath before he entered the threshold, Raghu got a final whiff of the sea salt air before it was replaced by the scent of jasmine from the vines that covered the back entrance of his house. The first thing he noticed was the commotion in the front yard. People were rushing; front and foremost among them was his mother in her saree of Tirunvelli silk.

Only one thing could make his prim and proper mother run.

So, he ran as well to the courtyard.

A procession of 12 carts crowded the wide verandah in front of his house. In the lead was a smiling figure, sunburnt black with windblown hair.

His father had come home.

His father wasn't alone, though. Alongside him sat strangers who were shrouded from head to toe and wore turbans of a myriad of colours, ranging from vibrant indigo to muted reds. All had curious hook noses and were decidedly tall and thin, looking exotic with their clean white robes, which were simultaneously functional and elegant. They couldn't look more different from his people's traditional dhotis and open-chested garbs.

With a loud yell, his father leapt out of the lead cart and yelled, "Nectar, I am home."

His baby brother, playing hoops in the front yard, had already leapt into his father's arms, who was now throwing him up in the air. Raghu felt a stab of jealousy seeing his father's doting attention on his baby brother. Like it or not, he was a man now and must act like one.

His mother had stopped at the foyer, her face partially covered with the sari, with only her downward eyes visible through the halo of jet-black hair that had escaped the wrap of the saree. Raghu could see that she had eyes only for his father.

His father gestured towards his family, the strangers who had gracefully alighted from the cart despite their flowing robes. Standing beside his father, they bowed deeply towards his mother and the rest of the family. Calling out to his wife, his father said, "Ponne, get Ganuta to take our guests to the khulam at the back so they can wash our travels' dust.

Raghu's mother nodded shyly in agreement and also asked Ganuta to cut out strips of neem twigs for the guests to brush their teeth.

Raghu waited until he got his father's attention, then walked stiffly towards him and touched his feet. Blessing him, his father lifted him up and held him out at arm's length. In spite of the long absence, Raghu still couldn't get even a ghost of a smile from him.

It would not do for the Karnuvar to be seen coddling the son who was to take up his mantle.

Quickly ignoring Raghu, his father welcomed the guests into the tharavad and personally escorted them around. He was joined by the rest of the family, who tagged along. Some out of politeness and the rest out of curiosity.

Raghu stayed behind, though.

Seeing his drooping face, old Abbas, with his touch of familiarity with the house, jumped out of the cart in spite of his age and clapped Raghu on his back. "Dropped our balls, I see."

There were a couple of shocked looks, especially from the priest, but the rest of the audience was used to sailors' salty language and didn't bat an eyelid.

Raghu laughed and hugged Abbas. His father trusted kappalottiya; the pilot had been with his father right from the beginning and was treated as a member of the family. After greeting Abbas, he looked at the rest of the crew of Kadalvar. Not all the men he knew were there; even some new faces were sitting with the rest.

Abbas yelled, "Didn't I tell you that your father is the best Nayakan in the trade? Look at what we have brought home."

It was then that he paid attention to the cargo in the overladen carts. The dabbas and barrels were closed but he didn't need to open them up to know what was inside. The heady perfume of pepper, cloves, and nutmeg filled the air now. Even more impressive were the steel boxes on his father's carriage. Abbas whispered in his ear the treasures they contained. Gold, silver, silk and much more.

A king's ransom's worth.

"So much and so soon? I thought it would be weeks before you would come back." Raghu said in wonder.

Abbas laughed. "That is a long story in itself, but I am hungry and tired, and the bushes over there look like they need some watering." And ran away to relieve himself.

Unique among the guests was a lone stranger in a kimono. Despite being an ethereal, he was unusually clumsy and tripped while getting out of the cart, dropping the books and maps he carried in a leather pouch.

Glancing at one of the open maps, Raghu yelped. " Are these the maps of the path of the Nile?"

"I have never seen one so detailed. It even shows the tributaries.

"Where did you even find them?"

The ethereal was surprised. "This is an original from the libraries of Alexandria and I have never met anyone else who could read it.

Raghu shrugged, "I have read every book and manuscript on maritime studies available in every library from Thanjavur to Chidambaram."

"I have studied maps like this before and many others."

A booming voice behind him asked aloud, "You can read those maps?"

Turning around, Raghu saw his father standing right behind him.

Filled with new-found confidence, Raghu squared back his shoulders, looked his father straight in the eyes, and simply said " Yes." He then demonstrated further by reading out the various markers listed on the map.

Looking up, he saw his father look at him ponderingly. After what seemed like forever, he reached out and grasped Raghu on his shoulder." We will have a talk later, but I think it's time you joined the crew."

Remembering wistfully, Raghunathan or Nathan Sentinel as he is known nowadays, wiped the tears from his eyes with both hands. In spite of his lengthy existence, Raghu still considered this memory as one of the proudest moments of his life.

| 18 |

Symptom of Being Human

Ramin woke up to the sound of bells.

The sirens of a medevac had come through the open windows along with the cold mountain air. The air still smelt faintly of sandalwood, just like the incense his ammachi used to light in the puja room every day. He inhaled deeply, remembering her sitting in the sunlit room with the white saree draped around her head, deep in prayer and at peace.

He still missed her after all these years.

In spite of the lights being turned off, he could clearly make out the room with just the light of the full moon coming through the silk-draped windows. Lounging in his king-sized bed, adorned in Phoenician linens, he gazed out at the breathtaking view of the Himalayas from his penthouse bedroom window. He stretched, luxuriating in the texture of the still-warm bed. He felt utterly relaxed and wished he could lounge in the comfort for a bit longer.

He considered going back to sleep but was shocked when he suddenly realised what exactly he was thinking.

That's unexpected

A habit he cultivated from his teens was that he got out of bed whenever he woke up, regardless of the hour.

It was just one of his rituals, and he never compromised on his rituals.

From his penthouse suite at Malavedan, the view of the Himalayas wasn't obscured by the skyline of the bludgeoning city, and he could just make out the snow-capped mountains from where he lay.

Looking down, he could see his taut tummy with its faint outline of his 6 pack abs, in spite of his prone position. Running a hand across his arms, he relished in the feeling of his firm and muscular forearms. Flexing it, he brought his hand close to his face and closely examined his fingers.

The tips of his fingernails showed more white than he would have preferred.

Better get Savatri to schedule a manicure.

Then realising what he had just done, he almost burst out laughing.

He closed his eyes and let his mind grow blank, trying to recall the last thing he could remember. His most recent memories were of the lab and the techs hovering about.

Must have worked then

He breathed in deeply, relaxing and feeling himself settle down.

He was feeling hungry, which was strange because he remembered having dinner just a couple of hours ago, and Ramin is not prone to snacking.

He wasn't just peckish; he was starving.

Really strange, but he thought he could put up with the urge for now.

The dissociative classes and training seemed to be helping. The sensations felt more natural, and in spite of Ramin's awareness of his situation, he couldn't sense any fear or panic.

Looking around his room, everything seemed familiar and as it should be.

Let's see if they have got everything then.

He walked over to the painting of the "Composition Book I + II" by Kurux Yakkha, which hung above a bureau of drawers near the window.

He was never much into art, particularly paintings, considering them chaotic and devoid of any logic or structure. That was till he saw this one at a small showing at Bolgatty house that Aunty Naina had organised.

It was the first painting that he had ever purchased.

Heading up to the painting, he turned up the brightness of the display LEDs and stared deep into it. Something about the straight lines, right angles, and primary colours evoked the same sense of order and balance within him, just like when he first saw it.

He remembered Dia, who showed the painting. He had only met her during the showing and while she was beautiful, what Ramin remembered the most was that she had really listened.

Associative memory, abstract appreciation check.

He headed to the stereo system and said aloud, "Savatri, play The Slickest by Roll the Ice."

As requested, the room was filled with loud bass drums as the popular opening lines blasted out: "There's some sick hoes in the club."

With his eyes closed, Ramin could feel his cheeks redden with annoyance the more he listened to the song.

Satisfied, he asked Savatri to turn the music off.

Neg Emotions and Personality Fidelity validated.

He suddenly realised that he was still naked save for a pair of tight briefs. Overwhelmingly he felt stirrings of something in his nether regions.

Just when he was about to reach down to investigate further, a booming voice said

"Hello, Ramin; how are you doing?"

Ramin didn't reply straight away but instead started walking down the corridor now to the kitchen at the end of the hallway. He was really hungry now, and he couldn't wait any longer.

Opening up the fridge, Ramin replied "Doing fine so far. I feel like me."

The cold air from the fridge chilled his legs and cooled him down in more ways than one.

"That's good to hear", the voice replied. "Things are looking great from here as well. Do you need a few minutes, or are you good to proceed with the review now?"

Ramin didn't answer and instead looked at the empty fridge and thought.

Black forest cake and vanilla milkshake.

With a shimmer, a large slice of chocolate and cherry sponge cake topped with whipped cream appeared beside a tall frosty glass of milkshake complete with a stripey straw and a single cherry with a stem on top—just like his favourite café in Besant Nagar.

Grabbing the dessert fork on the plate he sat down and cut a not insignificant slice, making sure to grab all the layers on the fork. The first bite was soft and melting into the mouth delicious.

Just like he remembered.

Continuing to eat, he smiled and said aloud, "I think I'm going to need a few more minutes."

It was a while before Ramin became aware of the booming voice again.

"Are you there? I haven't heard from you in a while. Is everything alright?"

He couldn't open his eyes and was surprised to find it felt quite sticky.

Touching it, he felt a mixture of revulsion and wonder as he found that his eyes were covered with what appeared to be cake frosting. Forcing them open, he blearily looked at the large table, which was now filled with bowls of kulfis, half-eaten burgers, chaat, jars of cocktails, lassis and cake.

Lots and lots of cake.

His lap was now covered with pretty much the entire menu, and his belly had grown to that of a woman about to give birth. In a daze, he could see that he was still eating, or at least that his hand was continuing to stuff handfuls of cake into his face. He willed it to stop but couldn't.

Still stuffing his mouth, his belly continued to grow till, with a pop, he could hear the waistband of his briefs snap.

Chocolate sauce is now dripping onto his chest.

And yet he kept eating.

"Help", he tried to whisper, his voice muffled between the cake fistfuls.

He couldn't speak and could barely make a sound.

With all force of will he could muster, he slammed his forehead against the table top. A small cut formed with the bruise of the first attack, and a streak of blood bloomed. He continued to slam

and slam, his face was now a mixture of blood and cream.
CLICK

A perfectly straight, thin line formed just below his nose and extended till it perfectly framed his eyes and nose. Without a sound, Ramin's eyes and nose detached themselves and hovered just in front of his face.

Starting with the table, the room around him dematerialised into a haze of static.

Turning away, disappointed from the screen, Ramin Contractor addressed the group of men and women in white lab coats just behind him. "Can someone explain to me what the badre just happened?" his voice was a controlled calm that belied the storm brewing beneath.

In a secluded lab far from the main ZyraCorp facilities, Ramin addressed the staff of scientists working on Nathan's special project.

After his conversation with Nathan, he decided to personally check on the progress of Project Aatmik and was furious that it was in far worse shape than he had expected. Kishore Rathore, his Chief Engineering officer, stepped up hesitantly with his tablet. Already rattled with the unexpected visit from Ramin, had been asked to provide an impromptu demonstration of the process. "We are still checking, Shri, but it looks like the Self-Management Module of Aatmik's AI wasn't reacting as we had hoped. The feedback from its emotional cores wasn't balanced with the primal desire modules. "

Ramin rubbed his eyes in frustration. "Or in plain Manglish it would have eaten itself till it exploded if it hadn't initiated the deactivation protocol. "

Kishore raised his hands in defence and said "The Aatmik modules scans work perfectly. This is just a hang-up from the bio side of things. "Shouldn't take us long to get this sorted out.

Instead of pacifying, it only made Ramin even more angry.

His voice going dangerously quiet, he asked, "But we are digital only now, so what exactly does the brain or 'bio', as you put it, be the root cause?"Based on your last report, I was under the impression that the Neuralyanser's algorithm was flawless. That you had accounted for every variable.

"Didn't we scan enough liabilities to get this right by now?

"All this cred lost, and you can't even get a working model?

"Failures. "

The word hung in the air; a guillotine poised to fall. Kishore swallowed hard, the weight of the word pressing down on his shoulders like the world itself. He had known Ramin ever since he was a child and was even in the hospital with his father to bring him and his sister into this world. Kishore however knew better than to show any form of familiarity with him.

Not after the last time he made the mistake of addressing him as "monne'.

Shuddering Kishore quietly accepted defeat and deferentially said. "We thought we had," he admitted, feeling the sting of each word. "But the human mind...it's not a machine, shri.

"It's a puzzle.

"Every time we think we've figured it all out, we find another hidden passage, another secret chamber. "

Once the dam was open, the flood of truth pouring out couldn't be stopped. He might as well let it all out. Throwing his hands up in the air, Kishore finally confessed. "The absolute truth is that we are really not sure how long it's going to take.

"It's true that the scanners work well, and we have been able to perfectly capture the essence of the subject's memory. You interacted with your Aatmik, and it validated all the tests.

"It was an exact version of you as of this afternoon. It had your same likes and dislikes. It could recall your childhood memories, and given time, it would have built its core memories.

"The Neuranalysers aren't the problem.

"The problem is the environment."

Ramin was a big-picture guy, and in spite of everything, he could see that they were really close, but the only way to truly gain control over Nathan was to get this guillotine hanging over his head safely dismantled as soon as possible.

Whatever it takes.

Mid explanation, Ramin stood up and beckoned Kishore to follow him to a small conference room at the back of the lab. Kishore silently followed and sat down at the proffered chair while Ramin shut the door and activated the privacy of the room.

Sitting at the other chair beside him, Ramin lounged back with his hands folded behind his back.

He waited a minute in silence to really get into the spirit of things. It had the desired effect; Kishore was now tapping his foot nervously, and his hands gripped the chair tightly.

Looks like he is prepped.

With a cough like a gunshot, Ramin stood up straight in his chair.

Hearing him, Kishore started and looked up straight into Ramin's eyes.

Their gaze locked, Kishore found himself unable to tear his eyes away from Ramin's own.

Ramin smiled now that he had really got Kishore's attention. All he needed to do was ask the right questions to guide Kishore's thoughts. "See, Kishore, for reasons of my own, I need this project to be wrapped up as soon as possible. So, if you can kindly tell me what the problem is and what is the fastest way to fix it," he said.

Like in a trance Kishore started. "It's not enough that we just scan an Aatmik, we need it to evolve, to grow organically as it would in the real world.

"So we need it to interact with other Aatmik's inside the Zyraverse sandbox.

"While we can create the foundation of the Aatmik's based on the subject's passkey, the fundamental digital ID for each person, the problem is that since each person is unique, their passkeys can't be perfectly replicated by the AI.

"Then there is the issue with the training seed."

Steeling his resolve, Ramin held Kishore's gaze and whispered. "And what exactly is a training seed?"

Kishore's eyes were starting to water, but he continued as if he didn't notice it. "For the Aatmiks to become sentient, we need them to be able to organically extend their boundaries, just as people would in the real world. However, they would need to self-regulate so that they don't exceed acceptable behaviour.

"Apart from the internal narrative, we also need a complementary regulatory system.

"This is easy for people. We have our own fundamental biochemical feedback system—our emotions, basically. We are, however, trying to replicate a human bio-emotional feedback system digitally.

"We can create an equivalent that all of the Aatmiks can use, but building all our best simulations will only be poor replicas of the real thing. Human emotions and cultures are too varied, so a wide range of conditions would need to be generated and reviewed.

"To properly simulate a digital equivalent of our own emotional system would require a large number of scenarios to be genuinely tuned.

"This is where the training seed would come in.

"It's a catalyst. A lock that can be unlocked only using the right keys from the Aatmik's core memories and become a true copy of their human.

"An Eden where the Aatmiks can be humanised."

Now we are getting somewhere,

Raising his voice but still crooning, Ramin asked, "What's missing, and what do we need to get this sorted?'

Kishore continued now, slightly twitching with the effort of looking into Ramin's eyes, streams of tears flowing down his face. "With the passkeys from ZyraVerse in theory, we have everything that we need to achieve true sentience for the Aatmik's model, but any new AI model still needs to have to build up its emotional core.

"We can do it but that will require constant feedback from a user over time for regular validation. "

Kishore stopped talking but was still staring at Ramin, a thin string of drool forming at the corner of his mouth.

Having already been updated on the increased baksheesh the IPS officers had demanded for assisting with recent inquiries into dead ZyraCorp employees, Ramin had an inkling of the truth but nevertheless asked, "And the Reloads?"

Kishore was now shuddering despite which his eyes still didn't break contact with Ramin's. "Devastating,"

"We've had reports of...suicides. The corrupted memories are driving them to madness.

"The memory overlays aren't just glitching; they're merging.

"The Aatmiks...

"They're receiving fragments of memories from the others. It's causing confusion, disorientation...and in the worst cases, a complete psychological breakdown.

"Reloading those memories blurred the lines between subjects. Now, we have some of them with memories of a life they never had.

"Without their fundamental identities, they have become untethered, living with the ghost memories of other people's lives."

Kishore now started convulsing, with the corners of his mouth now foaming.

Ramin blinked, releasing Kishore, who withdrew with a gasp.

Silence fell over the room, a heavy, oppressive thing that squeezed the air from Kishore's lungs.

Leaning back in his chair, Ramin's face remained impassive, with his fingers steepled deep in thought.

Ramin rarely pushed his hard. This wasn't just nudging people with hints and suggestions. Ramin did that all the time , subtly providing cues so that their subconscious would pick up on them and do what Ramin wanted. What Ramin was doing now, however, was forcing Kishore to make connections that he may have reasons not to subconsciously make. Usually, when it comes to ideas that could go against their inborn ethics and principles.

Their ego.

This, however, does have consequences.

Sigh, now I have to get a replacement for Kishore.

Kishore's head drooped down. He was aware now but he wanted Ramin to speak, to condemn, to rage—anything but the quiet that wrapped around him like chains.

Finally, Ramin spoke, his voice soft yet laced with graphene. "You understand the position this puts us in. If word of this gets out..."

Breathing in deeply, Ramin continued. "What's our risk of exposure on this one if it goes bad?"

Now released, it was as if Kishore was a battery of pent-up movements. In a burst, Kishore stood up, now wringing his hands so quickly that it may have caught fire if he wasn't sweating profusely at the same time. "The risk is absolutely minimal. We were quite careful to choose candidates whose profiles were those least likely to raise enquiries.

Smiling manically, Kishore yelled. "From where they are from, another dead body is not going to make much of a difference."

Ramin smiled a gentle smile now. He still needed Kishore a bit longer and needed to soothe him now.

Quite deliberately, Ramin smirked, and Kishore smirked in return and nodded in acknowledgement.

The tension lifting was quite visible, with Kishore's aura turning from a scared yellow to a more malleable soft pink.

Time to close this out.

With a straight look again into Kishore's eyes, Ramin asked, "So why don't we have a valid training seed, and what do you need to fix this?"

Kishore stared into Ramin's eyes again and again as if in a trance he said softly. "It's the sentience training seed. Getting one that is truly universal would take years unless.. unless..

There ,

Ramin had him. Now to coax it all out.

Pull the thread.

In the same soft but firm voice, Ramin said, "Continue."

Kishore continued, his foam of spittle forming back up again. "This needs to be fine-tuned and smoothened in the real world to get the feedback to perfect the catalyst. This would require a year of feedback though from a wide range of people all over the world to get a catalyst that would suit the full spectrum of the world.

"We are talking decades of feedback and there would be dire consequences if we take shortcuts.

Kishore paused, looking down remorsefully.

Ramin smiled, satisfied that he finally understood what needed to be done.

So that was the conundrum. Kishore is still thinking of getting his feedback ethically.

I can fix that.

Ramin blinked, releasing Kishore, who withdrew with a gasp and firmly asked, "How much time are you talking about."

Leaning back in his chair, Ramin's face remained impassive, and his fingers steepled. "So what you need is an AI system whose sole purpose is constantly to provide emotional feedback and be validated in the real world.

"You are talking about a fully sentient AI. An AI that is aware enough to actively use the emotional feedback of humans. An AI that is able to actually not just learn but to evolve to the point where it seems human itself.

"Nay

"Where it actually thinks that it may be human."

Ramin smiled now.

A very dangerous smile that sent chills down Kishore's spine without him understanding why.

Reminds of an AI that just lachuka pissed him off.

"I think I may have something for you, Kishore," said Ramin, smiling broadly. "Humor me with a hypothetical scenario. Assuming that you get one trained seed, how quickly can you get a working model together?"

Kishore, relieved to have gotten a smile out of Ramin and asked a question that he knew the answer to, chortled.

"In theory, we should be able to get working prototype within a year. That would be dangerous though. The feedback from the one seed would have a world view that is incredibly limited to a single aspect.

"That would taint all the seeds and could lead to unpredictable behaviours for Aatmiks far away from the profile. "

Ramin nodded and said grimly.

"That sounds like somebody else's problem, doesn't it?"

| 19 |

I Don't want to talk / Lets Nacho

Shaani ran with the generic focus that was typical of her as angry grey clouds threatened the sky.

The monsoons were still a month away, but this close to the equator, they wouldn't have mattered anyway. Heavy clouds this close to the sea would only mean thunderstorms.

The waves lashed at her feet.

Rather than getting annoyed by it, she relished it and ran like she always ran, with the abandonment and recklessness that is the stay of the young and the wistfulness of the old.

The sea breeze matted her hair, and the tight ponytail was like a whip on the back of her neck.

The barest slowing down in pace for her to catch her breath and then she was back at full throttle.

Blood pumping with adrenaline.

Senses heightened, every lungful of air brought the rich brine of the sea to her nose.

The heady bouquet of salt-encrusted fish rotting in the open air, freshly loosened seaweed, brought back a rush of memories of her childhood.

Shaani had always loved the sea, and some of her happiest moments were always by her side.

Running on the beach with their father and mother as a young boy, collecting seashells with their grandmother and fishing off the sea with their grandfather, feet knee-deep in the sea while they cast their line far out fishing for humour, basa and their favourite pomfret.

The Tshangla lagoon, which they called home, was isolated but had everything that they needed.

The sea provides.

No matter where she went around the world, her bond with the sea was always intimate, and even when walking on the most distant beaches, Shaani always felt at home.

She smiled, and her memories of a happier time seemed to lift her feet. Shaani felt like she was doused in Mithra's fire, guided by Anahita, and nothing would go wrong.

While she always ran for the sheer fun of it, she loved it best when she could incorporate work into it.

Nothing like being paid to do what I would do anyways
she thought with a smile.
Winner Winner Chicken Dinner.

The flame of the electric torch that she was carrying shone unwaveringly. The silver lettering on the side, which said 'Mazda' in Celtic script, gleams with a dull matt finish. Its sleek graphene handle, incorporating cutting-edge nanocomposites, barely warmed up by the intense flame and still felt cool in Shaani's hand in spite of being lit for over 29 days.

She was just carrying out the final assessment on the 6th iteration of the Mazda torch before it was sent across to the runners at Mannar as part of their run.

The torch, though sold at a nominal amount, was a marvel of modern technology, and many participated in the run simply to own a torch that was guaranteed to be windproof.

'Infused with ancient wisdom and digital enchantment, Mazda flickers with the essence of a thousand data streams, A beacon of connection between the past and the future, illuminating the path to transcendence in the midst of digital chaos.'

Or at least, that is what the marketing gurus came up with as the tagline for the torch's official launch.

Sponsored by, Koya Lodhi a prominent temple member from the tech community, it was taken on as a project to address concerns raised by the runners who carry out the regular Atash Behram runs on the Ram walkway. Emulating the run traditionally required them to run over the limestone rocks while holding aloft a wooden torch carrying the sacred flame, which should never be extinguished. In keeping with the times, the wooden torches were since upgraded to more reliable gas torches. However, they were still prone to being doused by the lashing waves.

Atash Behram was a legend, and even with modern technology, the runs were difficult and only attempted by the most dedicated pilgrims. The pilgrimage was considered completed when the sacred flame was carried from end to end, so true adherents went back to relight the sacred flame. With most participants barely able to make the entire stretch, the thought of carrying out multiple runs deterred even the most adherent believers.

When the WHO (World Heritage Organisation) decreed that the limestone steps that made up the walkway were crumbling, the local Padi community thought that this would be the end of their local business, which relied on the regular pilgrims for their trade. That was till an old, wise construction supervisor reminded them of the old adage.

Build it, and they will come.

So they built it.

With the surge of new attempts to run on the new Ram walkway, which at least protected them from the regular buffeting of water, the new challenge they faced was the fact that they still managed to extinguish their torches.

Koya personally took over the issue and insisted on developing a solution as part of his contribution to the agiaries. Owning a fledging asteroid mining company, he believed his team of scientists would be able to achieve this, and no expenses were spared in researching a product that would address the concerns raised by the runners. What they came up with was a torch that harnessed advanced plasma technology, emitting a luminous beam unaffected by harsh conditions. Its compact design integrated microreactors and ionised particles, providing a reliable source of illumination with unparalleled efficiency.

When questioned by the press drones on the amount spent for a seemingly trivial vanity project, Koya just shrugged and said

"Good thoughts, Good words, and Good actions. "

Later, it turned out that the research spent on developing the torches could be used to create new space drills, which, based on plasma technology, were perfect for working in the harsh conditions of space.

When afterwards, he was questioned by the press drones on why Koya won the vast majority of the contracts to supply his new space drills for the Shendu asteroid, he just shrugged and said

"Good thoughts, Good words, and Good actions. "

Incidentally, viral videos of his before-and-after shrugs became memes on VidMe and FlipFlop, which brought up his company stock price once it went mirchi.

An increase which bumped up his rankings on the daily arabpati rankings by 25 points at its peak.

Overwhelmed with all the attention he received, Koya declined further requests for a shrug.

Shaani's foot slipped a bit when it landed on the jagged rock. Barely perceptible aerogels of her Batata Malavedan absorbed and bent to mould around the tip of the rock like very fine clay . The thin nanoballs absorb the shock and adapt it to fit just right to the surface.

Another product she was testing, her expertise on the suitability of tech was slowly gaining traction and is already beginning to look like more than just a side hustle. With the release of Runtastic by ZyraCorp, there has been an increased uptick in running-related activities and the associated tech that they require.

Shaani was initially very disappointed about losing the contract for testing Runtastic when it first came out, especially since she thought she was perfect for the job, but the fact that she was a close contender actually provided suitable advertising for her brand, and they came in droves.

It was just enough to keep her afloat for now.

Afloat. Lol.. good one.

That's the only reason why she agreed to meet up with Karthik. To discuss another insane scheme to cause the great Renewal to happen.

Nothing else.

While it was supposed to be vague, with no exact date that it would occur, Karthik was absolutely convinced that it would happen during the next planetary parade when Mercury, Venus, Mars, Jupiter, and Saturn were all aligned with the Sun and the Moon.

The 'Great Syzygy'

It was also his firm belief that the 4 of them were destined to bring it about.

She should know. Its all he could talk about since they were children. She remembered when they were 4 boys just camped around the bonfire when Karthik first told of his plan to bring about the change.

So enamoured were they with him that they were carried along with the dream.

It seemed so impossible and so possible at the same time.

Shaani exhaled sadly.

That was then, and this is now.

With all their planning and scheming, they ended up here, where Shaani was the only person who spoke to the rest of them.

At least she was glad that Gaurav and Mahesh at least pinged each other once in a while. Still, considering that they have never met since that night makes her think that they still haven't forgiven each other.

She had no doubts, however, about their feelings towards Karthik.

Shaani paused at the edge of the narrow outbreak of rock, which looked like a long finger pointing somewhere. Just visible from the rock's edge was a narrow cove hidden in the cliff side and only visible to those in the know.

Her swimsuit, made of crafted NanoFlex, dynamically adjusts to the water's temperature, and its bioluminescent interlaced Nora-gel gives it a mesmerising glow underwater as she headed back towards the submarine docked underneath the cove.

With the grace of an eel, she swam closer to the cove, diving deep once she was close enough to peer into the underwater bedrooms.

Karthik hadn't bothered putting up the smart windows, and Shaani could see straight inside.

Last night may have been a mistake, but it was fun.

Though she may have to pay for it later, Shaani loved it when it was time to 222.

Though technically she was supposed to only party after the storming to commemorate the starting of the Norming phase she felt the need of a boost to fill her with good vibes and clear bad juju.

They were just forming at this stage. She was allowed to explore and experience any opportunity for pleasure.

What happens during 222, stays as a 222.

It helps to buffer the group when the inevitable storming happens.

Based on what has happened so far, it looks like there will be a thunderstorm both inside and outside the submarine. Encased in reinforced glass and sleek steel, the small bedroom gazes out into depths where shadows dance amidst the coral reefs.

Here, amidst the tranquil currents, Shaani finds respite from the chaos of the world above in the silent embrace of the underwater.

Entering the airlock, she walked, still in her swimsuit, the water wicked away by the smart fabric.

Heading up straight up to Karthik, she woke him up with a nudge to the shoulder.

Karthik turned with a snore. His giant frame made his feet pop out of the edge of the board despite his head hitting the headboard. The bed they slept in was meant for two normal-sized people.

Karthik wasn't normal, period.

At least she enjoyed the other abnormally large parts of him last night, so she put up with the snoring for an additional 10 seconds than she would have normally.

He looked way too peaceful, so unlike him when he was awake.

He is who he is.

Karthik may not be the fastest or smartest among the Banjaras, but he is the one with the most faith, and sometimes, that was all that was needed to give them the push they needed.

But sometimes, he does tend to push them a bit too much. Shaani understood. Having really known Karthik, she knew that it was actually something that he couldn't help. With his unwavering belief that he is always where he is meant to be, he consequently believes that he is never wrong.

The fact that an abnormally large number of things DID seem to always work out for him only seemed to further reinforce his belief that he was always right.

Ahh, you sweet, arrogant SOB.
What will we ever do with you?
What will we ever do without you?

Shani enjoyed her 10 seconds looking at Karthik when with a well flowed kick she got him off the bed.

With a groan, Karthik woke up scratching his head. "Abey yaar, I was having the best dream ever. I just managed to convince these 2hot chamaks to come with me when you woke me up. "

Shaani wasn't sure if Karthik expected her to be jealous. It was hard to tell with Karthik, and Shaani wasn't sure if Karthik was sure about them himself. Annoyed, Shaani said, "You have to head to the station; their carriage is in another hour. Don't give them another reason to get more pissed off with you by being late."

Karthik grunted. "I don't see what is the need to meet those badres at the station personally. Can't you just send one of the Relaxacabs to pick them up?

I will even pay for it."

Shani laughed out loud this time, 'And since when was the last time you actually paid for anything? You are the one who said to treat this with all seriousness, so let's do this properly."

Karthik sighed, and with a lazy stretch of his power arms, he said mid-yawn. "Fine, I am going. "

Karthik waited patiently at the Droid port. Shaani was the first piece of the puzzle, but they would have to work together to get the next 2 members of the team onboard. Each would boost the other until, combined, they could convince the other until they formed a unit.

A family.

It also doesn't help that apart from Shaani, he had seriously lachuched the relationships with the rest of them.

Karthik wasn't in a rush, though. He enjoyed chilling at the Hyperloop station's visitor's lounge. He often got glimpses of a life that he may have had had he chosen different paths, made different decisions, or just happened by chance, the dark matter of one's destiny.

He saw 2 kids being kids hanging out in the corner of the lounge. While he watched, the older boy, about 11, went on tippie-toes with his black patent leather shoes. He paused in the stance, savouring the elegance of the moment. Then, in one smooth slide, he begins smoothly gliding backwards, defying gravity with each step. His feet seemed to slide across the floor effortlessly, creating an illusion of walking on the moon.

Karthik almost slapped his head.

That's why they call it that.

He had seen the vids on FlipFlop of the 'Moonwalk', the latest craze to hit the waves.

The kid had the costume down to a pat: an open brown leather jacket, a V-necked T-shirt showing a bit of his chest, and dark blue denim jeans. He even took the effort to wear thick, padded white gloves, which perfected the contrast required for the move. With one final twirl, the kid was again on tippie toes, but this time with one arm outstretched in a power salute and the other grabbing an invisible microphone.

The little girl clapped and cheered, "My turn, Amu, my turn." Then, she proceeded to mimic the movements of her older brother. Clumsy with the last remnants of baby fat, she lacked the dexterity of the man her brother was going to be, and within the first few steps, she tripped and fell.

Karthik didn't move an inch and waited for the inevitable, and as expected, the girl fell straight into her brother's arms. Shocked, she was about to burst into a wail when Amu said. "Ui Ma!! Galti se mistake ho gaya" and laughed a big gleaming horsey-toothed smile.

The girl laughed a big toothy grin in return and stood up. "Thanks for catching me, bhai," she said. "Always Kittu," he said, hugging her tight.

Walking away, a random word blew into Karthik's mind: "Keewl".

It's not like Karthik didn't sometimes want a saadha life. His dad, being his dad, was the very definition of chaos, both good and bad. Even among the Banjaras, he had developed a reputation for being unpredictable. This included nights spent in the most amazing places on earth as well as in places that no child should ever see, let alone stay in.

His dad was the first to dream of being a legend by finding the 'Gift of the Magi', a dream that later in life he only found at the bottom of a bottle when he was drunk enough to reminisce about the past. If only his father had followed through with his promise to become Bodhiseva and stay sober, it may have saved him from heading to an early grave.

Karthik's last attempt at carrying on his father's legacy ended with his stint at Kallapani and the gang's breakup.

Karthik considered the irony of the web weaved by Anansi. The spider god of destiny. If it hadn't been for his time at Kallapani, he would have never found the next clue to the location of Amrtavipa and a reason to get the gang back together.

LATER

The badres were meant to be at Lounge A. Where the lachuka are they?

With a whoosh, the air was knocked out of his solar plexus. He was so stunned that he would have fallen to the ground if another fist to his cheek had not straightened him out.

Karthik opened his eyes to see Gaurav and Mahesh both rubbing their knuckles.

The bystanders around the trio were shocked by the sudden violence and retreated back as much as they could.

Karthik said aloud with a wave of a hand.

"It's okay. We are just 222 ing. "

With silent nods and shrugs, the bystanders resumed whatever they were doing before they were interrupted.

Rubbing his jaw, he squinted up at the rest of the gang.

"Hello boys. Been a while.

"Welcome to Goa. "

They didn't say a word.

They didn't say a word when they picked up their baggage.

TECHNOTANTRIC - 281

They didn't say a word when they hailed a relaxacab.

They didn't say a word when they drove to their destination.

Nestled along the sun-kissed shores, a haven of spiritual rejuvenation exists where seekers from across the globe converge for a pretty hefty price tag. Shaani, leveraging on her contacts at Batata Industries, managed to score some invites to their exclusive company retreat, where thousands of executives and their guests convene for their annual company Diwali party.

It took some effort, but she managed to get legitimate passes for all 4 of them, in spite of Gaurav's offer to forge the rest. She did however agree to his offer to add some preem upgrades for the before-party to really get them into the spirit of 222.

Not that she was expecting trouble. With the sheer number of people attending the various conferences at the venue, it was highly unlikely that they would be singled out.

I mean, surely the gang would be well-behaved. We are not kids any more, aren't we?

Hahahahaha...

hmmm??

Looking up, she saw a familiar Bat logo light up the night sky. With a yellow slash across it, it said 'Batata, You asked, we listened', and shortly followed up ", Pongal Sale Now On".

Driving up to the retreat in their cab, Shaani stopped breathing while taking in the view. No matter how many times she sees it, she is always blown away.

Nestled amidst a serene landscape adorned with sleek Egyptian motifs lies a sanctuary of opulence and rejuvenation – the pinnacle of luxury spas.

Svargaloka

Here, amidst the salty breeze and the soothing crash of waves, it awaits visitors seeking solace and rejuvenation.

They didn't say a word when they authenticated themselves at the reception.

They didn't say a word when they were led to their individual rooms.

They didn't say a word when they were led by the Welcomebot to the Fight Club.

They enter the Kalari ring. Blindfolds on. With a syncing of their flow in unison, they yell

IPPO

They were no ritual of checking each other's flow. No gliding, slipping, or sliding.

This was pure fisticuffs.

Just like when they were kids.

Their breaths were heavy with anticipation and unresolved tension. With his towering frame and bulging muscles, Karthik exuded raw power as he clenched his fists. Mahesh, the unpredictable drunken master, swayed slightly, a weary grin playing on his lips. Gaurav, the master of mahrams, stood calm and collected, his fingers twitching with precision. Shaani, the elusive flow fighter, exuded an aura of fluidity and grace, ready to dance through the chaos.

Blindfolded, they relied solely on instinct and memory as they lunged forward, their fists colliding in a flurry of strikes and counters. Karthik's brute force clashed with Mahesh's unpredictable sways, while Gaurav's calculated strikes targeted vulnerable points with deadly accuracy. Shaani, relying on her intuition and agility, weaved through the chaos, delivering precise blows with deceptive speed.

Amidst the chaos, a strange harmony emerged amidst the blood and bruises. Each blow exchanged was a testament to years of friendship tainted by betrayal and misunderstanding. As they grappled and stumbled, they found themselves navigating the intricate dance of conflict and reconciliation.

In the midst of the chaos, a moment of clarity dawned upon them. Beneath the blindfolds, they recognised the familiar rhythm of their movements, the echoes of laughter shared in better days. With each strike, they shed layers of resentment and pride, inching closer to understanding and forgiveness.

Shaani, in her sweet, tingling voice, was the one to yell out to them.

PODDUM. Enough

Lying panting on the ring, they slowly unfold their blindfolds and crack the first smile.

All wasn't forgotten or forgiven, but they can start now, and sometimes that is enough.

'Lachukabadre', said Gaurav, thumping Karthik, who winced with a bit too strong friendly pat on his bruised back. Gaurav, however, didn't see; ignoring him for now, he joined Mahesh in hugging and fussing over Shaani. Gently touching her single bruise, they both rushed to grab the ice pack for her before waiting to treat their own wounds.

Sulking, Karthik went to grab a lot more ice packs to treat his broken nose and double black eyes. The bruises on his back would just blend into the lattice of scars already present, and he didn't even bother looking at them.

"Ohh, how I missed you boys", said Shaani, who now started fussing over Gaurav and Mahesh. Shaani had a good, long look at Mahesh. While Gaurav looked well, Mahesh seemed to be the one who seemed to be most conflicted.

Agreeing with Karthik's plan that working deep cover at ZyraCorp was the way to his Legend, his time spent as a saada had made him despondent and aloof. Shaani even noted the lack of his trademark Sarod anywhere.

He has even stopped playing. I had no idea it was this bad.
Damn you, Karthik.
Looks like we need this 222 for more reasons than one.

Hearing the laughter, the Welcomebot sensed the end of the first part of the 222 session and returned to the gang. With a namaste, it requested they follow it to the next part of their itinerary.

The massage parlour exuded an air of opulence, with richly embroidered tapestries adorning the walls and intricately carved wooden screens separating private chambers. The strains of the tabla and sitar filled the air, mingling with the intoxicating fragrance of cardamon and lavender. In the centre of the room, 4 plush massage tables awaited, draped in cashmere silk and adorned with cushions with purple tassels at the corners of each. Each table is surrounded by flickering candles, casting a warm, golden glow over the space.

The masseuses, dressed in elegant saris embroidered with gold-edged borders, lead them to their respective massage tables, where they are invited to recline and relax.

Slowly but surely, they apply the coconut oil infused with herbs on their bare body, kneading and manipulating muscles with precision and care, easing the sprains and bruises incurred.

Ahh, Karthik sighed.

Nothing like a Marma Kizhi after a good punch-up.

Whoosh

The air was knocked out of his solar plexus for the second time today.

Shocked initially by the weight on his shoulders, once the realisation hit, he melted into the massage table as the smooth, strong feet glided their way over his body, lathering with fragrant sandalwood and tea tree oil.

Unless it's a Chavutti Thirumal, Ahhh...

The ancient massage therapy used by Kalari warriors to repair their bodies and to prepare and strengthen for the next day when they were grateful to do it all over again.

Blissful tranquillity,

drifting on waves of pure relaxation.

Can it be any more relaxing?

Tending their wounds with Ayurvedic potions made from secret, ancient recipes, the masseuses left the gang slumbering.

Karthik wasn't sure how long it was, minutes/hours.

Time seemed to bend and be as light as he felt.

The gentle strains of 'A Horizon Over' gradually filled the room. The helpful Welcomebot had returned with the alarm activated.

"I am so sorry to disturb your sleep, my Shris, but it's time for the next part of our scheduled program. "In a daze, Karthik and the rest followed the bot to a discrete door that simply said

The Pharaoh's Oasis.

Oh yes, it can!!!!

The Pharaoh's Oasis was not merely a cigar lounge; it was a sanctuary where guests converged to bask in a realm where the hustle of the outside world faded into mere echoes. Upon entering, patrons were immediately enveloped in an atmosphere that transported them to the banks of the Nile, under the watchful eyes of the gods of old.

The interior was adorned with lavish tapestries and gold leaf, illuminated by the soft glow of lights that flickered in imitation of the stars that guided the ancient Egyptians. The walls were adorned with holographic hieroglyphics and a towering obelisk stood at the centre of the lounge with a moving kaleidoscope of coloured bubbles constantly morphing and swirling.

The air was thick with the rich and heady scent of cannabis, mingling with the undercurrents of incense that seemed to whisper of hidden chambers and divine mysteries. The smoke curled upwards in lazy spirals, each puff a meditation, a momentary journey into the realm of the gods.

Silent as the desert night, waiters moved with a grace that belied their earthly tether.

Ethereals, adorned with intricately crafted earrings, necklaces, bracelets, and anklets, each designed to accentuate their natural curves. Their elegant linen garments flow gracefully around their bodies to move like water. Each Ethereal bore the insignia of the deity they served. Even Karthik was able to recognise Anubis, the guardian of the afterlife and Isis, with her wings subtly embroidered, their gestures as fluid as the Nile itself.

In this hallowed space, words were unnecessary and, by unspoken agreement, almost considered sacrilegious. The patrons, ensconced in leather chairs that embraced them like thrones, were pharaohs in their own right, ruling over unseen but no less potent domains. Though they may be corporate foes or on opposite sides of the law, here, in the silence, they found a camaraderie that transcended the need for speech, a fellowship sanctified by the smoke of their cigars and the shared reverence for the ancient world.

Communication in the Pharaoh's Oasis was an art form, a ballet of silence and gesture that spoke volumes. With their snow-silver hair and sides shaved and tattooed with elaborate depictions of animals and mythological symbols, budtenders looked around with kohl-lined eyes for patrons looking for service. Offering an array of premium marijuana joints and accessories, they picked up the slightest hint of the guests' wants and appeared as if like ghosts with their very desires. Patrons, initiated into this silent world, requested their cigars with the subtlety befitting the lounge's ambience. A slight tilt of the head, a gesture towards the humidor, and the budtender would understand, responding with a nod or a hand sign that confirmed the choice. The cigars, each a masterpiece of craftsmanship, were presented on silver trays, their aromatic promise wafting through the air like a whispered secret.

Like the sprites they were, 2 waiters appeared in front of the gang. Their hands folded in a namaste, and their hands flowed into beckoning to a cosy corner where four high-backed red leather chairs were placed. Aware of their request that this be a 222 session, the servers activated the privacy barriers. With a hum, invisible sound barriers switched on, which, while still allowing them to move freely, blocked all sound, allowing them to converse freely without intruding on the privacy of the other patrons.

A budtender stood to the side with a silver tray and waited for the gang to be seated before placing the cloth-covered tray at the centre of the table. With a furl, he unveiled the signature cigar of the Pharaoh's Lounge.

The Kili Poyi

Considered the epoch of the vortex of joint engineering, the fabled cross joint was one large cigar with 4 smaller joints attached to it in the middle. One for each of them to activate and engage. With all 4 of them reverentially touching it, the budtender selects a double-blade guillotine and neatly snips the ends of the large cigar. Lighting it with a silver blowtorch, he places it back on the pedestal before discreetly retreating.

Gaurav was the first to take it and light the first joint, inhaling deeply and holding the smoke in before passing it on to the others. After each participant had partaken, all 4 exhaled, the smoke covering them and confined within their booth.

Shaani was the first to break, her laughter a shimmering stream of giggles. She was followed by Gaurav, who started chortling, and Karthik, who started laughing deep from within his belly. Mahesh, however, only silently smiled, which, though pleasant enough, still didn't reach his eyes.

With each inhale, barriers dissolve, and truths emerge, revealing the misunderstood intentions that had sown discord among them. Laughter intertwined with tears as they laid bare everything —every hurt, every misunderstanding—until finally, the group found solace in the understanding of their shared pain.

Except for Mahesh.

While he publicly blamed Karthik for turning away from his Banjara ways and forcing him to work deep cover, the truth is that he was planning on doing that anyway. No matter how much he loved being a domo, he unfortunately was never able to make much money out of it. Unlike some other domos, Mahesh was extremely shy, and the prospect of working in the filmi world dismayed him. He was well aware of how successful some of his kin were, with regular reminders with all the filmi posters everywhere. Having long given up any hope of working in Filimistaan, he thought some time working as a Saadha would give him just a taste of what it would be like to have the comforts of a house and live a king-size life in the big city.

That was 2 years ago and stint as a corporate desk jockey had taken a toll on him. The constant pressure of maintaining his cover and the isolation and loneliness had plunged him into a deep melancholy. The carefree days of his childhood gnawed at his insides, the laughter and camaraderie shared with his troupe and friends. Those days felt like a distant dream now, overshadowed by the darkness that enveloped his present reality.

The others, though, seemed suitably unburdened. The laughter in their eyes indicated the ease with which they felt at each other's company. At the conclusion of their session, the isolation barriers lifted, silently indicating that it was time to move on to the next session.

Energised with their renewed relationship, Karthik yelled out even before the Welcomebot could utter anything.

"Alright boys and girl.

"Let's Nacho!!!"

The gang didn't wait to find out the impact of the outburst in the tomb-like room before being shuffled to the adjoining room. Passing the sound airlock, another discreet door opened up into the full belting of the latest Balti EDM.

Strobe lights filled the room, and patrons dressed in bell bottom pants with wide collar shirts danced under shiny disco balls with their chest hair toupees and dark sunglasses.

Gaurav, Shaani, and Karthik made their way deep into the dance floor, where servers circulated with trays filled with cocktails in various rainbow colours.

Mahesh stayed at the periphery, however. Availing himself of one of the colour cocktails carried around by the servers around him, He gulped down the drink and grabbed another and another. He stopped after a while when he had lost count. Conversations had started to become dim, and topics jumped from one fancy to another.

He didn't like this part of the drinking. This was the part where he started to shrink. Some people expand and become all-encompassing with love and affection for one and all. Others get sullen and occasionally rough enough to get into actual fisticuffs. He, however, was usually a member of the other tribe, who shrink-huddled into his drink and the next until there was a sign to leave.

Something, however, shifted slightly within him, and he craved companionship, although not from his friends. Unable to bear the weight of his thoughts any longer and the reminders brought back by his friends, Mahesh decided to join the strangers at a private party of what appears to be desk jockeys as well on a company retreat.

Although he did not really know anyone among them, surrounded by discussions around typical office gossip, Mahesh found himself relating more to the corporate saadhas than he thought possible. Brimming with liquid courage, Mahesh stepped onto their dance floor with a slow shuffle, overestimated his current ability to dance, and stumbled and fell on his rump on the kaleidoscope dance floor.

Biting his lip, he prayed that the ground would swallow him up or, if not, that he might suffer a quick and merciful heart attack. No such luck. He remained solidly among the living with his rump still on the floor.

His solitary rapid consumption of drinks eventually drew the attention of a stranger who was observing him,

The man, who appeared to have a stern demeanour, was sitting apart from the rest of the group and had been a silent observer until now. Likely a senior manager, he appeared to be the only one who was sober.

And annoyed.

Shaking his head, he walked towards Mahesh all while never taking his eyes of even once attention.

Damn a comptroller.

As the gatekeeper for his team's accounts, Mahesh could see the question in the eyes of the designated manager.

Who exactly is Mahesh, and what is he doing mooching off MY party?

Stuck at the moment with the stranger, Mahesh had just enough time to read the name off the helpful 'Intro tag' on his shoulder lapel before he blurted out,

"Hey, you are Richard, right? 'The Fallout' fan. How's it going?"

The mention of the performance band sparked a glimmer of a smile on Richard's impassive face.

Bingo.

A skill of all domos, banjaras so entrenched in the performance arts, Mahesh could instantly identify a favourite song of any person almost instinctively just by looking at them.

The smile wasn't big but still a smile, so Mahesh breathed a sigh of relief.

Having worked long enough in Corpo, Mahesh was also able to reasonably guess that Richard's desk would likely be filled with memorabilia related to the band.

Including Fallout Boobleheads.

The little bobble-headed dolls with the oversized wobbling heads were a current mirchi craze, and many corpo saddas, in order to impose their identity into the workspace, had taken to getting personalised versions of their favourite influencers to decorate their dock stations.

To Mahesh, it seemed almost weird, creepily fascinating that prim and proper saddhas would resort to fisticuffs to get the ultra rare ones, leading some to compete in the HR-sanctioned thumb wars for the chance to gamble and win swag.

Having personally never collected them, he had listened to enough water cooler chats to quickly mention to Richard how his non-existent son had found a pseudo-rhinestone-encrusted version just lying around at a hyperloop station bench.

"I have been meaning to ask every time I pass your desk, but are they meant to be rare or something? Maybe I can bring them around the next time I swing by.

Mahesh had no idea that the version he described actually existed, but having seen enough random videos of VidTubers who scored rich with pretty rare finds of Bobbleheads, he was fairly confident that this should theoretically exist.

The smile that now filled Richard went all the way from the end of one ear to the other.

He doesn't just like them; he's a 'Deep Fan'. This should be easy.

Too embarrassed to question a person who obviously seemed to know him and may actually have something that he needs, Richard instead asked Mahesh if he was okay and offered him from the packet of HR-issued stims to stabilise the effects of the excess alcohol.

Shaking his head, Mahesh was actually energised by the near miss and moved further into the crowd of dancers.

This party, was looking like it was just beginning as more and more of the DJs moved to the dance floor.

He scanned the crowd for familiar faces and noticed Stella dancing with Steve from Finance. With her arms around his shoulders and hips moving in unison, they stared intently at each other with easy smiles of knowing.

Mahesh was surprised by the open display of intimacy, especially with Richard around.

Richard himself was with Carolyn, and though she did the typical "CLUB" moves of swaying provocatively and whipping her head, Richard actually had some surprisingly structured and complex dance moves.

Mahesh had seen enough vids at Corpo of shared vids of colleagues' kids and knew way more of the current mirchi crazes on "Flipflop" than he would have liked.

The more he looked at Richard, the more he actually recognised some of the moves. There was the "Fringe" with its signature hip thrusts and hand wags, the "Void Break" with its mix of Saturday night arm flicks followed by the headshake and thrusted arms.

Richard didn't seem to be the sort of person who kept up with the current trends on social media, let alone practice them, but here he was. Mahesh assumed that he had a family and enquired as such when Richard wound up next to him during a break.

"You have got some moves," said Mahesh appreciatively.

Richard, panting, replied. "Used to. Not anymore. ".

With a flick, he extended his cheek jowls into the puffed-up white hard beard of Kathakali dancers.

Judging by the reactions of the rest of his colleagues, no one appeared to be shocked.

A companion tribe to the Domos, Mahesh was surprised to find a surprising sense of commandership beyond the façade that he had put up earlier.

"You are a Kathak? What are you doing here?"

Richard shrugged, curling the beard back in place.

"I don't know, to be honest. First, it was the cred, then it was simply easier to do, and next thing you know, you are supervising a company-mandated relaxation trip."

With the company trip officially ended and staff on their personal time, any liaisons that occurred was unofficial and unspoken. Already, the amorous members of the group had paired up, and having settled on a partner for the night were moving well beyond mere flirting. In this brief respite from the drudgery of their daily lives, kindred spirits found companionship in shared miseries.

Team building, filled with regret.

What happens at company retreats stays at company retreats.

Mahesh could clearly see both sides of the coin of Corpo and suddenly wasn't sure if this was what he wanted. To be honest with himself, he really didn't know what he wanted, but for once, he actually knew what he didn't want, and that's more than he knew earlier. For now maybe rather than choosing which side of the coin he wanted to land on, he instead he didn't want the coin at all.

The alternative seemed equally dangerous, but surprisingly, it was something that Mahesh actually wanted.

Nay, actually needed.

Without a word, Mahesh slipped away in search of his friends. Wandering away from the dance floor , he activated a solitary Welcomebot and asked it to guide him to his friends. The Welcomebot obliged and guided Mahesh outside, the echoes of the music fading away the further Mahesh walked.

With a decision made, Mahesh was finally able to breathe easy. What the decision entails the voices didn't say but for now, he was glad that the world was quiet.

The Welcomebot ended up on an isolated part of the beach where he was greeted by the sight of his friends gathered around a bonfire, their faces illuminated by the flickering flames.

Just like that night.

"Lachuka!!!" yelled out Karthik, and just like that, it was as if he was back there that night. 4 boys basking in the bliss of that was great and unexpected.

The most intoxicating of victories and to be experienced by ones so young only created a bond that would have the greatest chance of grinding of time.

The air was rich with the scent of burning wood mingling with the cool night breeze from the sea. The gang, now settled into a comfortable silence, was basking in the glow of the fire and the afterglow of their reconciliation. It was a moment of peace, a much-needed respite from the storms they had weathered both individually and together.

Sleepy now with the effects of the night, Mahesh closed his eyes.

His legs seemed to turn to jelly and he collapsed in a heap on a wooden log. He forgot why he was here but that was okay. He had been living for so long with this pain that it was only while listening and drifting that he tended to forget.

Those stolen moments of bliss.

The strains of a beat kept him from falling deeper, however. Something primal within him awoke. Something prodded him, bringing him back from the edge of sleep.

That doesn't seem very nice. Knock it off silly billy.

Something shook inside him. Happier now, Mahesh didn't mind too much.

Hey it would be considered rude for you do that.

but she did it again and this time the shaking was quite incessant.

"Just leave me alone!" he wanted to yell, but his tongue felt like it weighed a ton, and his mouth filled with cotton.

At least open your eyes.

and this time he awoke.

A sarod hidden behind the stage. Crafted from sleek chrome and luminescent synthetic wood, emanating ethereal melodies that danced through the air, weaving tales of distant galaxies and cosmic wonders. Like in a dream, he walks to it, and with trembling hands, he lifts it up, his fingers finding their way across the strings, and old muscle memory finally remembering. He strummed and trummed the sarod. The notes wafted in the breeze, jagged and broken, shimmering in the air.

He took another gentle puff, and his gaze began to soften. His goofy grin was now even more pronounced and he felt happy for the first time in days/weeks/months he wasn't sure.

Years?

His fingers moved on their own accord. It took him to realise that he was strumming the Chemeen Ponne , a tune filled with nostalgia and the warmth of sunnier days.

The melody unfurled around them as he played, a soft reminder of shared histories and simpler times. With the realization came the twist of the hips, the tapping of the feet, and old '60s hip. Slight subtle nods, nothing major.

As the music filled the air, Mahesh felt a sense of liberation wash over him, a cathartic release of pent-up emotions. With each strum and pluck of the strings, Mahesh poured his heart and soul into the music, the melodies weaving a tapestry of healing and redemption.

As the final notes echoed into the night, he felt a weight lift off his shoulders, a sense of peace settling over him like a warm embrace.

In that moment, amidst the flickering flames and the gentle rustle of the breeze, Mahesh knew that he had found his way back to himself. With a smile on his face and a song in his heart, he joined his friends in laughter and celebration, ready to embrace the journey that lay ahead.

He was still smiling when a while later when Karthik looked around and, in all seriousness, said.

"Alright, boys and girl. Now that we have sorted that out, let's chat."

| 20 |

LE7LS / Secrets

While waiting at the platform, Tara couldn't help but have second thoughts about the whole thing.

The interstate Trans-Ind Hyperloop for Filmistaan was running late and Tara had nothing to do but think. Though it felt good to work out in the field again, she didn't know whether it was the right thing to do.

It felt like the right thing to do, though.

Go with the flow, Jaanu.

Having always had a knack for detective work, even among more aggressive members of the IPS, she had a grudging reputation for ooham resolution with minimal trauma. In the past, as part of her job, Tara has been known to skirt on the edge, sometimes relying purely on instinct and adrenaline during the heat of an investigation. Rituals that she had slowly given up over time to rely on the requirements of the duty bound. Even back then, though, she was always able to know where to draw the line and made practised efforts not to break any rules.

Which also included the rule that IPS officers should not get personally involved in any case.

Admit it, Tara, this is not normal, period.

This is well in the realm of uncharted territory for you.

Technically, with the case still open, she could always state that she was simply gathering evidence—a statement that would be demolished in the first instance if she had to face the Vishadgami during an inquisition, but she actually shrugged it off.

Ehh.. so the bloody things can read my thoughts. What's the worst that they could do?

Tara knew the real answer to that question all too well, but she also realized that she didn't care.

I have already been through your worst.

After a long time, she felt she was doing something right, and it felt better.

Better is better than feeling worse so...

Besides all I am doing is catching up with an old friend while I am on vaccay and we happened to be discussing certain topics of interest.

The fact that it would also help my case is just a bonus.

So, with the clarity of thought that accompanies a greater sense of purpose, Tara reflected on why she was really doing what she was doing.

Ever since Fasil's passing, she had become less sure of herself. She now had plenty of time, and she had been spending a lot of it taking a long, hard look at her life. With great reluctance, she admitted that she agreed with Fasil, and the admission tasted like tamarinds—bittersweet.

The law doesn't always get it right.

Born with an innate sense of right and wrong and a keen desire for order, the smartly dressed IPS officers, with the restrained control of their abilities, seemed to have all the answers and sense of belonging that she craved as a child. At first glance, they seemed like kindred spirits with the same innate values, and Tara was desperate to fit in anywhere. However, Her turbulent childhood offered few opportunities for her to relate with anybody apart from her mom, and knowingly or unknowingly, joining the Police Force seemed like a fantasy to take her away from the harshness of reality.

She took a deep breath, letting the cool raindrops wash away some of her frustration.

Breathe. Out

For the enquiries that she was currently making, she would need expertise that she could trust outside of the system. Fortunately, or unfortunately, Nithya was the only one she could think of. Tara was glad in a way. It's been a while, but she finally had a legitimate reason to catch up with Nithya.

It's definitely not from wanting to. Having known Nithya ever since she was a scrappy kid from the streets, Tara was actually very proud of Nithya and what she had made of her life. This is not something that Tara would ever admit to anyone else, and she would barely admit it, even to herself. Fasil knew and always quietly encouraged her attempts to keep tabs on Nithya's new companies and the solid reputation that she had built through her own efforts. That was only carried out from afar, though and with their history, even a phone call was a line that she would not cross lightly.

Nithya, though surprised to receive Tara's call, immediately offered to clear up her schedule and asked Tara to head over straight away to Filmistaan. Tara may be getting out of touch with technology, but she knew enough about her digital trails to know that a conversation like this should only be had face-to-face.

Despite the turmoil, acknowledging her current state—a blend of sorrow and determination that propelled her forward—was strangely comforting.

Looks like this show is already on the road.

Tara tapped her foot impatiently.

While she usually travels by express, all the trains seemed to be unusually busy today, and she had to settle for the slow train to cover the 1500 KM journey from Agra to Filmistaan. She was among the few who seemed to be in a rush to go. While it is expected that Hyperloop to Filmistaan would have its share of film enthusiasts, the platform seemed to be like the waiting room of ComicSymp. A lot of the passengers appeared to be vibing with the Filmistaan spirit dressed in a myriad of fantastical costumes, most of them from the iconic films released by RRR Studios.

In comparison her sombre plain green churidar, only further contrasted the world away from the grayscale routine of her existence within the system. She could, however, ignore the cacophony around her.

Tara had good practice in choosing to see only what she wanted.

Stepping into the crowded train, she pinged Nithya that she would arrive in about 2 hours. Tara leaned back in her seat and stared out of the window. With most of the hyperloop track underground, the view from the windows was only a line of screens with advertisements that stretched outside. It was quite easy to ignore them till they just became white noise. Damn, if she is actually going to watch recommendations of shampoo from Edifer Glover and his dyed green hair.

Why did you have to go Fasil?

She wasn't really expecting to find a partner, least of all a soul mate, even when she literally bumped into Fasil.

Fasil and his unique perspective of things.

You silly, mad, and frustrating man. Ohh, how I miss you.

However frustrating and passionate some of their discussions ended up, he always seemed to have an alternative view, which still made her think. If it wasn't for her bruised ego, Tara even dared to admit to herself that he was more often right than she had given him credit for.

Now that he was gone, all that she had left were memories of him and time.

And now she could see better.

Justice is still justice, but the law, however, isn't always just.

Tara has accepted that the system is the system, and players here will always play to win no matter how high the cost others have to pay. Though she was a great player, she realised it didn't mean she had to play it the same way to still win. Her innate sense of justice was, is, and will always be strong, and as of now, she couldn't see herself far removed from the system. Still, it doesn't stop her from seeking justice on her own terms.

She thinks she could live with it for now.

With a slight smile of comfort, Tara turned to pay attention to the life around her and felt an unexpected stir of nostalgia—a longing for simpler times when the world seemed vast and filled with wonder.

It was the annual open day at RRR studios, and the pilgrimage of fans who were heading to Filmistaan to celebrate would be non-stop for the next couple of days. Celebrating their epic films, many of her fellow passengers were dressed in the iconic dresses of the popular stars in Filmistaan. There was Santhali with technology-infused muscles and eyes alight with faux fire. Nearby, a group clad as the Malaryan shared laughter, their outfits a homage to the epic heroes, from Paliyan's crossbow to Ralte's power hammer.

Though she still felt like an outsider, the atmosphere, charged with the passengers' collective enthusiasm for Filmistaan's cinematic magic, stirred something within her: a forgotten memory of childhoods spent watching the temple processions on her father's shoulders.

Tara scowled, her mood darkening again. As always, as soon as she had a pleasant memory of her father, she blocked it out, refusing to associate any sort of happy thoughts with the man who had made her life a living hell.

Her introspection was briefly interrupted when a child dressed in peacock feathers and a guitar passed by. "Are you here to save us?" the girl asked, repeating the famous one-liner from 'Kabhi Dilwale ' innocence and playfulness sparkled in her eyes. Tara, taken aback, offered a gentle smile and a nod, touched despite herself by the unexpected encounter. A shower of fine, sparkling glitter from the costume dusted Tara's dress and hair, leaving her momentarily enveloped in a cascade of light. "Anointed by the magic of Filmistaan, huh?"

As the child scampered away, laughter trailing behind her, Tara wished for the days when she was carefree enough to laugh with a stranger.

One woman, draped just in a white silk sari reminiscent of Yamuna Rani's iconic look, moved with a grace that made the fabric seem like cascading water. Nearby, another channelled the extravagance of Zenkha in the '80s, her outfit a dazzling array of lakmé and bold makeup, shoulders exaggerated to make a statement that was as much about confidence as it was about style. Inspired by Priya Mahali's iconic dress from Krantiveer, a younger attendee wore a slinky black dress and the iconic headdress riot of feathers and sequins - the quintessential item girl.

Tara shook her head, a faint smile playing on her lips, as she settled into her seat.

That's Filmistaan for you.

Shaking the glitter out of her hair, she stepped out into the waiting lounge. She considered taking a Relaxacab to Nithya's place and put on her peripheral to grab the co-ods to her place. A message from Nithya was waiting for her.

'At the lounge already. Waiting for you.'

No sooner than she had read the message, Tara heard an exuberant

"TARA!!!!"

Ignoring the throngs of people around her, Nithya bounded towards Tara, her right hand already outstretched to touch Tara's feet. Too late to stop her, Tara stretched her arms to lift Nithya before she touched her feet. Lifting her up fully, she replied in the traditional reply of respected elders.

Jeete Raho.

Now that formalities were over, Nithya didn't waste any time hugging Tara as tight as she could, her leather rider jacket squeaking. "It's so good to meet you, Tara Shri finally. It's been far too long." Tara nodded, although her controlled restraint didn't reveal how touched she really felt. It felt good to feel wanted again, even if it was for just a little while. Grabbing her hand, Nithya guided her through the throng of people. Feeling lost, Tara allowed herself to be led and followed Nithya.

Tara was initially worried when she saw Nithya's exuberance. She didn't really know how to talk to her, having only dealt with her professionally in the past. Tara didn't have to worry, though. Nithya spoke nonstop all the way to her car, and Tara didn't think she could have gotten a word in edgewise even if she wanted to. Nithya herself seemed quite happy with Tara's monosyllabic responses.

Heading up to a waiting valet, Nithya grabbed the keys and unlocked her sports car.

The car in holographic mirror chrome was a compact and sleek.

Tara didn't know much about cars but knew the MeiTei was expensive.

Very expensive.

I knew she was doing well, but I had no idea she was this well-to-do.

Good on her.

One wouldn't think it with the way Nithya casually threw her bag onto the ultra-luxury mushroom and apple leather seats, though. The dings on the side of the car, which even its self-repair modules couldn't fix, confirmed her thoughts that Nithya really just treated the car as a car. Again, hiding her pride, Tara carefully entered the car with far greater care than Nithya, who had leapt in without bothering to open the door.

Thanking the valet bot, Nithya switched to manual and smoothly eased into the outgoing traffic. Focussing on the road and driving the car, Nithya finally lost her steam on the conversation, and they drove for a bit in companionable silence. Tara had yet to tell Nithya the real reason she was here after so many years, but she was hesitant to broach the subject.

Almost as if reading her mind, Nithya flicked a strand of platinum white hair and switched the car to auto. Without any hesitation, she looked directly at Tara.

"Now that the pleasantries are out of the way, how can I help you, Tara Shri?"

Tara started hesitantly at first but delved deeper and deeper the longer Nithya drove. Nithya did not interrupt her once but only nodded in acknowledgement. Without planning to, Tara told Nithya everything she knew, from Vaishali's background to the coroner's feedback. She even vented about Deepak and the deep-rooted corruption that most people almost took as a way of life.

Finishing in a huff, Tara concluded with everything. The car was silent again as she tried to catch her breath. For the first time, Tara realised how truly lonely she felt and how good it felt to talk to someone on a personal level.

Nithya thought hard and long and said out loud, "So let me get this straight. You would like me to hack into Zyra-Corp, find out about this secret project, which is more than likely to have the backing of some very heavy hitters, and potentially make me a target myself, not to mention jeopardising my company and all future work."

Nithya smiled, a big, wide smile that couldn't get any more genuine." That sounds like fun. I'll get on to it straight away."

Tara was surprised and relieved. She didn't realise how much she had asked from Nithya until she summarised it. And she agreed in spite of everything.

Tara asked. "Just like that?"

Nithya nodded, and Tara again saw her mettle behind her eyes, the same that she had seen in her as a kid, and it was what told her that she would be okay. "This is just not right, and somebody has to do something about it. I don't know how much I can help, but anything I can, I will do." Nithya said grimly.

They didn't speak to each other until they pulled up in front of Nithya's house, each lost in thought as they realised the magnitude of the work they had just decided to undertake. The house appeared to be deceptively old. Tara wouldn't be surprised if it were even heritage-listed, given the effort taken to maintain the external façade. Entering the front door, the interiors seemed to match the outside, and a very formal living room greeted Tara.

Tara was very surprised. The car made sense. It was expensive and fun. The house, though it had all the trappings of wealth, didn't really seem to suit Nithya.

Nithya didn't stop at any of the larger living rooms and instead led her down a narrow corridor to a recessed door. Palming a scanner, a door slid with a whoosh, revealing a room that was a stark contrast to the living room.

This room was dripping with so much tech that Tara would have thought it could add legs and simply walk to where it wanted to.

The lights were turned off, but it didn't matter. Holographic displays flicker across walls lined with crystalline data storage units, pulsing with vibrant neon hues. The air hums with the low, constant drone of quantum processors working in unison, their cooling systems emitting a faint mist that lends a surreal, almost mystical atmosphere.

At the centre stands a sleek, black monolith of a control console, its surface alive with shifting patterns of encrypted codes. The operator's console was a sleek, ergonomic throne made of black alloy and bio-luminescent fibres that responded to touch. Next to the seat were neatly stacked boxes of, from the smell of it, leftover biriyani and something pineapple and a blanket with a flaming skull.

Apart from the mess next to the seat, the room was bare of furniture or any other personal effects. The sole exception seemed to be a wall with HackerThon trophies all surrounding a single framed piece of paper. It appeared to be oddly familiar, as if it were from a distant memory. Approaching it, Tara saw that it was an old-fashioned FIR register sheet. The weathered piece of paper was ripped in half at some point in time. At the bottom was a handwritten note.

DO BETTER

Well, no wonder it seemed familiar. She was the one who wrote it.

Tara eyes started itching for no particular reason, and that was the only reason she had to rub them. Once she could compose herself, she spoke aloud without turning around.

"You actually kept it after all these years."

Nithya matter-of-factly replied, "Of course, Shri. I wouldn't be here if it weren't for you."

Tara was touched but curious, though. "Wouldn't this be bad for business? You just put a sign declaring that you have a police record."

Nithya laughed out loud. "Tara ji, to the people who I normally allow down here, that FIR would be very tame compared to what they have done."

"I put it up simply as a reminder. Every time I feel that life is getting tough and I can't take it anymore, I look at that note and imagine how my life would have turned out if it hadn't been for you on that day. "

"Things always seem to get easier after that. "

Her eyes were itchy as well Nithya said, "Now I am a bit short on preem tissue papers, so why don't I have a little poke around and see what I can find on Vaishali."

Immersing herself in her console, Nithya put on her headset of flaming yellow and red, becoming flow-personified, a digital trailblazer in the vast wilderness of the global net.

From Tara's vantage point, the screens were a blur of rapidly changing text and images, incomprehensible yet somehow mesmerising. Tara couldn't shake the feeling that there was much more happening on those screens than met the eye. She observed Nithya's fingers moving swiftly over the keyboard, a silent ballet of keystrokes that Tara was quite familiar with. However, the results seemed more like a mysterious ritual than any form of work she was used to. The detective knew that Nithya employed various software tools to probe and navigate through ZyraCorp's defences, though the specifics—encrypted tunnels, masking of activity, exploitation of vulnerabilities—were akin to a foreign language.

To Tara, the world Nithya operated in was one of the abstract concepts and invisible trails. She understood that, at a fundamental level, it was exactly what she was trained to do all her life. Nithya was accessing data, perhaps searching for evidence and making a decision based on that. It was surely a form of detective work, but one that Tara felt comfortably alienated from. The tools of her trade—interviews, physical evidence, the instincts honed over years of fieldwork—still had their value and still had to be carried out in the real world.

An added caveat was that rather than tracking all her actions, Nithya was doing the exact opposite. Yet the way she did it, deleting logs and erasing evidence of her intrusion, seemed too clean and bloodless to quiet Tara's conscience quite quickly. The concentration on Nithya's face as she worked was quite familiar, though, having seen the same expression in the mirror when she was deep in reviewing case files and during undercover operations, though the silence of this digital hunt was a stark contrast to the adrenaline of physical surveillance.

With a sigh, Nithya finally leaned back and pointed at the screen. "There are absolutely no records anywhere but I managed to find an archive that looks it was stored incorrectly. This is all I can find on the girl. "

On the screen, Tara saw an employee profile with the same photo of Vaishali as her ID card.

Personnel Name: Vaishali Tracy.

Classification: Privileged Access R&D Lab 2.

Project: Aatmik.

Authorisation: Kishore Karbi

On a hunch, Tara took an old Instagraph and rattled out a couple more names.

Lara Chopra, Priyanka Rao…

Knowing what to look for this time, Nithya quickly pulled up the details she could find.

Lara Chipra <user deleted>

Priyanka Rai <user deleted>

…..

Tara was pensive. Looking straight at Nithya, she asked. "Does this mean what I think it means?"

Nithya turned around with a horrified expression and nodded. "They were all ex-employees of ZyraCorp, and they have now been deleted. "

Tara may not know much about computers, but she knew enough about police procedures that this wasn't evidence enough to warrant further investigation. So that's exactly what she needs to do.

Gather evidence.

Turning to look at Nithya, she asked. "Is that all you can get?"

Nithya shook her head ruefully. "Unfortunately, yes. ZyraCorp may have something on the archive servers where we can pull up the deleted logs, but those Xyphor servers are accessible only within the building itself."

"We would need to phreak into ZyraCorp from the inside.

Tara never remembered the time when she was travelling. Her spirit form moving through a realm of pure feeling and colour was as elusive from waking thoughts as a dream.

Now, however, she remembered the swirling patterns of the rainbow collecting like the clouds in the sky. A great big mandala of colour with hidden patterns, connections, and oohams starting to swirl and settle around something which reminded Tara of a heart-shaped upala.

Just wait and watch, jaanu.

Tara wasn't surprised when, with a flick of her white fringe, Nithya tapped her nose and said, "Tara Shri, if you had met me on any other day, I would have said that this was all I could do, but I may be able to help you in more than you know.

"How would you like to be my Plus one for a party?"

| 21 |

Narcissistic Cannibal

The black glass building rose defiantly against the urban skyline, its once sleek façade now marred by the stains of neglect and time. Once a symbol of modernity and opulence, it now stands as a testament to abandonment and decay. The broken windows, once polished to perfection, now darkly reflect the modern cityscape around them like a black mirror.

At the pinnacle of this forsaken tower, the penthouse stands like a solitary sentinel. Its black glass walls offer a panoramic view of the desolation below, a stark reminder of the building's faded grandeur.

Inside, the corridors echo with the ghosts of its former glory. Empty rooms, their doors hanging off hinges, old witnesses to the lives that once thrived within these walls. Dust motes dance in the shafts of light that filter through shattered windows, casting eerie shadows on the cracked marble floors. The bare carpet stank of rot and mould. Although it was bone dry now in the summer heat, the stench remained.

In this black glass building, where shadows dance, and secrets lie hidden, Aparicita awakes from sleep, dreaming of the sea again. They wake up knowing that it was always the same dream, or so they thought. Pieces of a life from so long ago sometimes they feel that in itself is a dream.

The fear that they felt in the first few seconds of waking up was the same, though, and it remained unmitigated in spite of all this time.

The waves above him crashing and him swimming.

The ship below him crashing and him floating.

They still never went into the water.

That was all the fear that they allowed themselves, and once past it, they arose, shorn of all self-doubt and indecision.

Here, amidst the ruins of a forgotten empire, Aparicita has made their sanctuary. Hidden from the world below, they watch from behind the tinted glass, a silent observer of the lives unfolding around them. Their presence is not even a whisper in the wind, and they are a shadow in the night. Their face was darkness personified.

Slipping on a thick fur-lined dressing robe, they walked closer to the windows to look out at the world. The room was never lit. Used to darkness, the streetlights through the windows were sufficient for their purposes.

They stared out at the world, watching the multi-hued light show that was the world that they saw as always now, the rich smorgasbord of flavours drafting in the night air.

Their preference was for negs, the dark red aura that particularly wafted from the apartments of families in conflict.

The rage and the hurt. The lies and the betrayals,
They particularly savoured the salty tears of young ones.
Little drops of nectar.

Tonight though, something was niggling at them. It wasn't inside them but external, so rather than looking inwards for answers, they instead spread outwards.

SNIFF SNIFF.

It was from the nearby blue and white apartment complex. An aura of mustard yellow heavily tinged with green, the mix of curiosity with a generous serving of envy, looking towards him.

In spite of the significantly large number of apartments visible, they already knew them all really well, having viewed most of them quite intimately.

It must be murkha Mrs Heimlich with the telescope.

The busybody had just moved into the 50th floor of the complex a few months ago. Aparicita had viewed her as she had brazenly mounted the telescope on the balcony from the very first day and peered out into the world. The telescope was her only companion, but she was having the time of her life.

Although you couldn't tell by looking at her with the downward dip of her lips and her blue eyes still edging disappointment in the world and all its inhabitants.

Mrs Heimlich had convinced her oldest son that it was his idea for her to move to the city after Robert's death. She told him that it was to be close to the grandkids and that the house in the country was too big. Surprised the hell out of her kids, who had never known their mom to do anything nice for them.

The real reason, however, was the telescope that belonged to her second son.

Most people do not notice other people. Mrs. Heimlich did. Ever since she was a young girl, she noticed everyone. While she was fully abreast of the gossip about town, it was her greatest pleasure in life to be the first to discover a secret—the more hidden, the better.

With her husband dead for the past few years and her children out of her house, Mrs Heimlich found herself in the state she had always wanted. Free from the constant presence in her house, she was now able to indulge in her perfect pastime. She knew she was crossing a line when she set up the telescope in her house to check out her neighbours, but she told herself it was just to test it out.

Things might have turned out differently for Mrs Heimlich if the young jock who was visiting the Nihali's next door didn't happen to be showering at that exact moment with the windows open.

Suddenly, she felt the first stirrings in parts that she thought had long gone dormant, and she pleasured herself with a cucumber that she was saving for her salad.

Once you pop, you can't stop.

Soon, the first thing she did every morning was to 'check up on the neighbours'. Every day, she used to try viewing her neighbours from every room in the house, even daring to go up to the patio on occasion. Living in her large country home, though, here were only so many secrets to be had in a town where everybody knew everybody.

So, she decided to move to the city.

And now this kasmal dares to look at me

Play adult games.
Face adult consequences.

With a flicker of thought, Aparicita reaches out across the night, weaving tendrils of psychic energy that snake through the air like Naginis.

In the darkness of her solitude behind her beloved telescope, Mrs Heimlich feels the cold touch of their intrusion, a violation of her most sacred sanctuary. In a frenzy of fear and despair, she finds herself retreating to the edges of her mind, teetering on the precipice of sanity.

And then, with a silent scream that echoes through empty corridors, she opens her eyes and sees the jock.

She could see him clear as day, floating out right in front of her. For some reason, he was still soapy and wet. He turned and looked straight at her, beckoning.

Walking towards him, she was stopped by balcony railing. Annoyed, she grabbed one of her deck chairs and stood on it to get over the railing, and even ripped her housecoat a little bit.

That didn't matter, though.

She was hoping for a lot more of the housecoat being ripped off, judging by the way he was looking at her.

Maybe she was in shock, and her mind went into its default thought patterns, or maybe she died exactly the way that she lived.

As she was falling past the 23rd-storey of her apartment, Mrs Heimlich's last thoughts were not the sheer terror of falling or thoughts of her family.

t was about how many times she had told Shanti not to hang her laundry out on the balcony.

It's against the community bylaws. Somebody else will need to have a good chat with her.

Mrs Heimlich would have relished the opportunity to have a serious talk with Shanti and wipe the smile off her face, but she was a bit busy at the moment.

Certain behaviour is not dictated by humanity but by the most primal instincts of all living things.

Faced with imminent death, the most natural instinct would be to avoid it, however futile the gesture turns out.

Fight or flight.

Her body, working independently of her mind, fought back against the inevitable. Every part of her body tried to resist, with her arms and legs reaching out to the heavens and stretching out more than they had ever been in her last few years.

Even Mrs. Heimlich's salt-and-pepper hair streaked upwards in the rushing air and shaped her face into a halo, which almost looked beautiful—until you noticed the lips.

And now Shanti is watching her.

Bloody hell.

BLINK

Shanti had a ritual of only opening her blinds once the suprabhatam had played on the HMV and she had lit the lamp. That was the first truth they noted about her—that she only stepped out after lighting the lamp and listening to her morning chants.

A ritual Shanti carried on despite the many apartments that she has lived in.

Crawling through her mind, Aparicita viewed her as a newlywedded wife opening the blinds, her hair knotted in a thin khadi towel after her morning shower with the suprabhatam on the radio. Her happiness at the beginning of her new life with her husband was the start of a ritual she carried on all her life without knowing why.

Seeing through Shanti's eyes, they saw Mrs Heimlich falling but they allowed her to avert her eyes, catching the eyes of Mr Tripati.

BLINK

Mr Tripati had seen Shanti but quickly returned to watching the brunette on the 65th floor.

He had been staring up at her window for a while now, and she had just opened the blinds.

He saw her return with heavy bags last night. Yesterday must have been payday, which meant that tonight would be party time.

She was dressed in the black lingerie that she liked with a glass of something in her hand.

The little tease is putting on a show for him with the way that she tilted her head just the way he liked it and stroked her elbow, gazing far away.

She turned towards him, and he hid behind the curtain.

Does she know?

He froze. After all these months of staring at her, he always thought she had never noticed him. How could she? He always took great care to sit in the darkened room. The lights in every single room inside his house were switched off.

He looked again.

She looked directly at him and frowned.

BLINK

The old perv was at it again. She couldn't be bothered today; she had company over and touched her lips in anticipation.

WHOAA.

Hmmm, that's interesting.

BREATHE

They looked down, and it was breasts this time. Enhanced and quite perky. Actually, it's quite enhanced. They could feel more in this one.

She was wearing lingerie black and red, still connected to her peripheral.

Curious, they touched the top of one breast.

A flood of warmth and joy rushed in.

Sensory upgrades.

The world has changed a lot since they became them, but it does have its perks.

They arched her back till it hurt, relishing in the amplified pain. Curling her toes inwards till the tips touched the balls of her feet, they twisted and turned her neck while they gritted her teeth.

The pain caused a rush of endorphins, heightened by the chemical release of neural enhancers. With the release came a sweet rush of relief and a blissful silence of the mind.

Full spectrum, too. Curiouser and Curiouser.

DEEP BREATH.

STAY

Opening their eyes, they looked around the room.

The table had been set for 6 people. 6 glasses of wine were already poured with 6 inhalers of neural enhancers.

Looks like someone is having a party.

They walked to the kitchen and eyed the knife rack. It was a good selection, and they were all sharp.

They selected a carving knife, its folded steel rippling in the kitchen light. Rubbing a fingertip along the sharp blade, they licked the trickle of blood and smiled. A wave of endorphins again

This could be fun.

Even more surprising was the bedroom. Centred on the large bed was a fine collection of toys not marketed to children.

Hmmm.

Lying down in the bed, they relished the touch of silk against their legs. The weighted quilt was just the right, and combined with the climate-controlled room, They were nice and cosy enough to want to lie here forever.

This was a pleasant change to the last few trips. The last one in particular, they ended up in a hospital bed with the smell of sick death all around them.

Not very pleasant

they thought, with an upturn of the nose.

The discovery of the new, though. No matter how many times they have travelled, the first few moments were always thrilling. The awakening, the learning of the new treasure island filled with tiny pockets of stories to spy on.

But they also loved it when they found these little pockets of surprises. The unexpected among the ordinary. This tiny scar just above the heart. Who would have guessed that it was a slash from a lover's blade or a barely skimmed bullet? They thrived for the stories.

Stepping out to the balcony, they inhaled deeply.

Change was imminent, they felt.

They have always felt it, but tonight it was different.

More stronger.

More righter.

Maybe it was the chem enhancement or the general zeitgeist they felt, or maybe they were just weary.

The urge to settle down after so many, many years.

Still connected to the peripheral, they place a call.

A voice answered a cautious hello. The number was restricted, and only a select few had it. Still, one needs to vary in this day and age.

"Raghunathan. " said the voice crooning.

"Natha," Nathan replied in reverence.

"We grow weary Raghu. This wicked world needs us more than ever to show how things are to be.

"The child needs to be born."

Nathan stammered. "Not long now. The time of the Great Syzygy draws near and the hosts are being prepared.

"The child will be ready soon."

Aparicita didnt acknowledge what Nathan had said but instead croaked, "Organise for a clean-up crew to arrive at the phone's location tomorrow morning."

Smacking their lips, Aparicita said, "It looks like I will be having some friends for dinner.

Gravely nodding in acknowledgement, Nathan replied. "Thy will be done. Legion. "

| 22 |

Memories / Hit Sale

Nirukta silently glides through the dark abyss.
Named after the ancient Sanskrit discipline of etymology and semantics, Nirukta was as stealthy as the myths it was amongst.

The submarine's environmental scanning mode illuminated the path through holographic overlays. and Shaani guides her submarine with precision, relaying each command through her onboard neural link.

Staring out the front viewport, Mahesh, who had been landbound for most of his life, marvelled at the ancient ruins all around them and at the grace with which Shaani and Gaurav traversed the watery depths like mermaids.

Karthik, donning graphene-weaved diving gear, was occupied with configuring the integrated HUD displays and propulsion thrusters. This was not the first time that he had been through the legendary underwater city of Mohabbatein, and the ancient monuments had lost their charm.

Now that their paths were set, Shaani took a moment to give thanks to her forbearers, confident that Nirukta would be able to guide them for the rest of the way.

Stepping away from her seat, she walked to her bunk and opened up her Najum chest. Made from dark rosewood and light jackwood, she traced the motif of a deer head, its antlers curling into branches on top of the lid.

The box was her *sami-mootai*, her personal treasure box of keepsakes that she/he collected all their life. While the gang had seen the box itself, they were very mindful of the personal nature of the Yaadgaar, each having their own versions of the same and wouldn't dare touch the box, let alone open it. With reverence, she hovered both hands above the wooden box and touched the tips of her fingers to the corners of her eyes before opening it. She remembered choosing her box, one of the 12 that her family retained through generations, and her parents reverently replacing it with one that they had made themselves.

Opening up one of the smaller drawers at the bottom, Shaani withdrew the smaller box containing her googles and conch shells. Lovingly caressing it, she traced the letters that were carved into it, lingering on the K hand imprinted so long ago.

Breaking out of her reverie, Shaani opened the drawer next to it and withdrew Kamal, the ancient rectangular wooden board with the knotted ceremonial string. While the string was replaced regularly, the board itself was an original made for one of her ancestors and was adorned with encrypted symbols known only to Kadal Banjaras. Hand copied carefully by multiple generations, Shaani, however, being the first child of the first child, was handed the original to safeguard. Whispering her thanks, she spent a moment remembering the pride they felt when they were handed over the Kamal as part of their initiation ceremony.

Still following the maps put together by the ancient navigators of the river Padmavathi, she was still amazed at how accurately she could still use the old markers in spite of the river being underground for thousands of years.

Feeling the nuzzle of a cold nose, Shaani was tickled by an urgent pressing of fur at her knees. Laughing, she leaned down to pat Maya, mildly dislodging the catoms that made up the almost realistic fur. Still, only a working prototype, the claytronic companion wasn't fully stable as of yet, but she found its personality module more than made up for its apparent aesthetic shortcomings. Woofing around her ankles, it played till, with a sigh, it flipped for a belly rub, its tongue and eyes lolling in sheer pleasure with each scritch scritch. It always knew when Shaani needed to cheer up, and she was now back on track.

Nirukta beeped, letting her know that her markers have been met. They were close to their final destination. Shaani eased the submarine closer, the holographic overlays now highlighting the world above. Consulting the municipal maps, she reviewed them against the holographic view.

Right on target.

With hover mode engaged, the submarine idled near large open pipes, with a steady outflow of water turning the surroundings murky. With a deep intake of air, Shaani gave Gaurav a thumbs-up and opened the airlock.

Melding with Maya, Shaani willed it to morph and watched as, in a shimmer, it reassembled itself into a luminescent Nagini. Slithering its way to Karthik, it crawled into a transparent tube, which Karthik carefully placed on his back before he made his way to the submarine airlock.

Gliding through the murky depths, Karthik made his way close to the pipes, guided by his glowing green smart googles, which, along with Nirukata's sonar overview, allowed him to see better than on land. Karthik, with his hermetically sealed diving gear, was in no danger of contamination.

The turbine fans were supposed to be in sleep mode, but the blades were still spinning steadily. Karthik wasn't flustered though by the turbulent flow but instead watched the spinning blades calmly, relaying the images back to Nirukta. Taking a small bullet-shaped drone from his belt, Karthik released it and watched as it hovered, steading itself in the strong outflow.

Waiting.

Nirukta beeped to let them know that it had calculated the optimum path for the drone and with a push of a button, Karthik released it. and watched as it ducked and weaved through the blades, its microreactor-powered thrusters pushing through the current with ease till it stopped and hovered. Dropping its payload precisely where it was programmed to do so, the bullet-drone danced its way back into Karthik's waiting hand.

Karthik pushed out till he was well clear of the projected fallout and said "In position" into his headset.

"Copy that," acknowledged Gaurav, who carried out a final sweep to ensure that they were all in the clear. With a push of a button, he triggered the EMP that the drone had dropped earlier.

Exploding right on cue, the isolated blast knocked out the first lot of electronic equipment in the area, including the turbines.

Gaurav quickly reviewed the security report that Zarg had obtained. The blast was contained in an area with all of its sensors disabled. With the sizeable amount of debris floating around, the sensors were prone to frequent false alarms, so the maintenance crew had simply disabled them.

Gaurav looked on with satisfaction as the turbines slowed down, the calm of the water an expected and welcome change. Satisfied, Gaurav pressed the tab and asked, "Ready?"

"Ohhh, big boy. Are we getting nice and dirty at our large opening?" said Zarg with their usual cheekiness. Gaurav grinned in spite of himself. "I guess you can say that Zarg, good to go?"

Zarg acknowledged over the digital expanse, their excitement at the audacity of their actions a Parle-G kick.

Taking control over Maya, they guided the snake-like Maya to a tiny exhaust valve that led into the headquarters of ZyraCorp.

There was plenty of time to do what they needed to, and if all went as planned, they would be gone before ZyraCorp even realised that they had been hit.

Activating its self-guidance module, Zarg made sure that the maps were downloaded and readable before unleashing Maya.

Since Maya would be completely in comms isolation once it moved further up the pipes, all they could do was hope and pray that the schematics were accurate and, more importantly, that Maya would be able to reach their target through the labyrinth of pipes that made up the backbone of the building.

The clock ticked on.

1 minute.

Maya slithered its way to the pipes, occasionally disassembling itself to pass through vents and other impedance.

3 minutes.

Slowly but stealthily, it made its way to a large ballroom and to a familiar sensor at the top of the room.

5 minutes.

Reaching its destination, it merged into the sensor, and as programmed, Maya broke down and stretched, reassembling itself into a thread as thin as silk. Its catoms realigned until it followed its path backwards, still maintaining a connection to the sensor.

11 minutes.

At the entrance, Karthik waited till, with a ping on his HUD, he saw the glimmer of silver as the regenerated Maya poked its head out of the open exhaust pipe. Karthik smiled as he helped guide it to the base of the transmitter that he had rigged up. With a few quick adjustments, Karthik connected directly to the submarine successfully bypassing the Faraday cage.

Mahesh suited up and sat nervously in the airlock with Shaani. Sensing his discomfort, she gripped his hand tight. "We are okay," she smiled, and Mahesh nodded in acknowledgement. Together, they jumped into the murky depths. Using the self-propulsion system, they made their way to Karthik, passing schools of mackerel glimmering like jewels in the abyss.

The connection tested as stable; Karthik waited at the entrance of the pipes for Shaani and Mahesh to catch up with him. With time to reflect, he realised that despite everything, they were a lot closer to the seemingly impossible task of accessing Zyracorp than he ever thought possible.

Instead of feeling reassured by their success, Karthik actually experienced the opposite, and he started doubting himself. For all his external bravado and confidence, the truth of the matter was that he never really had a Plan.

He just really trusted that things would work out for him.

Humbled by the responsibility that he bore on his shoulders of leadership Karthik was starting to be wary that things were falling into place a bit too quickly. The others sometimes just said that it was pure luck, and while he never openly agreed with them, that was exactly what it was.

Sheer dumb luck. Good or bad, however, is something that takes time to find out.

Karthik had seen the look on their faces since he had got back. Mahesh, Gaurav and even Shaani. The disappointment that he could always sense in them now finally made him realise how badly his actions had on his nearest and dearest.

For the first time he started fearing that he was going to lachuka things up just when things were starting to work out.

And things were working out a lot.

Like Zarg, for instance. With the technical expertise required to actually break into ZyraCorp, Karthik highly doubted that any of them or even any of their contacts would have been able to do what Zarg did. And all they asked in return was to check out some missing Banjara girls—something he would have done anyway.

Hidden in the shadowed corners of his underground bunker, Zarg slipped on their headpiece while they sat in the device they dubbed Mastishk. The spherical chamber, made from pieces of discarded satellite dishes, was lined with a mosaic of processors, memory chips, and interface cards, all scavenged from the scrap yards of Mannar. While it didn't have a single quantum processor, nevertheless, through a patch of hacked server shares, a network of corporate processing bandwidth powered it, all repurposed as a distributed quantum computing grid.

The interface chair, cobbled together from an old pilot's ejector seat, connected to the system through a web of cables and jury-rigged connectors.

Using a neuro-interface helmet they made themselves, Mastishk was outfitted with an array of sensors pilfered from scrap medical equipment and gaming devices. Holographic displays, improvised from broken peripherals and tablet screens, were arranged in a dome to provide a fully immersive environment.

Fuelling this contraption was not the clean energy of zero-point modules but the erratic power siphoned from the city's grid, supplemented by an array of mismatched solar panels and bicycle generators.

Zarg relaxed in their seat. Their pride and joy, they were waiting for the right opportunity to truly test Mastishk's limits.

Game on ZyraCorp.

Now within range, Zarg pivoted off the sensor into the ZyraCorp corporate network. Activating the link from Maya, Zarg piggybacked off the local network and ran a custom script of their own design. Exploiting the synchronisation protocol of a server that accepts unauthenticated updates, Zarg deploys a series of malformed packets, triggering a buffer overflow in the server and granting Mastishk backdoor access to the Building Management server.

Once inside, Zarg deploys an AI-driven worm that silently navigates the network, blending with legitimate traffic. The AI worm autonomously spreads till it latches on to Mahesh's old employee profile and expands his authority.

Part of the IT department, Mahesh had already been granted limited access to most of the key jump hosts, including the Xyphor maintenance servers which controlled the building management system.

"Hmm. Can't give Mahesh's full admin just yet; that would trigger a system alert."

Looking through the list of company admins, Zarg randomly selected a user who would suit their purposes.

Zyana_admin remained highlighted, while Zarg cloned her admin profile and allocated it to Mahesh's profile. Subtly altering ancillary data, Zarg then obfuscates their actions to mimic routine database maintenance.

"We are in chokris." yelled Zarg in triumph

Upon receiving the signal, Karthik nearly whopped in his mask but maintained his stoicism while he guided Mahesh and Shaani to their secondary target, a small ladder affixed on the side of the pipe.

Climbing it, they waited by a disused maintenance hatch, part of the backup access system designed for emergency repairs. Now having full control of the system, Zarg opened the hatch and deployed a series of timed commands that temporarily deactivated the one-way valves and pressurised seals, creating a safe window for the team to enter.

With the flood prevention system momentarily neutralised, the hatch unlocked with a hiss, releasing a stream of bubbles.

Karthik, Mahesh, and Shaani slipped through the opening into a narrow, water-filled shaft. Swimming through the tunnel, they reached their destination: a heavily secured door labelled "Plant Room 12B."

"Alright, Zarg, we're at the entrance to the plant room," Karthik said through his peripheral, his diving suit dripping water on the already damp floor.

"On it," Zarg replied, executing another sequence of commands to override the internal doors.

Upon gaining access to ZyraCorp, Zarg hadn't stayed idle. With admin access to the security database, they were ready for Phase 3 and yet had plenty of time to do some additional digging in the personnel files for Kumari Sanu and the other missing children.

Whooa. This Zyana profile is pretty hectic. There is way more admin access than I expected, but hey, I'm not going to complain about a gift horse.

And in Zarg went as they as deep as they could go.

With a push of a button on Karthik's console, the plant room door swung open with a hiss. The room was noisy, and without their peripherals, it would have been impossible to hear each other. Ignoring the grunts, whistles, and swooshes as the chillers sucked in the seawater as part of the building's cooling system, the gang made their way down the warren of pipes and machinery to a giant service elevator.

"That should be it," said Zarg to all their peripherals.

"Mahesh's credentials have full access, and you should be clear all the way to the top."

Nodding, Mahesh presented his periband, and the lift beeped and began its journey from the top down to the plant room.

Now, to look at the part.

Pausing at the elevator's entrance, Karthik, Shaani, and Mahesh shed their diving suits, peeling away the layers of neoprene to reveal the finery that lay beneath.

Karthik's kurta was a light shade of grey, almost blending with the shadows, while Mahesh's was a more flamboyant peacock green and blue. Both were impeccably tailored to their athletic frames. Giving Shaani privacy while she adjusted her sari, Karthik and Mahesh busied themselves tweaking their kurtas.

"So boys can't decide what look to go for? Care to share an opinion."

Turning around, they had a good look at Shaani, draped in an elegant sari in a delicate weave of gold and midnight blue that seemed to shimmer with every movement. Hugging her curves, the sari flowed like water down her body to match her hair, which now cascaded down her shoulders in waves.

Rapidly, Shaani's appearance flicked through the options on her peripheral, her face changing to suit the filter she selected.

Failing to get a response, she looked up. Both Karthik and Mahesh were still gaping at her. With a sly smile and a wiggle of the shoulders, she settled for metallic gold and vibrant neon accents that highlighted her features.

LED lashes cast a glow around her captivating eyes.

With a gulp, Karthik put on his cowboy hat. Taking a deep breath he addressed them. "This is it, no turning back now guys. You know what we are getting ourselves into but you also know what is at stake.

"I ask you one final time,

"are you sure you want to go ahead?"

Looking around, Karthik could see a resolution on their faces but still waited for them to nod in acknowledgement. Relieved and with consent received, he pressed the button to take them to the top.

As the elevator made its way to the surface, Zarg piped again on the broadcast channel.

"Lady and Gents. This lift goes all the way to the top.

I have got eyes, ears and a whole lot of other sensations going on here.

Welcome to the main event. "

With an almost planned flourish, the lift doors opened with a hiss as it opened up into a warm garden with a clearly visible sign in front.

"Welcome to Founders Day X"

Opening at the side entrance of the ZyraCorp corporate grounds, they joined the throng of people walking up to the stairs to the official Founders Day Launch Party. Adding to the chaos of the crowd were they paparazzi drones as they buzzed and clicked around the throng of guests.

Grabbing Shaani's and Mahesh's hands, Karthik guided them up the stairs till, with a halt, he hit an iron wall. Armoured sentry bots in red and gold, these in humanoid form in line with the event's visibility.

Extending a robotic arm, a helpful screen popped up on his chest in 15 languages, requesting their invitations.

Submitting his periband, Karthik ran through the names of all the great ones in quick succession,

Anansi, Lagor, Jaladhar.....

"Access Granted" popped on the Sentrybot's screen, and with a sigh of relief, Karthik guided the rest of them into joining the queue. Having never been to a Filmistaan party before, Karthik couldn't help but be a little awestruck by the whole thing—the thong of celebrities, drones, and the throngs and throngs of fans outside the gates.

He couldn't help but wonder if the people on the inside even knew what it was to be in the real world.

Take a look at that chromatic MeiTei. Its mirror wrap reflecting the paparazzi drones making it sparkle like diamonds. The white-haired young'un and the fit matron types looked well suited to the filmi and corporate world they obviously looked like they belonged to.

With a cringe, he noted. "Ha, the cougar just throws her limited edition Pengo around as if it was worth nothing. "

Badre Badre Badre.

Tara hated being photographed and here were a thousand drones whose sole job was to just do that. So flustered was she when she got out of Nithya's MeiTei that she even dropped the purse that she had lent her. Tara had specifically asked for the cheapest one, so she hoped Nithya didn't get annoyed with her chamal. Nithya, sympathetic to Tara's nervousness, instead held her hand and together, hand in hand, they entered the party.

Neon lights bathed the space in a kaleidoscope of colours, reflecting off the polished bronze and glass surfaces that dominated the décor. Holographic projections of intricate mandalas floated in the air, constantly shifting and morphing, creating an almost hypnotic effect. Above, a ceiling of transparent glass revealed a breathtaking view of the starry night sky, augmented by holographic constellations that shifted and changed. The floor pulsed gently, responding to the movement of people, creating a fluid, ever-changing mosaic of light.

The air was filled with a subtle, fragrant mist, infused with Oud and lavender, creating an atmosphere of calm amidst the vibrant energy.

At the center of the ballroom, a massive stage was set, where key products were concealed beneath a shimmering veil of nanomaterial. The air buzzed with snippets of conversation, a mix of languages and dialects.

Guests arrived adorned in variations of traditional sarees and sherwanis augmented with subtle, bio-luminescent designs. Jewellery, both heirloom and high-tech, sparkled everywhere, casting tiny rainbows around their wearers. Food and drink on automated hover trays floated between the guests, ducking and weaving in anticipation of the crowd's movement, only to alight with refreshments at a wave of hand.

Nithya moved through the crowd with ease, exchanging pleasantries but not engaging in any deep discussions. Her aim was to blend in. A voice chirped in her peripheral. "Ahh, welcome to the party, Nithya. I see you have brought a friend. She looks nice."

Nithya looked around. She still had no clue who her mysterious benefactor was or the purpose of this secret meeting, but her instincts strangely told her to trust them.

"Where are you?" Nithya said out loud.

The voice continued. "All in good time. I am setting up the war room. With the crowds of people here, that floor would be unoccupied, so we can discuss our matters in private.

I am glad that you have brought a friend along. I understand that some things are easier to process with friends. I will touch base with you shortly and give you the directions once ready.

Till then. Why don't you enjoy yourselves." signed off the voice with a laugh.

Enjoy yourself huh?

Looking around, Nithya could find quite a few potential distractions, and not all of them were floating about.

Well, if I have to

she thought and eagerly looked around for her next mistake.

Like the hard badre with the cowboy hat.

Kollam. He looks like he has potential.

Oh, never mind. It looks like he has already taken it, with the way he is shepherding the chokri he is with, full to paghal.

Karthik was getting nervous. Going with the flow is one thing, but things seem to be going at a rocket's pace now.

Steady. Steady. Nice and easy.

Shaani and Mahesh seemed to be blending in nicely. Both in their element, they seemed a bit too friendly for Karthik's liking. With the amount of attention Shaani seemed to be drawing, Karthik was sure that she would blow their cover. He didn't seem to mind that Mahesh seemed to be getting just as much attention himself, though.

His doma spirit free, Mahesh started blending into the crowd. Really blending in. In and out, he ducked out of conversation, his features and conversations merging in line with the audience. Stealthy making his way through the crowd, Mahesh activated his glove; the smart gel started to realign itself to become a copy of Ramin's hand.

Having heard of Ramin's dislike of handshakes, Mahesh had been worried that even if he had managed to get Ramin to shake it, it wouldn't be long enough for him to have his glove learn Ramin's hand. Luckily, the glove had picked up enough for Gaurav to build a perfect replica of it.

The Way is powerful, but Mahesh didn't think that any domo would be able to mould themselves to fool fingerprint scanners.

Behaviourals, though, was another matter.

Few outside of the doma really knew the power of the 'Way'. Many thought it was just really good mimicry, but it was much more than that.

For a few moments, Mahesh can choose to be truly somebody else.

On the way to the lift, Mahesh started the transformation. Recalling Ramin back to the meeting room, he recalled every frown, line, laugh, and smile till it became one with the memory of his body.

Mahesh was glad that he was able to neg Ramin on. The full spectrum of emotions, including anger and displeasure, was needed to truly become someone. The brochure was money well spent, and just appearing unfit and wearing the blue turban was enough for most of the negs to come through.

The request for the handshake was enough for the rest of them, and Mahesh shuddered in the memory of the fury behind the smile.

Moving in a manner so superbly cool and subtle, that nobody noticed anything at all, Karthik , Shaani and Mahesh gathered at the elevators at the back of the room.

It was now or never, and they have never been so close to their prize.

Patching a direct link to Zarg, Karthik asked them to drive them straight to their final destination.

The war room.

Karthik and Shaani waited with bated breath, watching as the person in front of them turned out to be somewhat like Ramin.

Mahesh breathed. He needed to be focused.

To become Ramin.

I am Ramin.

"I am Ramin "he said louder to reinforce this belief as the lift doors opened.

"I know Ramin, and you are not Ramin, came Zyana's prompt response.

A gamut of emotions ran through Karthik and the gang's faces.

Staring right at them was a young woman in a traditional white saree with a golden border. On her forehead was a tilak of sandalwood, and a garland of jasmine flowers hung from her ponytailed hair. Despite her extended arms, she seemed to be retro-ing, wearing spectacles instead of a peripheral or any other wearables.

Without waiting for them to alight from the lift, Zyana opened the folded leaf she was holding and taking the paste of sandalwood and ash, she marked a tilak on all 3 of their foreheads.

If Zyana was puzzled by their bemused expressions, she didn't acknowledge it. "You must be the special guests that Indra was talking about. I believe we are meeting in the war room."

Shaani and Mahesh looked around at Karthik who followed Zyana, his feet seemingly having a mind of their own. At the far end of the corridor, another lift opened up and in walked Tara and Nithya guided by Indra.

Across the hallway, Karthik could hear the platinum blonde talk aloud in her peripheral.

"Yes, thanks for this, but it would be great if you could at least let me know who I am meeting," said Nithya.

"Yes, I am patient but you can understand how a person can get a bit annoyed.

"What do you mean you are not exactly a person?

"What's going on here?"

Almost as if it was timed, both parties stood in front of the war room while Zyana opened the doors to look at the cameras. In they walked into the conference room and sat at opposite ends sizing each other up.

Zyana said out loud "Ahh, Indra, I trust you are in the room ambient? I had a look at the claytronic emitter while I was in Palaghat, and I was able to fix the processing overflow buffer.

"You should be more stable now."

And so saying Zyana flicked a disc at the center of the table.

In a blue-grey haze, Indra appeared in claytronic form; her flickering form settled into that of a young woman with short blue hair and a prominent aquiline nose.

Seated opposite Mahesh, Tara had a long look at him.

I have seen that flickering aura before.
It reminds me of the domo at the basti, only much calmer.
No, it can't be.
Agra is over 2000Kms from here. What are the chances?
But they are so rare.
Could it be?

Mahesh actually had to use all his will not to look at Tara.

A favour for Kannan, he had visited Habibayada Basti just before heading to Filmistaan to talk to Vaishali, one of the friends of the dead Banjara twins.He had disappeared quite quickly when her mother identified Tara as a police officer.

How the lachubadre did the police follow me all the way here?
Hang on, why is he always in her civvies?

Nithya wasn't paying attention to any of the commotion around her. Instead, she stared at Indra's projection as she seemed to stare back at Nithya in a knowing way.

There is something familiar about the girl.
Why does her face remind me of someone long gone?

Both Gaurav and Shaani stared at the safe, both had the same thought.

The safe was large enough to store maybe a few books and definitely not the 'Gift of the Magi.'

With a cough, Zyana continued as normal and stood up. "Now, if I remember correctly, introductions are customary as per protocol.

As the chair, I will lead, and I believe it's ladies first. I am Zyana Contractor, head of R&D Zyracorp. "

Pointing to Tara, who sat closest to her, she smiled—maybe a bit too wide or a bit too narrow for some people, but a polite smile nonetheless.

It clicked at that moment for Mahesh and Tara. They stood up and pointed at each other in unison. "You were there at the Basti that day. "

Nithya stood up and pointed at Indra. "Why does your assistant look like my father?"

Both Shaani and Gaurav pointed at the safe." You said it was here in the war room. This has all been for nothing. "

Through all this, Zarg seemed to be going mad with power.

On and on, they were rattling on in Karthik's ear about missing Basti people and links to dead Chokri girls.

Walking on a knife's edge of tension, all of this was just a bit too much for Karthik, who stood up with a yell.

"CAN SOMEONE EXPLAIN WHAT THE BADRE IS GOING ON HERE?"

**DIGITAL AMRUT
COMING SOON**

I

Vienna/ Planet Zero

ELSEWHERE
Tara pulled up the co-ods on her peripheral again. Her final destination was deep in a protected rain forest and so remote that the paths leading there weren't even coded and had to be driven manually about 10 Km into the deep forest.

The rental was pretty decent for once. She didn't skimp this time and went for a mid-size model. This car even had cultured leather seats and a SoundWave just like Nithya's.

The display around the car, pulsed in time with her drive, the music and surrounding display keeping in time with the velocity (both speed and direction ;) of the car. Each turn, acceleration, and halt played into the Sound-Wave system, changing the melody to ebb and flow with the motion of the car. The display, wrapping around her like a cocoon, pulsed with waves of light, radiating outward, mirroring the rhythm of the forest and the music born from her drive.

Tara, being both conductor and audience, was the only witness to her symphony.

She pulled up to what seemed like a log cabin. She had only seen them in old cowboy videos and didn't even know that they existed in real life anymore. When she went in a group was already gathered around an old lady in a kimono.

The room was quiet as if waiting for somebody.

At her entrance, the old lady with kind almond eyes looked up and smiled. "We can begin now. "

She led them down a well-beaten path deep into the forest, and they silently followed. There among the mountains were mighty redwood trees amid the native conifers. In a large clearing, which though it appeared purposely made, was surrounded by ancient hemlocks. The old lady stood in the centre and waited until the group silently formed a circle around her.

She pointed to tiny paths through the grove of trees and gently said

"Go and tell"

Tara wanted to protest. The whole thing seemed strange and cult-like, but so far, she couldn't see anything illegal, so she just followed. She was getting a bit agitated, so she tried being analytical about it. Logically, none of this seemed dangerous. It's not like she really had anything else to do today, so she might as well see this through. The thing was that...

All this silence was overbearing.

The more Tara walked deeper into the path, the calmer she became about the whole thing. The intoxicating forest aroma of sycamore and jasmine seemed to soothe her soul. She walked until she came to an old banyan tree. Older than any of the other trees, the giant branches were so tall that they formed a cool, dark canopy with supports growing deep into the ground.

The trunk shouldn't be glowing red deep in the shadow of the grove, but it did. Beckoning her.

She touched the trunk and remembered Fasil. She hadn't thought about him willingly for so long that she could actually feel it as an old but familiar thought, like seeing an old photograph.

Tara tasted tamarinds and lemons.

She remembered his smile. Wide and innocent.

She remembered the blood. Bright Red and everywhere.

She remembered his touch. Soft and sensual.

She remembered the stench. Putrid and gagging.

She remembered his gaze. Hers and hers alone.

She wept. Openly and uncontrollably.

She thought she heard laughter.

She thought she heard screams.

She wasn't sure it wasn't hers.

She walked back calmly with her shoulders back and head pensive.

The old lady in the kimono met her at the entrance just when she was leaving, smiling "I see that our trees have lifted your spirits for now. Would you like to join me in the kitchen? I would like your help with something. "

Tara, never one for actually cooking, nevertheless silently followed the old lady into a small kitchen. On a table, a couple of bowls were already laid out with something soaking in them. Upon closer inspection, Tara saw that they contained Bora daan rice and a bowl of black sesame seeds.

Just like her mother used to leave it.

Walking over the old lay guided Tara while she scooped up the softened glutinous grains, preparing them to be ground into a fine powder. This rice flour, the foundation of their Pithas, was mixed with water to create a batter of just the right consistency, neither too thick nor too runny, ready to cradle the heart of the dish.

Lighting a skillet, the old lady dry-roasted black sesame seeds, the air instantly filling with the nutty aroma. Grinding the sesame seeds with pods of black cardamon, she poured the mixture into a large bowl.

Gently taking Tara's hands, she placed them into the bowl. Together, they mixed the filling, infusing the mixture with the sweet, earthy richness of jaggery and the subtle warmth of crushed cardamom seeds, ensuring that the flavours melded together in perfect harmony.

Just like she used to do with her mother.

As Tara watched, the old lady expertly poured and spread the batter on a seasoned skillet, transforming it into a thin crepe. A generous line of the sesame and jaggery filling was placed in the centre. With a practised hand, the crepe was rolled, enclosing the filling in a warm embrace, and then carefully removed from the skillet once firm.

Pouring from a pot of chai, its spiced aroma weaves through the air, a perfect companion to the sweet richness of the Til Pithas. Sitting down to savour their creations, Tara found each bite infused with memories, the sweetness of the Pithas mingling with the spiced warmth of the chai to bring solace and healing.

Feel free to return at any time if you would like to join another one of our sessions said the lady when she bid farewell to Tara with a package of Til Pithas to take back home.

Tara thought about it.

Tara knew that she should find this whole thing strange and alien, having never been here before or ever having done this before, but she didn't.

She thought about how she felt. She wasn't exactly happier. She definitely didn't forget what happened with Fasil but she did feel lighter.

That seemed like a start.

She looked up at the lady, smiled, and said. "Yes. Yes, I think I just might. "

The old lady waited until Tara had turned down the path before smiling. "See you soon, Tara."

Turning around, the old lady entered a room with a giant banner of a deer, its antlers blending into sycamore and entwined conifers floating above the island of Amrtavipa.

With a gentle thud, the giant double doors swung close behind her.